The Dreaming Circle in Time

Kim Murphy

Published by Coachlight Press

Copyright © 2017 by Kim Murphy

All rights reserved. No part of this book may be reproduced or transmitted in any form or by any means, electronic or mechanical, including photocopying, recording, or by any information storage and retrieval system, without permission in writing from the copyright owner.

Published by Coachlight Press March 2017

Coachlight Press, LLC
1704 Craigs Store Road
Afton, Virginia 22920
http://www.coachlightpress.com

Printed in the United States of America
Cover design by Roberta J. Marley

This is a work of fiction. Names, characters, places, and incidents either are the product of the author's imagination or are used fictitiously, and any resemblance to any actual persons, living or dead, events, or locales is entirely coincidental.

Library of Congress Control Number: 2017932271
ISBN 978-1-936785-22-3

To the memory of my mom and Isabella

Also by Kim Murphy

Nonfiction

I Had Rather Die: Rape in the Civil War

Fiction

The Dreaming: Walks Through Mist
The Dreaming: Wind Talker
Whispers from the Grave
Whispers Through Time
Promise & Honor
Honor & Glory
Glory & Promise

1

Phoebe

July 1645

"PHOEBE, I'M BLEEDING."

I gazed upon Meg's countenance, which was etched in despair. "Are you certain?"

She placed her hands upon her abdomen. "I'm going to lose it, aren't I?"

The year afore, my friend had married my brother Charging Bear. When she had discovered she was with child, she had been ecstatic. If the blood loss had come earlier in her pregnancy, there would have been less cause for concern, but as near as we could tell, she had entered her fourth month. Both of us were cunning women, or healers. At this stage, we knew that bleeding was not a good sign. "Have you had any cramping or passed any clots?" I asked.

Meg shook her head.

"Then we wait and see."

"What should I tell Charging Bear?"

"Naught, 'til we know more."

Meg gave a weak nod, but fear remained in her eyes.

I squeezed her shoulder in reassurance. "I shall inform the others that we must postpone our return."

"Thanks, Phoebe."

As I helped Meg to the house, my throat pinched, for I had once lost a babe that I carried. I had painted my face black and wailed my sorrow. Whether Meg had lived amongst the Appamattuck long enough to follow tradition, I didn't know, but she would be surrounded by those who loved her and had knowledge in the ways of *wisakon*. The art of healing.

The men traded near the barn and failed to notice our approach. Hoping to delay any questions 'til later, I circled round them. We neared the pitched-roof house, and I scrambled along a straight path for the door. Afore I reached it, Wind Talker joined us. "What's the hurry? Is everything all right?" he asked.

"Meg isn't feeling well."

He glanced from me to Meg, then back again. Afore I had wed him, he had been a detective in the twenty-first century and could generally surmise what was left unsaid. Silently telling him that I would inform him later, my gaze rested upon his. With a slight bow, he backed away.

I aided Meg inside where Elenor, my grown daughter from my first marriage, greeted us. "Momma?"

"Meg's not well."

"Phoebe, there's no need to spare my feelings." Meg looked in Elenor's direction. "I'm having a miscarriage."

"I'll fetch Bess and inform the men of the events."

Whilst Elenor went after Bess, I helped Meg to the bed. I stripped her down to her shift and gave her a linen pad for the bleeding. Once she was comfortable, I went to Elenor's herb cabinet. I would wait to give Meg the medicine to aid in birthing 'til we were certain, but all of my instincts warned me of what Meg already knew. I searched through the glass jars, locating blue cohosh, black cohosh, and cotton root bark. I carefully measured the roots and readied them for making tea.

"Phoebe." I turned to my former servant Bess. She hailed from Africa, and her prominent cheekbones were adorned with tribal scars. "I'll make the tea, whilst you sit with Meg."

"Thank you, Bess." As I sat on the edge of the bed, Meg gave a satiric laugh. "I never thought of the consequences of miscarrying in this time. Where I come from, women get a D&C."

I'd had enough nursing courses in the twenty-first century to realize that dilation and curettage was a surgical procedure, but I had ne'er understood the concept of rushing into surgery if a body could heal itself. "That shan't be necessary."

Meg pressed a hand to her abdomen and groaned. 'Twas the first sign of cramping. I helped her to the pisspot. She squatted and passed a bloody clot. No doubt remained. My friend would lose her babe. When she returned to bed, Bess brought her the cohosh tea to encourage labor pains. O'er the next few hours, her pains got worse. Meg moaned. "This is worse than childbirth."

More often than not, she sat on the pisspot, bleeding and dropping clot after clot. I remained with her throughout, with Bess or Elenor usually at my side. Once Meg got up and her legs buckled. I caught her afore she fell. "Don't attempt to get up without one of us helping you," I said.

"I felt something pop. Something is coming out."

I helped Meg to the pisspot. She squatted. Out slid a tiny babe that I caught in my hands. A boy—he was perfectly formed, but there was no caul. A navel cord came from his belly, and I could see his backbone and ribs. E'en his fingers and toes were fully formed. So tiny, about the size of a plum, he had died weeks afore.

With the passing of her babe, Meg's cramping and bleeding halted. Tears streaked her cheeks, and I gently placed the babe in her hands. She cupped him and cried.

We gave her a few minutes to mourn her babe afore Bess offered her more cohosh tea. "You need to pass the caul."

Whilst Meg drank, I carefully placed the babe in a copper urn.

Her cramping began anew along with more bleeding. I aided her to the pisspot where she passed a clot the size of my fist. 'Twas followed by gushing blood.

"I feel dizzy," Meg muttered.

"Just rest."

She laughed. "What I wouldn't give for a modern toilet."

I brushed her black hair away from her face, and she laid her head upon my thigh. She picked up her head, but lowered it again. Whilst she rested, blood dripped into the pisspot. After a while, she breathed deeply. "I'd like to go back to bed now."

With my aid, she stood. I helped her clean the blood from her legs, and she climbed into bed. Afore long, she was up again, scrambling for the pisspot. I tried to get a grip on her arm to aid her, but she fell straight forward afore I could catch her. Her face thumped the floor with a loud whack.

"Meg..." I dropped to her side and touched her gently. Her arms and legs twitched. Her jerky muscles weren't as violent as someone who had suffered a fit, but I dared not move her. "I'm here, Meg. I'm sorry. I should have caught you."

She slowly came round but lay there awhile longer. "My face hurts." She pressed a hand to her lip. "Ow."

Beth and Elenor joined us, and we spoke softly to Meg, reassuring her. I pressed cool cloths to her back and neck. When she was strong enough, we rolled her onto her back and placed a pillow neath her head. "I don't think I can get up without fainting again," she said.

Her lips had swollen from the fall, but her bleeding had slowed.

Elenor's six-year-old daughter, Elsa, poked her head in the room. "What's Miss Meg doing on the floor?"

Elenor hurried o'er to Elsa and escorted her from the room. Bess gave Meg a tincture of yarrow root and Shepherd's Purse to slow her bleeding. I washed her bruises with Solomon's Seal and checked her womb by pressing down near her navel. 'Twasn't firm, so I massaged her abdomen by cupping my hand and moving in a circular motion.

More blood gushed and Bess took o'er. Her fingers reached into Meg's womb whilst her right hand pressed down on the abdomen. Meg groaned.

"Her womb has contracted," Bess said, "but she still must pass the caul."

Meg shivered. "I'm cold."

Elenor returned with a blanket and drew it o'er Meg, whilst I continued to knead her womb. She relaxed. "I'm feeling better now."

Meg was too faint to use the birthing stool. "Let's get her to the bed," I said.

"I don't think I can make it."

"You won't have to. We'll carry you." With Elenor and Bess's aid, I spread the blanket neath her. Betwixt the three of us, we lifted her and carried her to the bed. "Are you more at ease?"

Meg stretched and laid her head against the pillow. "My feet are cold."

Elenor got some heavy wool socks, and I kneaded her feet. I washed the blood away, but more gushed. Once again, Bess reached inside Meg's womb and placed pressure on her abdomen with the other. Another labor pain came forth. " 'Tis the caul."

Meg's bleeding slowed, but weak from blood loss, she slumped. The previous year, using Meg's knowledge, Elenor and Bess had given a transfusion to Wind Talker's brother. The action had saved his life. Could they do the same and save Meg's life too? "Meg, what is your blood type?"

"Blood type?" she asked with her voice barely a whisper. "O . . . O positive."

"She needs a transfusion," I said to the others.

Elenor gasped. "Wind Talker made it very clear that we could not perform such a procedure without knowledge of a donor's blood type."

"I was typed in the twenty-first century. Whilst I'm A positive and cannot give, Meg has the same blood type as Wind Talker."

"How can a man give blood to a woman?"

"I don't understand it completely myself, but blood type is not based upon the sex of a person. They both have the same type; therefore, Wind Talker can give his blood to Meg."

"Then we shall. Momma, if you would fetch Wind Talker, Bess and I will prepare in here."

I hurried outside where the men were gathered. They no longer traded and kept watch o'er the children, whilst waiting for word about Meg. "How is she?" Charging Bear asked.

My brother maintained a solemn countenance, but I was aware he shed his tears inside. He had lost two children during a smallpox outbreak and his first wife after birthing their son Strong Bow. "The babe was born too soon," I replied. "Meg has lost a lot of blood, but she need not die." I looked to Wind Talker. "She is O positive."

He straightened. "I'll do whatever is necessary."

"Good." I grasped his hand and headed to the house.

"Walks Through Mist," Charging Bear called after me, using my Algonquian name. "May I see her?"

"After the transfusion. There is too little space in the room. We must move quickly for the procedure to be a success." Charging Bear frowned but remained behind. I showed Wind Talker to the room where Meg lay. Her eyes were glazed but she breathed.

"Momma," Elenor said, "because Meg hails from the twenty-first century, she understands what we're about to do." She motioned for Wind Talker to lie on one of the children's cots near the bed. "I shall draw Wind Talker's blood, whilst Bess injects his blood into Meg."

"Nay, Elenor, you're trying to spare me, but I shall see to Wind Talker."

"Very well." She turned to Bess, who nodded in agreement. "Bess shall flush the syringes." Elenor stepped aside me and explained how we would carry out the transfusion. Because I'd been a cunning woman and had nursing courses, I had become experienced in drawing blood into a syringe. I needed to adapt my skills to seventeenth-century tools.

Finally, I held the coiled-iron fleam in my hand. Wind Talker lay on the too-small bed below me with his feet hanging o'er the edge. He uttered not a word of discomfort. I glanced o'er at the others, and they nodded that they were ready. I rolled up the wool sleeve of Wind Talker's shirt. "Are you ready to proceed?"

"I am," he replied.

With the sharp end of the fleam, I pierced the crook of his arm. I placed a penetrating quill into his vein, then put a brass syringe inside the quill and drew some blood. When the syringe was full, I handed it to Elenor, and Bess gave me a clean syringe. I withdrew more blood. More than anything, I dared not lose count of how many syringes I filled, or I would risk Wind Talker's life. After I had filled ten syringes, his dark brown eyes showed discomfort. "Shall I continue?"

He nodded. "I'm fine."

I continued drawing his blood. Upon reaching fifteen syringe fills, I asked him how he fared. Again, he repeated that he was fine.

Circle in Time 11

Sixteen, seventeen. The previous time, Elenor had taken thirty-five syringe fills. Meg had estimated the amount as well below two pints. Who would have e'er guessed we would now be using the same method to save her life? I worried about the accuracy of the measurements but kept my concern to myself. Wind Talker had been fine on the previous occasion. I carried on. Twenty, twenty-one. E'ery so often, I asked him how he was. Twenty-nine, thirty. We neared the end.

After I drew the last syringe and handed it to Elenor, I put a clean linen cloth on Wind Talker's arm and bent it to staunch the blood flow. "How are you feeling?"

"I think I'm okay. And Meg?"

Whilst Bess handed Wind Talker a flagon filled with water, I looked o'er at Meg. Elenor injected the final syringe fill into Meg's arm. She withdrew the quill and placed the padded cloth on Meg's arm afore bending it. "How is she?" I asked.

Elenor checked Meg's pulse. "Already she's stronger. Her heartbeat is no longer flighty, and her breathing steadies."

I turned back to Wind Talker and smiled. "You've saved her, my love. Now we need to get you something to eat to restore your energy." But Bess was ahead of me. She handed him a fresh berry mixture laden with cream.

Welcoming the fruit, he eagerly spooned the berry mixture to his mouth. After he finished, he attempted to sit up but swayed. "You would have thought I'd have remembered from the last time."

Bess and I grasped his arms to help steady him. "Rest now," I said.

Content to obey my command, he laid back with our help. "Just keep me up to date on how Meg is."

"I shall," I vowed and sat on the cot aside him. Meg would grieve for the loss of her babe, but she had been saved. I whispered his Algonquian name, "Kesutanowas Wesin." Wind Talker. I gripped his hand, and afore my eyes his countenance faded 'til I could no longer see him on the bed.

2

Wind Talker

Phoebe withdrew her hand from mine like her fingers had been scalded. "Phoebe?" I switched to Algonquian, "Walks Through Mist." But she still didn't answer. Something had happened. Too exhausted to inquire further, I breathed out and laid my head back.

By the time I woke, Charging Bear sat on the opposite bed beside Meg. He held her hand, then looked over in my direction. "Thank you, brother."

"You would have done the same." He nodded. "How is she?" I asked.

"It will take her awhile to heal, but she will be fine."

Over the next few days, although I tired easily, I regained much of my strength. Meg took longer to recover. Fortunately, we weren't in any hurry to return home to the Appamattuck. Normally, I enjoyed visiting with Phoebe's daughter and family, but I needed to walk the land that originally had belonged to the Paspahegh. Elenor's seven-year-old son had led me along the route the first time. We had roamed the woods, keeping watch for bears and woodpeckers, when he had shown me an arrowhead.

I navigated the trail through the forest to the place where he had taken me until coming to a section that had smaller growth than the surrounding trees. No matter how often I visited, I still got chills running up and down my spine. While the Appamattuck had taken me in and accepted me as one of their own, I was Paspahegh by birth. I stood in the spot where the massacre of my people had taken place.

Guns fired and smoke billowed. Death screams came from every direction. This was where my mother had died. As children, Phoebe and I had barely survived. I moved in the direction of a fallen cypress tree. Brambles caught on the fabric of my wool shirt, but for the most part, I remained unscathed. I made my way through the overgrowth. More panic-stricken screams and shouts pierced my mind. I spotted part of a femur and a bony hand. Ribs, jaw bones, arms—most were partially buried in the loose soil.

These bones were what was left of my people, and my mother was among them. More than thirty years had passed since they had been mass murdered. Most of the warriors had been away on a hunting trip. The town had been left all but defenseless. Elderly men, women, and children had died and been buried in one stinking mass grave.

Only because of a freak of nature, I hadn't been buried with them. Instead, for some inexplicable reason, I had traveled through time to the twentieth century, where I had grown up and eventually became a detective. But my mother had been buried here. I had promised that I would find some way to give my tribe a proper reburial, but I was no closer as to how to go about doing so than when I had returned to the seventeenth century.

The flapping of wings came from nearby. A crow settled on a branch that swayed in the gentle breeze. At first I was uncertain whether it was a real bird or a spirit. When it made a series of clicks and rattles, I knew.

Wind Talker.

The words weren't English or Algonquian, but I heard them in my head.

More rattles. *You will be challenged in the days ahead.*

"In what way?"

Allow me to give you a glimpse.

The jet black bird took flight and I followed. Fog engulfed me. In the beginning, I had needed Phoebe's assistance, along with a candle, to help me focus to enter the dreaming. Now, traveling through the realms came easily. Crow was my spirit guide and led me on my journeys.

In the swirling mist, Crow cawed. I tried to locate the sound, and the wind picked up, reminding me of my true heritage. As a child, I had been known as Crow in the Woods. Because I had been absent from the seventeenth century for most of my life, I had received my adult name, Wind Talker, the year before. At the time, I was informed that I possessed the capabilities of speaking to the wind as easily as I did Crow. Such prophecies continued to elude me.

Out of the mist, a man with the top half of his head painted black approached me. He wore a loincloth, deer-hide leggings, and a bear claw necklace. The right side of his head was shaved, and on the left side his black hair was tied in a knot and held an osprey feather. His prominent cheekbones and the shape of his nose and mouth had an uncanny resemblance to me.

"*Nows*," I said. Father.

Black Owl stretched his arm and intertwined his index finger with mine in an Indian handshake, then he pulled me close and embraced me. "My son, if you're not careful, you will soon join me in the afterlife."

Although I was no stranger in facing death, I would heed any warning. "What should I be on the lookout for?"

"I'm uncertain of the circumstances. You will know when the time comes."

Having delivered his message, Black Owl was swallowed by the mist. Crow cawed, and I moved toward the sound and emerged from the fog. Waves rolled beneath me and wood creaked. My hands and feet were chained to a wooden post. With each sway, groans surrounded me. I was below deck of a sailing ship. Other warriors were chained as I was. I counted at least thirty of us.

The boat met rolling waves that pounded against the fore section and sent a shudder through the hull. The frame vibrated like it was about to be torn apart. The ship pitched, and then all was calm again. Men in armor carrying flintlocks descended upon us. One soldier unlocked my shackles, but clamped them around my wrists again as soon as I was free of the post. Like cattle, we were herded from the bowels of the ship. I nearly stumbled on the steep wooden steps leading to the next deck. After climbing two more decks, light pierced my eyes. I squinted back the brightness.

When I reached the upper deck, my vision gradually adjusted to the light. The soldiers guided us to a gangplank and toward a marshy island. Before I stepped onto the gangplank, mist captured me.

"Wind Talker..."

I blinked back the effects of the dreaming and stood beside the mass grave. Phoebe, with our daughter Heather in her arms, stepped toward me.

"I thought I'd find you here."

Heather was now two, the same age I was when my tribe had been massacred. I scooped her into my arms. She laughed with delight and said, "Poppa." Her two-word sentences were equally fluent in English or Algonquian, and she rarely mixed the two languages. She also imitated many bird calls, as well as barking dogs and animals in the forest.

"You appear bewildered," Phoebe said.

Before returning to the seventeenth century, I had visions of a skeleton that I thought was me, and I had withheld my fear from Phoebe. In reality, the skeleton had been Black Owl, and I had promised myself if I ever faced a similar situation again, I would be upfront with her. "Black Owl came to me with a warning."

"A warning?"

"He says if I'm not careful, I will join him and my mother in the afterlife."

As Phoebe sucked in her breath, Heather squirmed in my arms to be put down. I lowered her to the ground but kept a firm grip on her hand. "Did he give you any clue as to what might happen?"

"No, but afterward I saw myself on a ship..." I told Phoebe about my experience during the dreaming.

When I finished, she said, "We shall continue to seek answers through the dreaming."

The first time Phoebe had mentioned the dreaming, I had been skeptical. In time, traveling through realms had become second nature. Unlike when the skeleton had been uncovered, I didn't fear what lay ahead. Eventually, I would find answers, and I refused to let Heather suffer what I had at her age.

3

Phoebe

THE MEN HAD MADE A TINY PINE CASKET for Meg and Charging Bear's babe. Because he had been born so small, they hadn't needed to dig very deep in order to bury him. Charging Bear lowered the casket into the sandy earth, whilst Elenor said a prayer. Afterwards, he offered the babe an Appamattuck blessing, allowing him to return to the afterlife where he would grow into manhood.

Tears streaked Meg's cheeks, and I placed my arm round her waist. Together, we said a round of "amens," and the men started to shovel dirt to cover the casket. Meg gripped me and wept upon my shoulder. "I didn't even get a chance to know him."

My tears mixed with hers as I recalled the babe I had lost.

Meg's six-year-old daughter Tiffany clenched her momma's hand. "You still have me, Mommy."

My friend cried harder and clutched Tiffany to her breast. "Thank God, and Mommy will always love you."

Wind Talker came o'er to me carrying Heather. Of late, he spent a lot of time with her. Aware that he was vexed about what his fate might be, I realized my own vision of him vanishing was interconnected with his father's warning. In the days to come, we would explore the answers through the dreaming, but for now, we would grieve with Meg and Charging Bear.

The last shovelful of dirt covered the babe's casket, and we returned to the house where Elenor and Bess served dry cornbread and wine. My momma had told me about such gatherings after funerals, but because I had been raised by Indians, I had ne'er partaken. E'en then, Elenor made due with what was available in Virginia as corn originated from this side of the Atlantic.

When the gathering ended, I held Wind Talker's hand and turned to leave. On the morrow, we would return to the Appamattuck.

Afore our journey in the morn, I broke my fast amongst my family and friends. Wind Talker had awoken afore dawn and taken a trail leading from the house. I was certain he traveled to the grave site of his tribe for reflection. 'Twas the only way he would e'er come to terms with what had happened. E'en I recalled the horror, but 'twasn't my family who had died.

Meg said little during our meal, and her countenance was etched in sorrow. Aware that she didn't wish to say goodbye to the babe she had buried, I remained near her side in case she wanted to unburden her grief. On her other side sat my brother. Like so many warriors, Charging Bear remained stoic and refused to shed any tears.

After the meal, we gathered outside. Wind Talker had yet to reappear. Though I would likely interrupt him at the grave, I informed the others I would seek him.

"Momma," Elenor said, "pray leave Heather with me. I'd like to visit with my sister a while longer."

Leaving Heather in Elenor's trusted care, I followed the path to the grave site. Afore I reached the sacred ground, I heard a rich tenor voice. I had so rarely heard Wind Talker sing that at first I didn't recognize him. He greeted the new day in the manner of his people. I waited at a distance, allowing him the chance to finish.

As he sang, he raised his hands to the sky. Instead of the light of day, I saw darkness surround him. His black hair turned gray and deep wrinkles formed on his face. Instead of the muscular body of his youth, he was frail and stooped. His brown flesh shriveled 'til only bleached bones remained.

When I gasped, he turned to me. "Phoebe?"

I blinked. Once again, his hair was black and no wrinkles riddled his countenance. He had changed so much since returning to his people. At one time his hair had been short, now 'twas shoulder length and tied back. "I didn't wish to disturb you again."

He frowned. "I promised them a proper burial, but I haven't figured out a way to go about it."

"Mayhap, you will in time."

He simply nodded. Together, we returned to the house where the others waited. Afore we left, I gripped Elenor's hand and said, "I shall miss you." We hugged, then I embraced Bess. Charging Bear, Meg, and her daughter joined us, and we waved goodbye afore setting off on our journey. We followed a forest trail. Because colonists had encroached on more and more Indian land, we walked farther along the path than when I had first brought Elenor as a small lass to the plantation. With Heather and Tiffany presently alongside us, the trip was slow going. Nearly a day passed afore we arrived at the section of the riverbank where we had left our dugout.

Charging Bear and Wind Talker tossed ferns aside to reveal the boat hidden underneath. I gathered Heather in my arms as the men shoved the canoe from the bank, then they helped Meg, Tiffany, and me inside. Alongside the men, I helped paddle. Tiffany curled up to her momma, hoping to lift her spirits, and Heather pointed at the herons that fished near us.

Paddling upriver, I soon felt the ache in my muscles. 'Twould take twice as long as the journey downriver, but we rowed in a steady rhythm. Once, we spotted a colonial ship and came ashore 'til it was well out of sight, and near sunset, we landed for the night.

Meg and I gathered firewood, whilst the men caught some fish. Afterward, we shared parched cornmeal with the roasted fish. Heather slept betwixt us, when Wind Talker and I collapsed into worn-out heaps. The next morn, we followed tradition and cleansed ourselves in the river, then set out shortly after dawn. A couple of times when we encountered swifter currents, the men tied lines to the dugout, and we walked alongside on the banks.

Near sunset, we arrived at the Appamattuck town of arched houses with woven mats. Some of the women rushed out to greet us, and after a while the men gathered as well. We showed them the gifts of our trade, which included cotton cloth, wool blankets, copper, metal tools, and ammunition for the few flintlocks the men possessed. 'Twas difficult getting such goods because the English had placed death penalties on trading with the Indians after paramount chief Opechancanough's attack the previous year, and I feared for Elenor and her family's lives if they were discovered.

Some of the women shared their food with us. Grateful for their hospitality, I was thankful that 'twould be unnecessary to prepare a meal so late in the day. The eves were warm enough that we ate outside. We told the others about our trip, leaving out what had happened to Meg's babe. After the meal, the men passed a pipe.

All the while, Meg remained despondent, and when we went inside, she said, "Thank you."

"For what?" I asked.

"For not telling them about my baby."

"Should you wish anyone to know, 'tis your place to tell them."

"I also want to thank you for not saying that I can always have another baby."

"Each has a special place in our heart, no matter how long they live."

A hint of a smile crossed Meg's countenance. "They do indeed, but I should have known you would understand. After all, you've lost an older son as well as a baby."

"And I'm comforted they have come of age in the afterlife."

Meg shook her head. "I'm still not certain how many of the Appamattuck philosophies that I believe, but it sounds nice. I'll try to keep that in mind."

Drums beat in a rhythm outside. 'Twas the traditional dance in the eves. "Shall we join them?"

"I'd like that."

We guided Tiffany and Heather to the dance circle. E'en as young as the lasses were, they joined the others as men, women, and children danced to the tempo of the drums round a fire. For the moment, I felt blessed, but then I recalled the vision of Wind Talker vanishing afore my eyes. I made the dance steps, but my heart was no longer in them.

When the dancing ended, I tucked Heather in on the sleeping platform. I often slept with her, but on this night, she preferred Tiffany's company. E'er since returning to the seventeenth century, Wind Talker and I had shared a house with Charging Bear, Meg, and my brother's son Strong Bow. In that time, Heather had come to view Tiffany as an older sister.

Barely were the lasses settled when Charging Bear and Strong Bow returned. I looked past them, hoping to see Wind Talker. Concerned, I glanced at Meg. "Go ahead," she said. "You know I'll look after Heather."

"Thank you." I made my way outside, where the town was now quiet. The moon cast enough light to see by, and when I reached the river, I spotted Wind Talker sitting on the bank, staring out upon the water. "Wind Talker," I said in Algonquian. "I know you're troubled by what you've seen."

He stood and faced me. "It's not just that. I've been asked by the Kiskiack if I can help as an interpreter."

Since our return to this time, he often carried the responsibility of being a mediator betwixt the tribes and colonists. E'en though he was uncertain if he could change the future, he viewed the role as his mission in order to try and save our people. In these tense times and after the vision of him vanishing, I feared for his safety. As his wife, I would ne'er admit as much aloud. "Mayhap the dreaming can give you answers."

He smiled slightly. "You've read my mind."

"How could I read...?"

He kissed me on the lips afore I could finish. "Never mind, it appears I've used another twenty-first-century phrase that you haven't heard. I would like to enter the dreaming with you at my side."

The first time I had shown him the dreaming, he had difficulty concentrating on anything but carrying me to the bedroom. His smile widened to a grin. Aware that he was contemplating the same now, I grasped his hands. "You asked to enter the dreaming, not make love."

"I thought you didn't read my mind."

"Whilst I fail to comprehend the phrase, your thoughts are evident."

To this, he laughed and drew me into his arms. "Phoebe, I love you."

"Later, my love. Let us find the answers you seek."

He kissed me once again and lowered his arms, keeping a firm grip upon my hands. "The dreaming."

On our first venture, I used a candle in order to help him concentrate. In spite of his distraction, such formalities were unnecessary now. I recalled my first journey. A magnificent, sleek white hound stood afore us. His long legs were well muscled, and his frame was made for coursing. Faster than the wind, the dog raced through the forest with his feet barely touching the ground.

The mist swirled round us and grew thicker and thicker. As we walked, I felt smaller. When I emerged from the fog, I stood on a sandy bank. Wind Talker was nowhere nearby. Nearly naked except for a doe-hide apron, I inspected my body. My arms were bony, and I had no breasts of a woman. I was but a lass again. A lad scribbled lines in the sand with his fingers, and I overheard a woman's laughter.

A crow cawed, but 'twasn't a bird making the sound. The lad was Crow in the Woods. At the time, I had no idea that he would become Wind Talker. E'en at two years, he could mimic most animal sounds. I glanced o'er my shoulder. Two women gathered herbs and placed them in a leather satchel. Snow Bird had her long black hair pulled back in a single braid, and she had bangs. She was Crow in the Woods's momma, and I hadn't seen her since . . . I caught my breath. She had died in the Paspahegh massacre.

Aside Snow Bird stood my momma. Her hair was blonde and like Snow Bird's, it was braided down the back. She wore a deerskin skirt and shell-bead necklace. Dogwood blossom tattoos encircled her upper arms. "Momma," I said aloud.

She looked o'er at me. "Is something wrong, Red Dog?"

At the sound of my childhood name, I smiled at her in fondness, for she had died later in life from the smallpox.

She motioned for me to check on Crow in the Woods. Instead of scribbling in the sand, he covered himself in dirt. Momma laughed. I was supposed to have been watching him and would be the one responsible for cleaning him. "Crow in the Woods," I said in a stern voice.

The lad continued pouring sand upon himself, and momma laughed harder. When I went o'er to stop him, he shot off like an arrow. I chased after him along the river bank. Just as I about reached him, he pulled up short. At the end of the trail stood a man in a woolen shirt, breechclout, and moccasins. His black hair was tied back, and he had dark brown eyes and brown skin. He wore a deer-antler arrowhead round his neck. "Wind Talker."

I blinked. Except for the light of the moon, darkness surrounded me once more, and I held Wind Talker's hands.

An impish grin crossed his countenance. "I'm sorry that I caused you so much difficulty when I was little."

I shrugged. " 'Twas naught."

He shook his head. "But I don't understand. Why were we seeing me as both an adult and a child? We only saw you as a young girl."

"I *was* the lass in the dreaming. Which one were you?"

"Me, as I am now."

I contemplated the meaning. Except to relive a more peaceful time, I could not fathom why I would view myself as a child. " 'Tis puzzling, but 'tis the way of the dreaming. In time, we shall learn what it means." For some reason, I shivered. I could not shake the sudden feeling of doom. My trembling increased.

Wind Talker rubbed my arms. "What's wrong?"

I caught myself, then reached up to stroke his cheek. " 'Tis naught."

"Are you sure?"

"Aye." I pressed my hips next to his, and he bent down to kiss me. Thankful that I had distracted him, I reciprocated with a kiss of my own. In his arms, I had always felt safe, and as he explored my body, I could pretend the dire vision had not been a warning.

4

Wind Talker

AFTER MAKING LOVE WITH PHOEBE, I was more relaxed than I had been in a long time. Hand in hand, we returned to the *yi-hakan*. House. Everyone else was already asleep, and there we made love again. Upon my return to the seventeenth century, I had gradually adjusted to the concept that absolute privacy was a thing of my past. Most *yi-hakans* had more than one family living in them. For convenience sake, Charging Bear shared his home with Phoebe and me.

At night there was no light, except for the fire embers in the center, and this gave some solitude. Meg had the greatest difficulty adjusting to the new lifestyle and hung a blanket between their personal area and ours. The living space almost made it seem like dormitory life in college.

In the morning, following the daily ritual of bathing in the river, I met with William Carter. The year before, he had been an indentured servant who had run off from an abusive master. He had aided my family and me on more than one occasion. As a result, he had been welcomed by the Appamattuck, even though he had yet to officially join the tribe. Not that anyone was terribly concerned, as he contributed in any way that he could, making him and his girlfriend Chloe honored guests. Thankfully, though, for everyone near him, he had forsaken the colonial habit of not bathing. I still recalled the stench that emanated from him when we first met.

"I've been asked by the Kiskiack to help as an interpreter and was hoping you would join me," I said.

" 'Tis a long journey. 'Tis also near where I originally lived."

"It'll likely take us a few days to get there. My brother, Wildcat, will meet us, but if you think it's too risky that your former master will find you—"

"Nay, I'll join you. Let me inform Chloe."

Like I had so often done when I was a detective in the twenty-first century, I kissed my family and waved goodbye. Only now, the separation would be measured in days, rather than hours. Our journey started by boat. We rowed along the Appomattox River until we joined with the James, where we continued for several miles. Instead of traveling as far as Elenor's, we passed a river branch and brought the dugout up on the bank.

We gathered our packs loaded with supplies and placed them on our backs. Part of me regretted not taking Charging Bear up on his offer to accompany us for this portion of the trip, but Wildcat was supposed to meet us, and Meg still needed Charging Bear's presence. I tried not to dwell on what would happen if Wildcat missed connections with us, as neither William nor I knew exactly where we were going.

For midsummer, the air was cool. For that saving grace, I was grateful. At least traveling with William, I didn't have difficulty keeping pace. Even though he was nineteen, and I, thirty-eight, his physical endurance failed to match the native people, including mine. We walked along a palisade where the timbers were lopsided and others lay on the ground. After the paramount chief Opechancanough's attack the previous year, new forts had been built, and others, like this wall, were no longer considered necessary and falling to ruin.

"Chloe wants to get married," William said, breaking our silence.

Thankful for his distraction, I asked, "That's a good thing, isn't it?"

"She wants a Christian ceremony."

I detected more that he wasn't telling me, but such sidestepping was a common occurrence with William. He had taken a long time to trust anyone. Not that I could blame him, but he was one of the few in this century that I could call a friend. "Do you want the same?"

Circle in Time 25

"I don't know. These days..."

I placed my hand on his arm and gestured to the trail ahead of us. He nodded that he saw the traveler. The man's body was painted black, and his long black hair was tied in a knot. As he approached us, I smiled and moved toward him. When we met, we intertwined index fingers in greeting. "Good to see you, brother."

Wildcat smiled and turned to William and gave him the same Indian handshake. "It's good to see both of you."

Relieved that Wildcat had joined us, I felt certain we would arrive safely at our destination without getting lost. We talked about our first journey together, where I had traveled to the Northern Neck region to meet the rest of my family for the first time. On that trip, we had also met William. Although he had grown accustomed to wearing moccasins, he continued to wear linen shirts and wool breeches. In some way, he reminded me of myself at his age and being caught between cultures. The tug between the two was likely more apparent with Chloe's recent request.

Now that Wildcat accompanied us, William and I had difficulty keeping pace. I placed my pack on my brother's back. This only slightly slowed Wildcat, and he continued to outdistance us. Oftentimes, he doubled back just to make certain nothing had happened to us. Unlike other trips, in this one we came across no travelers. Most of the tribal people had moved further west, and the majority of the colonists had yet to move inland. I found myself missing the tradition of stopping for a chat and passing a pipe.

As we walked by bushes with ripe fruit, we picked raspberries and blackberries. At night, we roasted a fish that William had caught earlier in the day. Afterward, we passed the pipe and brought each other up to date since our last meeting. Wildcat's and my sister, New Moon, had given birth to another son in the spring. She already had twins around the age of four, and I presumed they kept her very busy.

Finally, we bedded down for the night. No matter how often I slept on the hard ground, I never got used to it. While I tossed and turned, William snored. In the distance, the haunting trill of a screech owl swept through the forest. On similar nights, I would rise and attempt to enter the dreaming. Why not? I got to my feet and tried to envision the flame of the candle in my mind.

Nothing. Even the wind was quiet. The owl got closer. During the great assault, warriors had mimicked the call. Except for present company, there were likely no warriors in the area now. When the owl quit trilling, only the buzz of some insect remained.

"Wind Talker..."

Startled by Wildcat's voice, I turned toward where the sound had come from. The night was so dark that I couldn't see him. "I was unable to sleep," I said. I went on to tell him about the vision I had of our father's warning.

"Then we shall proceed with caution."

"I'd prefer if you'd continue on home after we reach the Kiskiack."

"Wind Talker, we're brothers. We shall remain united in whatever awaits us."

I should have known he would take that stance. I would have done the same had our situation been reversed. "Then promise me you won't take any foolish risks. I've already given one transfusion this month. I can't easily give another so soon."

Even though I couldn't see his face, I knew he smiled. "Your lifeblood runs through me. I'm forever grateful. I'll take measures to prevent such conditions from arising again."

"Good. Shall we try and get some sleep?"

We returned to the campsite where William continued to snore. Once again, I stretched out on the ground. Sleep eluded me, and the night dragged. When dawn arrived, I struggled to my feet. I had a sudden craving for a strong pot of coffee. When I was a detective, I had practically survived on caffeine. Until now, the desire had been snuffed for over a year.

With no river or pond nearby, we had to forgo our daily bath, but I had grown accustomed to giving thanks and saying prayers to welcome the new day. Wildcat offered us some dry, chewy meat that looked like jerky. I had no idea what it was and didn't care to. After the quick bite, we set out for the day. The rest of the day passed without event, and when the sun got low in the sky, we approached the Kiskiack town. All was quiet. Too quiet for my liking. No warriors greeted us, and no children played. No women scurried about preparing meals.

Wildcat readied his bow, and William's face creased with worry. When we reached the clearing, scorched ruins greeted us. Houses had been reduced to charcoal. Ashes no longer smoldered and were long cold. Even so, firing guns pierced my mind. I envisioned a woman with her black hair pulled back in a single braid. She screamed and fell to the ground. I swayed unsteadily on my feet.

"Wind Talker..."

At the sound of Wildcat's voice, I blinked back the vision of my town being burned and my mother murdered.

"They escaped," he said. "There are no bodies."

Both Wildcat and William had a grip on my arms to help support me. I looked around at the blackened timbers. "No bodies?"

"They escaped," Wildcat repeated. "We need to see if we can discover where they might have fled to."

Blinking back the vision, I shook my head and began sifting through the debris. I wished I had a forensic team to aid in the search. Such a group wouldn't come into existence for at least another century, and many more years would pass before they reached the level to which I was accustomed. Still, I had been a detective long enough to have a reasonable grasp of studying the evidence for clues.

I tossed aside what was left of a mat that had served as a wall for a house. Beneath it, I found a tiny charred body in the typical burned-body pose of flexed elbows and knees with clenched fists. "Not all of them made it out alive." Sick to my stomach, I reached for the small child. There was no way to tell if the corpse was a boy or a girl, but something inside told me she was a girl. I thought of Heather. If circumstances had been different, the toddler could have been her. I let out an anguished cry. "When does it end? They destroy towns, murder, and rape."

"We'll bury the child," William said. "I'll find some digging tools."

As I turned to him, I caught a tortured expression on Wildcat's face. As a father too, he understood my grief. With sticks and hands, the three of us dug into the scorched ground. Finally, the hole was big enough, and we carefully placed the remains inside. We covered her with dirt. When we finished, I sang and the others joined me.

A child so young—the belief that she would grow to adulthood in the afterlife failed to comfort me.

A crow flew overhead and landed on a nearby branch. While it wasn't the dozen or more that had joined me when my father had died, I was pleased to see the lone bird. The bird cawed in a raspy tone as if it were giving a speech, then finally it flew off. Paying my final respects, I stood beside the grave a while longer and said a silent prayer. Wildcat and William had already moved off. I started in their direction, when I heard a branch snap in the woods.

I turned toward the sound. A brown-haired man in a tattered shirt and breeches aimed a pistol. Before I could react, I reeled to the ground. Blinding pain radiated through my head and gunfire surrounded me. Something warm ran in my eye.

The brown-haired man stood over me. "You're not so tough now, savage."

Drifting, I fought through the layers of fog. "Wildcat and William?"

"This one speaks English," the man shouted over his shoulder.

His face remained a blur. Fog sucked me under, and my head thumped back. Rough hands jerked me to my feet. If they hadn't maintained a solid grip on my arms, I would have fallen again. Faces shimmered in and out of focus. As darkness engulfed me, I thought of Phoebe.

5

Phoebe

MY HEART POUNDED AND I BROKE into a cold sweat. *Wind Talker.* I had the overwhelming feeling that he was in danger. As the sensation gradually faded, I breathed easier. When he had nearly died, the feeling had failed to pass, and when he had traveled through time, I had heard him summon me. This experience was neither. I could make no sense of the meaning and continued applying a jewelweed poultice to Charging Bear's son's leg. Strong Bow scratched the poison ivy rash. "Don't scratch," I said. "You'll make it worse."

The boy followed my command, and I finished wrapping the poultice round his leg, whilst Meg looked on. "So you crush the leaves for the poultice?" she asked.

"Aye." At least a spark was beginning to return to my friend's eyes, and she was again taking an interest in learning a cunning woman's ways. "Not only does it soothe, it prevents the rash from spreading." Then, I felt it again. My heart pounded so hard, it seemed like it had drifted to my throat. I sucked in my breath.

"Phoebe?"

Once again, the sense of danger passed, and I nodded to Meg that I was all right. Throughout the day and into the next as I went about my chores, I kept receiving brief sensations about Wind Talker being in peril. In the eve, when I put Heather to bed, I overheard excited voices. I poked my head out of the house to discover what the commotion was about. When I spied William, I knew. I moved towards him. "He's dead."

He shook his head. "Not when I last saw him, but the colonists have taken him. Wildcat and I managed to escape. He's following the trail to find out where they've taken Wind Talker. I returned to tell you what has happened."

"Tell me all you know."

William told me of their journey and meeting Wildcat, and of sifting through the burned Kiskiack town. He relayed the finding of a child in the ash, and I choked back a sob. After they buried her, Wind Talker had been taken by the colonists. "He was wounded," William said, "but I couldn't tell if 'twas serious. Wildcat and I barely escaped."

"Thank you for telling me." I thought o'er the predicament.

"Wildcat says he'll meet me at Elenor's plantation."

"Then I shall go with you."

In the morn, I said goodbye to my family and friends. Heather saw the trip as a great adventure, whilst William and I sailed down the James River. 'Twas much faster than our earlier journey upriver. Though the two of us had the same skin tone as the colonists, Heather and the dugout would give away our association with Indians. As a result, more than once, we dodged colonial ships and came ashore.

By nightfall, we arrived at Elenor's. She was pleased to see us 'til we told her what had happened. Her husband Christopher listened to our story and mulled it o'er. "On the morrow, I'll go into James Towne and see if I can find out what has happened."

"I shall go with you," I said.

"Nay. You cannot. You've already been tried twice for being a witch and escaped."

"I shall disguise myself. They'll ne'er know who I really am, but I must learn what has become of Wind Talker." O'ernight, using black walnut, I dyed my red hair a dark brown and donned a skirt and leather shoes. I pinned my hair back and placed a cap o'er it. We went out to the dock, where I kissed Heather goodbye. Elenor clutched her hand, and Christopher shoved the boat away from the dock and guided it towards James Towne. I helped Christopher row. Plantations passed. Since my arrival in 1609, more and more colonists had reached Virginia's shores. In the fields, Africans worked alongside those who hailed from England.

One servant waved as we went by. I returned the wave, and we continued downriver. After several hours, we neared the island. Other boats were on the river, and up ahead, near the port, sizable sailing ships were anchored. I swallowed. The first time I had been tried for witchcraft, I was sentenced to return to England. I had escaped afore the sentence came about. If I were caught again, the authorities would not go easy on me.

Instead of rowing directly to the port, Christopher turned into the bay, where the current was less swift, making rowing much easier. Though many years had passed since I had lived here, I recognized the landmarks. We avoided the mud flats and rounded some sandy banks. The bay narrowed, and we entered the Back River. Less than a mile later, we rowed towards shore.

Near the bank, Christopher waved for me to stay put and got out of the boat. "No need for you to get wet afore necessary." He sloshed through the swamp and brought the boat onto the bank. After I got out, he gestured the direction. "This way."

As the sun slipped in the sky, we traveled through the cypress and pine forest. In the twenty-first century, Wind Talker had brought me here to the National Park that celebrated the first successful English settlement. E'en though the park had attempted to reconstruct the original colony, I had seen little resemblance to the settlement of my first memories, but then I had been a mere lass when I'd first arrived.

The water swirled round my knees as we waded through the swamp. We startled a buck, and he dodged amongst the trees for a better hiding place. Finally, we reached dry land. A double-pitched frame house came into view. We skirted the governor's house and reached a rutted lane known as Back Street. We passed a wattle and daub house. People gathered near the riverfront. I gasped. A cow pen contained not livestock, but Indians.

Christopher and I moved towards them. In the fading daylight, I couldn't see how many the enclosure contained, but 'twas a group of men, women, and children. Guards with flintlocks were stationed at strategic corners, and the mob outside pointed at the captives and jeered. I checked the sullen countenances to see if Wind Talker was amongst them.

"Christopher," I whispered.

He hushed me. "I know what you're going to suggest, but 'tis beyond our capabilities."

Though I didn't want to make such a confession to myself, I knew he spoke the truth. Two of us against many—we could ne'er find a way of releasing all of them. I kept searching the faces and spied mommas consoling their children as well as warriors filled with rage. They stood ready to assault their captors should the opportunity arise.

A woman with a small lad in her arms came up to the rails and pleaded, "*Mammahe sucawahum.*"

She had asked for water. E'ery bone in my body ached, but I pretended not to understand her words. I continued looking at the countenances—more and more of them. There must have been at least fifty in the overcrowded pen. The stench of human waste assaulted my nostrils. Nauseated, I pressed a hand to my belly. Christopher lent me a steadying hand. I nodded that I would be fine and continued searching amongst sunken faces and withered hands. I had no doubt that food was in as short of supply as water.

Amongst a cluster of arms and legs, none had enough space to truly stretch out. Some curled on the hard ground, whilst babes cried their share of tears. I spied a warrior lying on the ground. His head was wrapped in a bloodstained cloth. At first, I didn't recognize him, then I closed my eyes to keep the tears at bay.

Taking a deep breath, I rounded the pen and moved towards Wind Talker with Christopher bearing down upon my heels. "Phoebe," he said in a loud whisper. "Pray don't do anything foolish."

Outside the rail, I came to a halt a few feet away from Wind Talker. Careful not to alert the guards, I checked o'er my shoulder. With their constant surveillance, I had to remain cautious, but I needed to know how badly injured he was. "Kesutanowas Wesin." He failed to move as if he had not heard me. I repeated his name.

He angled his head in my direction and blinked, but his gaze remained fixed and unable to focus.

My heart thumped. The guards had not overheard me, so I tried again. "Wind Talker." I detected bewilderment in his eyes.

"Elenor?"

With his question, I recalled my dark hair and whispered, "Nay. Wind Talker, how badly have you been hurt?"

"I think it's a graze. Now, go away. There's nothing you can do to help."

As I was about to protest, Christopher grasped my arm and led me away. We strolled along the riverfront. "You've lingered too long. The guards were growing suspicious."

"We need to help him."

"Phoebe, I shall make inquiries, but I fear Wind Talker is right. There may be naught we can do to help any of them."

"Naught? Christopher..."

"Pray let me check into the circumstances."

If I could do naught else, I would find a way to make Wind Talker and the others more comfortable.

6
Wind Talker

Though my head hurt like hell, I was lucky the wound had been a graze. I had no idea how much time had passed. Had I really seen Phoebe? I had been unable to clearly see who the man was that accompanied her, but he must have been William or Christopher. Suddenly less groggy, I sat up. The world around me spun. I placed a hand to my head until the swirling motion halted, then I struggled to my feet. When I swayed, a woman latched onto my arm to help steady me. I nodded that I was fine and thanked her.

Most of the other captives were Pamunkey, but a few other tribes were represented. Part of me hoped I'd see Phoebe again. At the same time, I didn't want her risking her life by remaining in Jamestown. I staggered along the perimeter of the fence, noting the guards in key positions. Exhausted before I returned to where I had begun, I reseated myself on the ground before I fell. My vision blurred, and I lowered my aching head to the hard ground and closed my eyes.

"Are you Wind Talker?" came a colonial accent.

"Who's asking?" I asked without reopening my eyes.

I heard the sound of a pistol being cocked. "We need someone to translate for us. Since you indeed speak English, you must be who I'm looking for. If you fail to drop the pretense, no one will care that I shoot a disrespectful savage."

I gritted my teeth to keep from hurling the insulting curses that popped into my head. "I am Wind Talker," I said as evenly as possible.

"Then get up."

I gripped the rails of the enclosure to help keep me steady and got to my feet. The guard waved his pistol for me to head toward the gate. I moved in that direction. He opened the gate and motioned for me to keep moving. With my splitting headache and fuzzy vision, I shuffled along as best as I could. The narrow path led away from the riverfront, past a couple of gardens. Beans and squash—food that my own people could use—were being harvested by indentured servants. The guard brought me to a small house. Inside were a couple of tables and several chairs.

A gray-bearded, middle-aged man, wearing a slashed-sleeve doublet stood behind the nearest table. I had no doubt that he was a man of political importance in the colony. "You're Wind Talker?" he asked.

"I am."

"Master Stillwell," he said gruffly. "Are you Pamunkey?"

"No, I'm Paspahegh."

He looked at me in disbelief. "Paspahegh? I hadn't realized any survived."

My knees were weak and I felt dizzy. "I was a child at the time of the attack. I took refuge with another tribe. Do you mind if I sit down?"

Stillwell motioned for me to be seated, and I thankfully eased myself onto a chair. "What was your role in the massacre?"

Why were bloodbaths regarded as a massacre when Indians killed whites but not the other way around? Thinking better of voicing my question aloud, I responded, "I spoke to the Quiyoughcohannock to save colonists' lives."

"Were they saved?"

"All but one. Henry Wynne died in a barn fire when he tried to rescue the livestock."

He nodded that he knew of the incident. "A fire started by the savages?"

I refused to call my own people by that term. "The fire was started by the Quiyoughcohannock."

"An affirmative would have sufficed."

In my past life as a detective, I was used to being the interrogator, not the one being questioned. As a result, I was aware that remaining silent and waiting patiently for his questions would be less likely to piss him off.

"I have influence with the council," Stillwell finally continued. "Because you were not directly involved in the massacre and attempted to help, I may be able to keep you from being prosecuted along with the other prisoners. Would you be willing to aid us in translation?"

"Yes."

"Then I shall call you at the appropriate time." He waved at the guard to return me to the holding pen.

I stood. My head throbbed, but somehow I made my way to the door and back to the enclosure. With little shade, women and children sweltered in the midday summer sun. I turned to the guard. "Can you ask Master Stillwell for more water? The children are suffering."

He grunted a response, and I had my doubts that he would actually do anything to help. Like before, I found a spot on the ground. Rations were sparse, and late in the day, we received a small portion of gritty, weevil-infested cornbread. Some warriors managed to snare a couple of rats with their bare hands. After suffocating the rodents, they handed them over to the women for the children.

Catching vermin or being treated like one—I was uncertain which was worse. Outside the pen, colonists taunted us that we would be beheaded or burned at the stake. Occasionally, rotten tomatoes sailed over the rails, striking innocent victims. The guards merely laughed.

In spite of the distractions, all I wanted to do was sleep. With little space between my neighbors, I huddled on the ground. Like so many times before, I tossed and turned, but finally, I drifted.

"Wind Talker..."

I opened my eyes. This time though fuzzy, I could see Phoebe. I almost said her name but caught myself. She had gone to the trouble of dyeing her hair so she wouldn't be recognized. The last thing I needed to do was to give away her identity to the guards. We stared at one another, neither of us speaking. I longed to touch her, and almost felt we had been closer when we had been separated by four centuries. At least then, we could contact each other through the dreaming and feel as if we were together.

She glanced away, then looked at me again. With her eyes, she said goodbye and walked away.

Over the next few days, in spite of the lack of decent food, I surprisingly regained some of my strength. My head throbbed less and my vision improved. One of the women unwound the cloth around my head and told me that the wound looked much better. Unable to bathe and wishing I could cleanse the filth from my skin, I scratched at the fleas and lice.

Like a ghost, Phoebe reappeared several times. We never spoke and occasionally she joined the crowd to pretend she was part of them. Although I enjoyed seeing her, I hoped she didn't plan anything foolish. On a scorchingly hot day, sweat poured down my chest. She stood outside the rail, watching me. I nodded that I was fine, but a guard walked between us.

At first, he glanced at me, then over his shoulder at Phoebe. She rejoined the other colonists, jeering at the captives. "Stillwater wants to see ye," he said.

As I was escorted to the gate, I looked for Phoebe. She had vanished from the crowd. Again, I was taken to the same house a short distance from the riverfront. The same tables and chairs lined the room. Even though the room was hot and stuffy, I was relieved to be out of the sun for a short period.

Stillwater stood behind the table, and he motioned for me to be seated. "Wind Talker..."

I did as he instructed and waited for him to speak.

He cleared his throat. "I would like for you to speak to the men and find out how many colonists each of them has murdered."

"That's the translation you want me to aid you with?"

"It is."

Suddenly pissed, I no longer held back. "Let me get this straight, we've got women and children dying of heatstroke—"

"What pray tell is heatstroke?"

"Never mind. It doesn't seem to translate from the Algonquian," I lied. "I've been trying to make our concerns known to you, but the guards won't deliver my messages. Now, you want me to spy on my kinsmen."

"We can make life easier for you, Wind Talker. I have noticed that a woman visits you most days. I can't help wonder why."

I played innocent. "The only woman who has visited me is the one who tended to my head. She is locked in the same hog pen as I was."

"Very well, as you wish." He motioned to the guard.

I stood. "I suspect you've already made up your minds what you intend on doing to us—all of us."

"The council has yet to decide, but I held the belief you differed from the rest."

Ready to throw a punch, I clenched my hands. The guard glared at me, daring me, with a hand on his pistol. I relaxed and took a deep breath. He smirked and motioned for me to return to the holding pen. I complied.

By the time we reached the pen, a crowd had gathered as another captive was thrown inside. My heart sank upon seeing Wildcat. The gate locked behind us. Except for a few cuts and scratches, he looked in fair shape. With his eyes wide in a threat, he hissed at the guards. "It doesn't do any good, brother," I said.

He finally looked in my direction. "Wind Talker?"

I motioned for him to come away from the gate. The guards finally relaxed, and we found a spot out of earshot. Even though most colonists didn't speak Algonquian, I preferred not taking any chances. "I had hoped you'd be spared."

"I sent William to the Appamattuck to alert the others that you had been captured."

"They know. They've found me. Wildcat, why did you need to follow me? There was no reason for the both of us to be captured."

"I said we would remain united. I meant it."

I couldn't damn him for his loyalty. "You also promised me that you wouldn't take any foolish risks."

"I didn't. I surrendered before they could shoot me."

To what end? The colonists would likely execute all of us anyway.

* * *

A few days passed before Stillwell summoned me again. "I plead your case. The council has decided that the women and children will be sold. All men o'er eleven years of age will be sent on Sir William's ship to the western island, to prevent their returning to and strengthening their respective tribes."

So they weren't going to execute us outright.

When I failed to respond, he continued, "The council took into consideration your help during the massacre, but I fear that your refusal to continue with your aid has forced them to decide to send you along with the rest of the men to the western island."

I had no idea whether Western Island had a twenty-first century name that I might recognize, but I fully expected the treatment and merely nodded.

"Wind Talker, you will die there."

He almost sounded apologetic. "Then I will die with my kinsmen."

He shook his head. "I have ne'er understood such philosophy. Why do you prefer death? I still may be able to sway the council's opinion."

"I've already told you that I won't spy for you. Besides, what good is the information you sought now? You've already sentenced them to death—obviously a slow one."

"So be it. You have chosen your path. You leave on the morrow" Stillwater waved to the guard.

The guard grinned in triumph as he returned me to the hog pen. Once inside, I informed the others what fate awaited us. Some of the women clutched their children tighter. Others wept. Wildcat's and the other younger warriors' faces hardened, ready to renew hostilities with the colonists. Such a move would be futile. Outnumbered and outgunned, we could do little but accept our destiny. This event must be the one that Black Owl had warned me about, and I had failed miserably.

One warrior raised a fist and gave a whoop. He clambered over the fence rail. Before he reached the other side, a guard fired his flintlock. His body crumpled to the ground. As more warriors moved forward, a line of flintlocks raised.

"Wind Talker..."

I turned to see Phoebe near the fence. While Wildcat kept watch, the distraction gave me the opportunity to speak with her. I hurried with my message. "They're sending the men to Western Island. The women and children are being sold into slavery."

"Christopher can—"

"No, Phoebe. Don't ask him. It's too dangerous." She gripped the rail. The guards remained distracted, and I briefly caressed her hand. "I love you."

As her gaze met mine, her face filled with despair. "We mustn't let it end like this."

Wildcat tapped me on the arm. The guards had settled the commotion, and I drew away from Phoebe. "I don't think we have a choice."

One guard started toward us, and Phoebe moved into the crowd of colonists. I watched her until she vanished among the group. During the rest of the day, I paced. Phoebe lingered nearby, but thankfully, she didn't chance approaching me again. Throughout the night, sobs surrounded me. None of us could sleep, and voices whispered their goodbyes. On dawn's arrival, a few went through the motions of welcoming the day, but most faces were solemn in fear of what the day would bring.

We didn't wait long. The guards descended upon us, shackling the men with heavy chains. First Wildcat, then my turn came. I held out my arms, and the guard clamped the chains about my wrists. Afterward came my ankles. As soon as all of the men were chained, they motioned for us to move toward the gate. Wildcat and I walked together. Left behind, women wailed as we were herded away.

Outside the gate, men in armor escorted us through the Jamestown street. Sticks, stones, even horse excrement flew in our direction. A rock struck me in the ribs, but I kept walking with my head held high. Suddenly, I had the feeling that Phoebe was nearby. I glanced toward the crowd. Even though her hair remained dark brown, I saw red. How I longed to touch her silky skin and breathe in her herbal scent.

We reached the port, where a sailing ship, which reminded me of the replicas at one of the historical parks in the twenty-first century, was anchored. This ship was no replica and would be taking us to our fate. One last time, I searched the crowd. Phoebe remained among them. Before I stepped onto the gangplank, I whispered, "Goodbye."

7

Phoebe

WIND TALKER MOUTHED that fateful word, and my heart lurched. My eyes misted as I watched him and Wildcat stride up the gangplank. For some reason, I thought of the time when I had first shown him the dreaming. He had escorted me to his apartment in the twenty-first century, where I first viewed his Indian collection of arrowheads, medicine pouches, and blankets. At that time, I had been drawn to a dreamcatcher with a trail of beads and feathers and had informed him the sacred colors of white, red, yellow, and black represented the four winds. E'en then, I saw neath his exterior and what was in his heart. He had been cut off from his heritage.

Now, he reached the deck of the pinnace. He glanced o'er his shoulder afore being led below. I stood there waiting, hoping against hope that I was merely living through a nightmare, and he might reappear. The last of the warriors vanished below deck.

The summer morn already grew hot, yet I shivered. I rubbed my arms, but naught would rid me of the chill deep in my bones. I watched 'til the ship sailed. E'en when the pinnace grew distant, I could not look away.

"Phoebe..." Christopher gripped my arms to lead me away from the scene. Still, I resisted, but he managed to guide me from the main thoroughfare and away from the mob. "He's being taken to the western island," I said.

"Aye, I was able to learn that much. I know where it is. I can—"

"Wind Talker said not to ask you."

"You didn't," he replied.

"He said 'twas too dangerous."

"Phoebe, I don't know how many I can rescue with only a small shallop, but the western island has no fresh water. They won't survive for long."

" 'Tis in the bay?" I asked.

"Aye."

"Then we should enlist William's aid."

8

Wind Talker

WAVES ROLLED BENEATH ME and wood creaked. I had no idea how long I had been aboard the ship. Below deck and chained to a post, I couldn't actually see whether it was day or night, but I was certain several days must have passed. With each sway, groans surrounded me. My stomach churned, and for once, I was thankful we had been given few rations.

The boat met rolling waves that pounded against the fore section and sent a shudder through the hull. The frame vibrated like it was being torn apart. As the ship pitched, I realized that I was living the vision my father had warned about.

Concentrate. If only I could enter the dreaming, I'd be lifted from bleak reality into another realm—hopefully a better one. No matter how hard I focused my mind on the candle flame, I could not escape.

Beside my foot, a rat squeaked. If my stomach hadn't been queasy, I would have captured the rodent. After nearly a month being held captive in Jamestown, I was no longer too proud in joining the others in eating rats. Instead of killing the rat, I curled into a ball on the floor and closed my eyes.

Back and forth—the ship continued to rock. When would the pitching end? I thought of Phoebe. The way she tilted her head, or when she was angry, her face got as red as her hair. I almost laughed, but then I dreamed of her radiant smile of satisfaction after the last time we had made love.

My thoughts shifted to Heather. No matter how hard I tried to remain a presence in her life, I kept vanishing from it. Like me, she'd grow up thinking someone else was her father. At her birth, I had coached Phoebe through the pain. As a cop, I had helped another woman through childbirth, but the event was drastically different with my own wife.

At first Phoebe had thought my presence was bad luck, and she had to lay down her superstition about a man being present. Even so, she had circled the room and said a prayer in every corner to protect her and the baby against vengeful spirits.

When she lay on her side, the midwife massaged her legs, while I stroked her hair. "You're doing great, Phoebe."

A contraction caught Phoebe off guard. Her fingernails dug into my hand, but she refused to cry out. " 'Tis time to push." In Paspahegh fashion, she knelt.

The midwife placed absorbent pads on the floor, and Phoebe clenched my hand tighter. Her eyes brimmed with tears, but she still didn't cry out. I remained by her side. Her face wrinkled and she gritted her teeth. Blood ran down her legs, turning the pads red.

I urged her on.

The midwife applied warm towels to Phoebe's genitals and massaged the area, then motioned for me to be ready to catch the baby. The baby's head appeared between Phoebe's legs. Another push, and the baby's head was free. I held the head in my hands. Another contraction, and a blood-covered infant slid into my arms. I beamed with pride at the birth of our daughter.

But I wasn't attending Heather's birth. The memory had been a welcome distraction from where I really was. My wrists crusted with scabs from where the shackles chafed them, but thankfully, the ship sailed on calm waters again and made a gentle rocking motion, relieving my nausea. Time—it really had no meaning here. I had completely lost any sense of it.

The boat continued to sway, but forward motion seemed to have stopped. I couldn't be certain until pounding footsteps came from overhead. Armor-clad men carrying flintlocks descended upon us. One soldier unlocked my shackles, but clamped them around my wrists again as soon as I was free of the wooden post. Like livestock, we were herded from the bowels of the ship. My legs were weak from being left in the same spot for days, and I nearly stumbled on the steep steps leading to the next deck. Climbing two more decks was agonizing. I stumbled up the steps. Near the top, light pierced my eyes. I squinted against the glare and faltered.

My vision gradually adjusted to the light when I reached the upper deck. A soldier shoved me to keep me moving and I nearly fell. They guided us down the gangplank to a marshy island populated by tall loblolly pines. When all of the men were brought onto a beach, I finally saw Wildcat. We were ordered to wait in line, and I became the unofficial translator.

Seamen rolled a keg of water down the gangplank and informed us it was our only source of freshwater. After that, we would need to resort to catching rainwater. A satchel of moldy cornbread was tossed on the ground, and the colonists returned to their ship. We watched as they raised the gangplank and sailed away. Before long, the sails faded on the horizon.

There were nearly thirty of us, and we scouted the island in groups. It was about two miles wide and a couple of miles longer than it was wide. The southern end resembled a giant fish hook, bending to the east and sharply back to the north. A sizable marsh lay inside the fish hook with beaches on both sides. In the harbor, the water was a few inches deep, and crabs and minnows were plentiful. We would have no difficulty hunting for food. Beyond the marsh, waves rolled in from the bay, which I presumed was the Chesapeake, and coarse beach grass covered sand dunes.

As the group Wildcat and I were in walked along the beach, I decided to remove my moccasins. The gritty sand was cool beneath my feet. Besides our own, the only footprints belonged to water birds. Oystercatchers scolded us for coming too close, but they calmed when we moved farther down the beach.

The marsh was almost completely enclosed by dunes. For a few minutes, I sat on the sand, and Wildcat joined me without saying a word. Under different circumstances, I would have been in awe at the scenery and would have relaxed watching the herons and egrets dance as if they performed a ballet. Even then, the sounds of the surf and the wind rustling through the beach grasses were nearly hypnotic.

The other men seemed encouraged. The island provided sources for food, and for now, we had fresh water. Some had already made simple tools and begun fishing. As night approached, we bedded down on high ground. On other nights, there would have been the sound of the drums and dancing. I wondered how much of that way of life might already have been lost.

As usual, I had difficulty sleeping. I got up and perched on a sand dune, trying to concentrate on the flame. Unable to reach through to the other realm of the dreaming, I sat back and listened to the surf. Why was it that I had been able to reach Phoebe when we had been separated by centuries, but not now?

Days blended. Wildcat and I contributed to our share of the fishing—oysters, fish, and crabs were plentiful. Some constructed more tools, and due to our cooperative efforts, we survived. Each night, I attempted to enter the dreaming without any luck. The surroundings must have contributed to my failure, but I kept trying. One of the boys in our group was Swimming Beaver. He must have been twelve or thirteen and had yet to go through the grueling initiation of the *huskanaw* in order to become a man. One evening when I attempted to enter the dreaming, he watched curiously.

Etiquette kept him from asking questions, so I explained, "I've been attempting to enter the dreaming. My wife is a cunning woman. She taught me how to move between worlds."

He nodded in understanding. "Would you show me?"

"I'll show you, but so far, I've been unsuccessful entering the realm since we've arrived."

"It might be useful to know."

With that conversation, Swimming Beaver became my sidekick and almost seemed like the son I never had. I had guessed right. He was twelve and could already fish and hunt as well as most men. And when it came to the dreaming, he was a natural. On his first try with me alongside him, he entered the misty realm and visited his family. How I wished I could have reached my own, but I was truly happy for him.

As the days passed, the fresh water supply got lower. Rain water was collected, but not fast enough to sustain everyone. The warriors were used to hardships and knew better than to drink sea water. Thankfully, the nights were cool, but the days were hot. My head hurt like I had a severe hangover, and my mouth had become so dry that it felt like a wad of cotton had been stuffed into it.

A handful of the boys, including Swimming Beaver, could no longer resist and drank the salt water. I tried to lead him away from the marsh, but he drank in relief. His comfort was only temporary, and he darted out of my reach for more water. By the time I caught up with him, he had already indulged.

Temptation nearly got the best of me. I bent down, scooped the water into my hands, and poured it into my mouth. I rinsed the water around and nearly swallowed. Reason prevailed and I spat it out. Swimming Beaver had retreated to the shade. The dreaming was the one place where we could travel and not feel what we were currently enduring. "Would you like to enter the dreaming?" I asked.

He responded with a glassy-eyed look.

I tried to enter the dreaming by myself, but the tingling in my hands and legs made concentration impossible. I returned to the marsh. Again, I nearly drank the water, but somehow I managed to resist and swished it around my mouth for temporary relief. Wildcat grasped my arm, but it was too late. I swallowed and drank my fill.

Swimming Beaver laughed out loud at nothing in particular. "Wind Talker, I see the mist. I've entered the dreaming on my own." He spread his arms. "See, I can fly with the crow."

Delirium had set in. The other boys who had drunk the salt water showed similar hallucinations. They insisted they were home and started dancing to an invisible drum. Their movements were jerky and erratic.

Unless significant rain fell, there would be no turning back. All of us would die here. As if hearing my thoughts, a mist formed over the bay. Thunder and lightning raged. Instead of fearing the storm, I raised my arms to embrace it. Rain would bring us the water we so desperately needed. For some reason, the eerie atmosphere made me believe that I could finally enter the dreaming.

The wind howled with fury. I could hear its voice. *There is another way.*

The words were in my head. "What way?" I asked.

Circle in Time

You know the secret of traveling through time.

Like the boys, I must have been hallucinating, but I had traveled through time on two occasions. As a two-year-old, I had escaped the massacre of my people by traveling to the twentieth century, and the previous year, I had returned to the seventeenth. Phoebe had also traveled through time on two occasions. On her last trip, Meg had traveled with her. Could I save the others by leading the way?

The wind roared and I called to the others. They gathered around. "We'll find relief by traveling into the storm."

"There is no storm," Wildcat said. "Wind Talker, you drank the water and are seeing things that don't exist."

I gestured to the massive clouds. The battering wind nearly knocked me flat. I stepped forward and mist surrounded me.

"Wind Talker!" Swimming Beaver shouted.

I attempted to locate him. His voice had come from somewhere nearby, but the wind pushed me deeper and deeper. For the first time since my arrival on the island, I heard a crow caw. The mist cleared enough that I could see the crow flying overhead. My spirit guide would lead me to safety. I had to put my faith in that belief.

"Wind Talker!"

Swimming Beaver kept calling to me until his voice surrounded me. "Swimming Beaver, where are you?" He continued calling. I turned in circles trying to locate him. The mist only got thicker, and I fumbled through it.

The crow cawed. I followed the sound until the mist cleared slightly. The jet-black bird had perched on a branch overhead. "Can the other warriors join us?" I asked.

The bird spoke in clicks and rattles. *Only those who see me can follow you into the depths.*

Crow's message was understood, but I had drunk the saltwater. I could be hallucinating. I couldn't take the chance. "Swimming Beaver, if you see the crow, follow him. He'll lead us to safety."

Another series of clicks. *There's danger too.*

"Danger?"

You are seeking to escape, but the circle will repeat.

"Repeat?"

The circle will repeat. With the warning, crow gave an alarming cry and took flight.

Out of the mist, a plump woman walked toward me. She had shoulder-length blonde hair. I hadn't seen my first wife Shae since the previous year when I thought we had parted company for good. Though we had remained friends after our divorce, she was part of the twenty-first century and had stayed there. She grinned. "Lee," she said, using my English name, "it really is you. I didn't think I'd ever see you again."

"The feeling is mutual." Not knowing what to say, we stood staring at one another. Both of us opened our mouths and spoke at the same time, so I waved at her to go ahead.

"I was wondering how you are," she said.

"Funny, I was going to ask you the same thing."

She brought me up to date on how she and her husband Russ were, then frowned. "I can't believe that I've fallen for your distracting tricks again. Something's wrong, isn't it?"

"No, Shae," I lied. "Everything's fine."

"I know that look. What's really wrong?"

We shared too much history. I should have known better than to think I could fool her. I shook my head. "None of it is your concern anymore, and there's nothing you can do to help."

"Are you certain?"

"In case you've forgotten, we're nearly four hundred years apart."

"I haven't forgotten," she replied softly. Her brow furrowed. "I don't know if this means anything to you, but it popped into my head. The circle will repeat."

Before I could say anything else, the mist captured Shae and she vanished. I fumbled my way through the fog until I stood along the bank of the James River. I always seemed to return to the spot—the location of my birth. Was that what the crow had meant by the circle repeating? I laughed to myself. If I hadn't entered the dreaming, then I was having an incredible trip from drinking saltwater.

"Wind Talker!"

I looked around, trying to find Swimming Beaver. His voice echoed. The mist cleared, and Elenor's pitched-roof house was in the distance. A man with a slash-sleeve doublet and plumed hat stepped toward me. A sword was on his left hip and a pistol on his right. Phoebe's second husband, who had died the previous year during Opechancanough's attack. He had the dark brown hair of his youth. "Henry."

"Wind Talker, the circle will repeat."

"What circle?"

"Time."

"Time? Henry—" But the mist swallowed him as it had Shae. I continued walking and reached the door to Elenor's house. I hesitated before entering, then grasped the wrought-iron handle and went inside.

Instead of Elenor, Phoebe greeted me. Her arms went around my neck, and she kissed me on the mouth. "I thought you had died."

Closing my eyes, I drew her closer and returned her kisses. I wanted nothing more than to remain there forever and hold her in my arms. "Walks Through Mist," I said in Algonquian.

She reached a hand to my face and gazed into my eyes. "The circle will repeat."

And she was gone.

The mist engulfed me and I sank to the floor. What could it all mean? A cawing came from outside, calling me. Once again, I rose to my feet and followed the sound. Unable to see the bird through the fog, I fumbled along. I let the bird guide me until a man stood before me. His skin was brown like mine, and he wore deer-hide leggings and moccasins. Like Henry, my father had died the year before. Only in this realm he was much younger than the time of his death. "*Nows,*" I said.

"Crow in the Woods," he replied, using my childhood name.

"I'm Wind Talker now."

Black Owl nodded. "Wind Talker, you must choose a path."

"What path?"

"Either return and die as I warned you earlier, or continue forward, where the circle will repeat."

"And the others?"

"Some will die, others shall live. Your decision will not alter the outcome."

Although his message was cryptic, I presumed he spoke about the warriors stranded on the island. "Including Swimming Beaver?"

Anguish crossed his face. "Your decision will not alter the outcome," he repeated. The mist enveloped him, and he vanished. Once again, I was on my own.

A crow cawed. With the sound I realized my visions weren't hallucinations or the dreaming. If I moved forward, I would be stepping through time. But when? *The circle will repeat.* I shivered and thought about my life in the twenty-first century as a detective. Could I go back to that way of life? If Phoebe and Heather were with me, I could live anywhere. But any time? I stepped forward and walked through the mist. *Phoebe.*

9

Phoebe

WIND TALKER HAD CALLED MY NAME. Of that, I was certain. My heart raced, and the dread that had seized me so suddenly vanished as quickly as it had come upon me.

"Phoebe?" Christopher placed a hand on my shoulder to comfort me. "What's wrong?"

"He called to me."

"We'll be there in a few days."

Christopher had managed to trade his sturdy workboat for a larger shallop made of oak planks that were held together by wooden pegs. 'Twas a boat small enough to row, yet had enough space to carry any survivors we might find. I shuddered. Years afore I had vowed to ne'er set foot on a boat again. Too many times my pledge had been broken. This time was a necessity. I would not wait behind to discover Wind Talker's fate. With William's aid, we set out for the western island. The dank air gave way to dawn's light and a soft breeze that heated up the morn. Thankfully, the waters remained calm and James Towne faded behind us. We hugged land and came ashore as needed.

A day passed afore we entered the bay. Wind whipped my hair round my face, and the boat swayed gently. I counted my blessings for calm waters. As the day wore on, a haze appeared in the sky above the shore. By afternoon, puffy white clouds formed. Nights were warm, and we had no need to worry about getting chilled. The following day passed much the same with a clammy stillness and a southerly breeze. Late in the day, dark gray clouds rumbled. Fortunately, they remained in the distance. On the fourth day, we were close to the western island when waves furled and a sinister cloud blotted out the sun. Thunderheads had formed along the western bay.

"Hold on mates," Christopher said. "I thought we were having smooth sailing for this time of year. Time to drop the sail." William hopped up to aid Christopher in tying the sail to the mast. 'Twas obvious that we could not outrun the massive thunder squall. Instead Christopher guided us away from western island and round another. Once behind the tiny island and in shallow water, he dropped the anchor. "We'll ride it out here," he said.

Tucked behind our island shelter, we watched as black clouds rolled towards us. Water frothed as lines of wind raced across the waves. The waves got steeper and the boat rocked. Soon rain pounded down upon us. Waves rolled the boat to and fro. Sick to my stomach, I lowered my head. We covered ourselves with hemp cloth, the same material used for making sails, and waited out the storm. Betwixt the covering and our wool clothes, we stayed mostly dry.

After a couple of hours, the downpour changed to drizzle, but the waves continued to roll the boat. The sky brightened, but the sun got low in the sky. Only when the waves calmed did my stomach halt its lurching.

"We'll wait for the morrow to proceed," Christopher said.

On the morn when the sun returned, the men raised the sail, then lifted the anchor. No clouds were in the sky, and we sailed the short distance to the western island. A boggy island with a sandy beach came into view. My heart thumped as I thought of Wind Talker. I scanned the beach, hoping to catch a glimpse of him, but no one was about. I feared the worst.

Near the bank the men jumped from the boat, and with a hefty heave, they brought it onto solid ground. We walked along the beach, and I grew more and more vexed. Up ahead, I spied two shapes, lying on the beach as if sleeping. I pointed and Christopher and William nodded that they had seen them. We hurried forward. Afore reaching the lads, I halted. More and more bodies lined the beach. "Wind Talker," I whispered.

"Come," Christopher said, "some may be alive."

Whilst Christopher leaned over the first lad and shook his head, I crept forward. William had gone to the side of another and repeated the head shaking. All of the warriors dead? How could I have not felt Wind Talker's passing? Sorrow gripped me, and I nearly could not continue.

I knelt o'er one prone form and blinked. *Wildcat?* I placed my fingers upon his wrist. His pulse was uneven but definitely there. His eyes were sunken and his skin shriveled. His forehead was very warm to my touch. The cunning woman in me took charge. "Wildcat's alive. He needs water."

William ran back to the boat, and Christopher continued checking for other survivors. Though numb with grief, I stayed by Wildcat's side and whispered words of comfort. He muttered, but I could not make out his words. Occasionally, I looked up, only to see Christopher shaking his head at another he had found dead.

Afore long William returned with a wooden flask. For once I wished I had twenty-first medicine available. I could give Wildcat IV fluids, and he would most likely recover in a few hours. Instead, I placed the flask to his lips and let him sip the water. He choked, but I held his head. Finally, he managed to swallow. First, a few drops, then a trickle. He drank. "Walks Through Mist," he said in a choking, halting voice.

"Don't try to speak. Save your strength."

"But Wind Talker—"

Fearing that he would tell me Wind Talker had died, I hushed him once more.

"Phoebe!" Christopher waved at me that he had found another survivor.

"Let him drink," I said to William, "but slowly." I rushed towards Christopher, hoping against hope that he had found Wind Talker. 'Twas a lad of round twelve winters, not Wind Talker. I bent down to help as I had Wildcat.

Christopher gently touched my shoulder. "I'll let you know if I find him."

Grief stricken, I merely nodded and continued with my duties. The lad had the same withered skin and sunken eyes.

"William, I need water," I said.

William raced to my side and handed me the flask. "I'll go back to the boat and fetch more water."

"Thank you," I said, positioning the flask to the lad's mouth. Unable to swallow, he mumbled gibberish. "Pray drink."

The lad drank a few drops. I tried giving him a tiny bit more. Little by little, he was drinking. His nonsense talk continued. 'Twas Algonquian. That much I knew, but his words made no coherent sentences.

"Swimming Beaver," he said.

I presumed he was telling me his name as there were no beavers on the island. "I'm Walks Through Mist."

He muttered a string of words in a furious frenzy. When I failed to comprehend, the words came e'en faster. "Kesutanowas Wesin."

With my heart pounding, I raised my head. He had distinctly uttered Wind Talker's name. "Where is Wind Talker?" I asked. He uttered more gibberish, and I gazed across the bodies. Were these two the only ones left alive? I returned to my duties, but unlike Wildcat, the lad's eyes rolled up into his head, and his muscles quivered. I had arrived too late to save him.

When his fit ended, he grinned. "He and... Swimming Beaver walked... into the storm... and the wind... the wind carried them away."

"Wind Talker and Swimming Beaver?"

The lad's name wasn't Swimming Beaver. Another fit captured him and his body twisted. I told him how he would soon be entering the afterlife. Once there, he would meet his kinsmen, who had proceeded him. He would go through the *huskanaw* and become a man. Upon doing so, he would take his adult name and live in harmony.

His lashes fluttered one last time, and his muscles slackened. His eyes opened in the sightlessness of death. E'en though I wished to do naught more than to relieve my sorrow, I went to the next warrior that Christopher had found alive. By the end of the day, we aided three more survivors. In each of those faces, I hoped to find Wind Talker. We failed to discover him amongst the living or dead.

Whilst we prepared to deliver the living to the nearest tribe to recover, the lad's words echoed through my head. I returned to Wildcat's side. He looked less gaunt than afore, and I said, "The lad told me that Wind Talker and Swimming Beaver had walked into the storm and the wind carried them away."

He nodded. "That's what I tried to tell you. They vanished with the wind."

On two other occasions, Wind Talker had seemingly vanished—once when he was a small lad, and the other time, the year afore. He hadn't died but traveled through time. That's why he had called to me. When had he traveled to? I would enter the dreaming and find the answer.

10

Wind Talker

AS I EMERGED FROM THE FOG, THE CROW VANISHED. The sunshine and air were warm. The humidity felt lower than it had been on previous days. Instead of among sand dunes, I stood in a cypress and poplar forest. The trees were in full leaf, and the temperature was quite pleasant. Certain that I was no longer on the island, I turned in every direction. I guessed that it must be late spring or early summer. The land looked vaguely familiar. My throat remained scratchy and I felt dizzy. The first order of business was to find freshwater.

Staggering along like I had one too many beers, I heard a groan echo from a clump of trees. I moved closer. "Swimming Beaver?"

Another groan. I bent down and touched his forehead. He definitely ran a fever and moaned in pain. "Wind Talker—"

I hushed him. "Save your energy. Don't try to talk." His skin wrinkled like a seventy-year-old man, rather than a boy of twelve. Water—we both needed it. I placed his arm over my shoulder and helped him to his feet. We trudged through the forest. Barely able to support myself, let alone Swimming Beaver, I swayed. I continued onward. We reached a clearing, and I heard the sound of rushing water. I moved toward it.

The ground dipped to a stream. *Water.* In my excitement I stumbled over a branch and lost my grip on Swimming Beaver. He splashed head first into the water. I plunged into the current after him and pulled his head above water. He gasped, but thankfully, was breathing.

Tapping a reserve that I wasn't aware I had, I hoisted Swimming Beaver up and propped him against a tree. After making certain that he was steady, I dove into the stream and drank my fill. I cupped my hands with water and returned to Swimming Beaver's side. "Here, drink."

He sipped, slowly at first. Before long, I had to return to the stream for more water. Over the next few hours, he quenched his thirst. Exhausted of all energy, I curled near his side and fell asleep. Throughout the night, I fumbled to the stream for more water, hoping that no snakes lurked underneath the foliage ready to strike.

Morning arrived, and I felt slightly revived, then my stomach rumbled. Finding food was the next order of business.

"Wind Talker, where are we?"

Swimming Beaver's skin was less wrinkled and his eyes were no longer sunken. "I'm not certain," I answered. "But we're not on the island anymore."

"I recall the mist and a path. You spoke to a man."

"My father. He died last year."

"Then he was guiding us?"

"I believe so." I got to my feet and held out a hand. "Swimming Beaver, we need to find something to eat."

He grasped my hand, and I helped him to his feet. He swayed, and I put an arm around his waist to help steady him. Drawing his arm over my shoulder, I moved forward—one careful step at a time. Swimming Beaver leaned on me with most of his weight. We continued forward. As we walked along, I kept an eye out for anything edible.

Swimming Beaver needed frequent breaks, but by midday we passed through a grove of trees. The feeling of having been here before returned. Once again, I heard the sound of rushing water—only this time, it was much larger than a small stream. We made our way to the bank, and the expansive James River loomed before me.

Recognizing the landscape, I breathed out in relief. If we followed the river downstream for a couple of miles, we would arrive at Elenor's. She would give us something to eat and a comfortable place to recuperate. I guided Swimming Beaver in that direction, but the forest continued for longer than I had remembered. Another mile passed before the woods gave way to open ground. Instead of a familiar pitched-roof house, a town of arched houses covered with woven mats came into view. *On the James River?* There hadn't been any such dwellings since early in the seventeenth century. I clenched my hands. Once again, I had traveled through time, and this time, Swimming Beaver had accompanied me. Cautiously, I continued forward.

At the edge of town, a warrior aimed his bow at me. His crown hair stood upright, and the right side of his head was shaved. His black hair was tied in a knot and stretched the length of his back. He wore a loincloth and deer-hide leggings. With their bows at the ready, three other warriors joined him.

I held my free hand out with my palms up to show that I carried no weapons. "I'm unarmed," I said in Algonquian. "My friend needs help."

The lead man lowered his bow, but the others kept their weapons aimed at us. "I'm Silver Eagle," he said.

Silver Eagle? Suddenly short of breath, I lowered my arm. Silver Eagle was Phoebe's stepfather, and this town . . . this town was the one I had been born in. These people were my tribe. "I'm Wind Talker," I said, hoping the trembling in my voice wasn't noticeable. "And this is Swimming Beaver."

Silver Eagle stepped toward me, studying me closely, then gazed at me in what seemed like familiarity. "Where are you from, Wind Talker?"

I knew that I might eventually be able to share the truth, but for the time being, I needed to think of a plausible answer. "We were taken captive by the *tassantassas.*" The stranger.

"Let me help." He moved to the other side of Swimming Beaver and placed the boy's arm over his shoulder. "What tribe do you belong to?"

"Swimming Beaver is Pamunkey."

"And you?" Silver Eagle asked.

He had seen right through my half answer. No one would believe me if I said I was Paspahegh. I raised my hand with a gesture that I had been struck on the head. "Besides my name, I remember very little. I had hoped someone here might recognize me. Since

Swimming Beaver and I met in captivity, I can conclude that I'm not Pamunkey."

He glanced at the other warriors. They nodded, then Silver Eagle looked in my direction once more. "You bear a resemblance to Black Owl."

My father. He was alive. "I would like to meet Black Owl."

"You shall." He waved for the other men to accompany us, and we headed into the center of town.

Women prepared meals around cook fires, but they halted their work upon seeing us. One came over to us. "I shall see the boy gets the help he needs."

We brought him to a house. The women assured me they would see to his care. I trusted that Swimming Beaver was in good hands and continued on with Silver Eagle. Other women smiled and gave me warm welcomes. Hoping that I had arrived at a time before my birth, I tried not to look too closely at any of the faces.

I was escorted to a longhouse where a group of people were gathered and the *weroance,* or chief, greeted me. Wowinchapuncke made a round of introductions and offered me a copper band.

"Thank you," I said. "I'm honored."

He placed the band around my wrist. "You're a guest here and we welcome you. Silver Eagle will show you around the town while we prepare for the festivities."

As Silver Eagle led me from the longhouse, I thanked the chief again. We wandered through town, and he introduced me to the people, who stopped their work long enough to greet me. Finally, we came to another house. Out front, a white woman with blonde hair stirred the cook pot. *Phoebe's mother.* My heart pounded. Phoebe and her mother had only lived with the Paspahegh for a few months before the massacre. That meant the year was 1610. Phoebe would be a girl of ten, and I would be . . .

"My wife," Silver Eagle said. "Mother of the Red-Haired Lass." He motioned to me. "This is Wind Talker."

With a smile she looked up from her pot of stew and blinked. "Have we met afore?"

In the dreaming. "I'm not certain."

"Wind Talker has lost much of his memory," Silver Eagle explained. "He's trying to find someone who might know where he is from."

From inside the house, I detected movement. A girl scampered. My heart went through an odd thumping when I realized who she was. Phoebe poked her reddish-blonde head out the door and giggled. "Red Dog, pay proper respect to your elders," her mother chastised.

Red Dog had been Phoebe's girlhood name among the Paspahegh. I cleared my throat. "It's all right," I said. "I have a daughter too, but I don't know..." I almost said when. "...where."

With her head lowered Phoebe stepped out of the house accompanied by a mangy looking mongrel. She stole a peek in my direction, but quickly lowered her gaze once more. Even in that momentary eye contact, I detected a devilish gleam. Silver Eagle introduced us, and I became tongue-tied. *What did one say to a girl who would grow up and become my wife?*

For the moment, Phoebe spared me the bother. " 'Tis an honor to meet you," she said in English.

Once again, Phoebe's mother reprimanded her. "In Algonquian. Wind Talker does not—"

"I understand English." Everyone looked in my direction. "I learned the language when I was held captive."

They nodded in understanding, but Phoebe looked at me. Though she couldn't comprehend how we knew each other, I detected familiarity in her eyes. Silver Eagle motioned for us to continue.

By the time I met most of the town's inhabitants, the festivities had begun. Once again, I was escorted to the longhouse where the *weroance* resided. Inside, people lined the walls. Wowinchapuncke introduced me to those I had not met earlier in the day. Many intertwined index fingers with me. Finally, I came to a man whose prominent cheekbones and the shape of his nose resembled my own. He was much younger than I remembered, but there was no doubt in my mind who he was. *Black Owl.*

His gaze met mine, and again I spotted a hint of recognition. "You look like you could be a brother," he said.

When Wowinchapuncke introduced us, I wanted to tell Black Owl who I really was, but only grief could come from such a confession. I decided to play to my memory loss instead. "If you've never seen me before, then we must have an ancestor in common."

"I don't believe we've ever met." He interlocked his index finger with mine, then gestured to the woman standing next to him. "Please meet my wife Snow Bird."

My mother. I shifted my gaze. In her arms was a two-year-old boy. Chills ran up and down my spine. No matter how hard I tried, I couldn't look away. The boy was me. He struggled in Snow Bird's arms, and she lowered him to the ground, maintaining a firm grip on his hand to keep him from running off. "This is our son Crow in the Woods," she said.

Unable to look away, I kept staring. Had this meeting occurred before and I had no recollection because of my youth?

"Your friend," my mother continued, "will be fine with rest. I checked on him before coming here."

Her words barely registered, but of course, she had been a healer. "Thank . . ." I cleared my throat. "Thank you."

Wowinchapuncke distracted me by proceeding down the line of people, but I continued to glance back at my younger self. He peered in my direction. Our gazes met. I froze. Wowinchapuncke introduced me to another couple, breaking my paralysis. I dared not look back again, and as we went down the line, the tingling sensation vanished the further I moved away from myself. I was finally able to concentrate on the people before me. When we reached the end of the line, the chief took his place at the end wall of the house and sat on a wood frame. His wife sat beside him, and I was shown to a mat near the frame on his right. The others were seated in rows in front of the chief. In turn, each stood and welcomed me.

My stomach rumbled as people spoke. After the speeches, I finally satisfied my hunger as we feasted on squirrel, duck, and tuckahoe, a plant that was cooked for hours to make it edible and nontoxic. The taste, which had a hint of cocoa flavor, was worth the work involved. All guests were treated in a similar manner and given a lavish spread of food, even if the townspeople had little else. Following the meal, a pipe was passed around and stories were told.

When my turn came, I had to think quickly. I suspected that time travel would be an inappropriate topic of discussion. I had already resorted to the excuse that I had been taken captive by the colonists and decided to build on that story. As I recalled, the Europeans had sailed the coast a number of years before colonization. "I was taken captive by the *tassantassas* many winters ago." The tale worked as I told it to an intent audience. Not only that, the story explained my extensive knowledge of English, as well as a head injury giving me amnesia to other aspects of my life. I concluded by telling them how I had met Swimming Beaver on an island where around thirty of us had been abandoned. We had floated through the mist until finding our way to the Paspahegh.

After the pipe made a few rounds, the drums beat outside the longhouse. The evening dancing was beginning. With the others, I stepped into the open air where many of the townspeople had already assembled. Unlike the first time I had attended such a gathering, I was familiar with the routine. But why was I here? For now, did it truly matter? I was with my tribe once more. This time, I suffered no embarrassment as I knew the steps and along with the others, I danced to the rhythmic drums.

When the dancing ended, I was escorted to a guest house. In a polite way, I made it clear that I required no female companionship. I wanted no one besides Phoebe, and the Phoebe I knew was thirty-five years in the future. At least it wasn't four hundred years like the time before, but would I be able to contact her through the dreaming?

I sat next to the fire and cleared my head. With practice I had become more accomplished in the dreaming, but still no mist appeared before me. *Absorb the flame.* A gentle breeze ruffled my hair. With it, I thought I heard voices. *Phoebe.*

11

Phoebe

1645

I WOKE WITH A START AND SAT UP on my sleeping platform and hugged the blanket next to me. "Wind Talker..." Any sense of his presence had vanished. Had hearing his voice only been wishful thinking? Embers from the fire were my only source of light. I rose from the platform and wandered outside. The night was warm, and crickets chirped a chorus. No one lingered about as all had retired to their rest. I entered the neighboring *yi-hakan*.

E'en breathing of deep slumber surrounded me. Why had I come here? Wildcat was recovering. He no longer needed my aide, and since we had returned the three survivors from the western island to the Sekakawon, there were many healers who could assist in their recuperation.

I made my way into the open air and meandered the town. When an owl hooted, I halted. 'Twas not the cry of a crow. "Wind Talker, pray speak to me again."

"Phoebe..."

I turned to him. "Kesutanowas Wesin."

"Nay, Phoebe. 'Tis only me," said Christopher.

"I heard him."

"I don't doubt that you did." He stepped closer. "Phoebe, we need to return to the plantation. You will not find your answers here. Of that, I'm certain."

"Aye."

"Then we shall return on the morrow, but first, let us get some sleep." He held out his hand.

I grasped his fingers and he led the way to the *yi-hakan*. He held open the mat covering the door. "Thank you, Christopher." I stepped inside the guest house, where I had lived for the past week. Sleep. But I could not. I stirred the embers and added a log. Soon, the fire burned brightly. I sat cross-legged afore the fire. "Wind Talker, show me when you have traveled to."

My hound stood afore me, and mist engulfed me. When the dog raced through the fog, I had difficulty keeping up with him. He returned to my side and whined. "Find Wind Talker," I said. He ran off once more.

In the distance, I heard hands clapping. The mist faded, and I stood in a grand hall surrounded by people. 'Twas similar to a movie theater that Wind Talker had taken me to in the twenty-first century, only in the center was a stage. I had ne'er been to a play whilst growing up in Dorset and wondered why the dreaming had brought me to this place. As the room darkened, except for the stage, the crowd hushed. They seated themselves in the chairs behind. I followed their lead.

Children came onto the stage and pretended to sail the ocean on a paper ship labeled the Mayflower. E'en in make believe, I felt the rocking waves. The lads were dressed in black with white collars and floppy hats, and the lasses were in black skirts with white caps. One lad pointed. "Land!"

The children brought the ship ashore. As the play continued, the children collected food, but not enough for the coming winter. Many grew ill. In the spring, a brown-skinned, black-haired lad, wearing a headdress with blue and red feathers, entered the stage.

The woman next to me leaned o'er my way and whispered, "That's my son."

"You must be very proud," I replied.

On stage, the lad said to the other children dressed in black, "I am the chief and I want to help."

I blinked with a feeling that I knew the lad.

More children dressed in pretend deerskin and feathered bands round their heads entered the stage. Whilst numerous Englishmen had been adopted by tribes, I had ne'er seen as many as depicted in the play. Why was there only one native-born amongst the group?

Once more, the woman angled in my direction. "Which one is yours?"

"Which one?" I asked.

"Which child is yours?"

"None. My daughter is not here today."

"Lee didn't want to take part either, but the principal threatened to expel him if he didn't participate. Lee thought they portrayed the Native Americans all wrong for Thanksgiving. After all, he is Native himself."

Lee? I gasped. The lad on the stage afore me was none other than Wind Talker. "I would like to meet your son. My daughter is—" I almost said Paspahegh. "—Native." I sat back and watched the rest of the play. The Indians showed the English how to grow food, and after the harvest, they feasted. At the end, the audience stood once more and applauded. Though the play had most likely depicted Thanksgiving incorrectly, I rose to my feet and joined them.

When the lights returned to the great hall, I recognized the woman who sat aside me. Though her hair wasn't completely gray as it had been when I had known her in the twenty-first century, she was Natalie Crowley—Lee's adopted momma. "Nat," I said without thinking.

"Have we met before?"

I had cared for her in her final days, helping to mend the kinship betwixt her and her son. "Nay," I said, thinking quickly, "other mommas have told me about you and your Native son."

Her eyes narrowed. "I don't like the way they whisper things about him."

I placed a gentle hand on hers, and she immediately calmed.

Her gaze met mine. "You do understand."

"Aye."

Along with the rest of the crowd, we got to our feet. I accompanied Nat backstage where other parents had gathered with their children. Most beamed with pride. One young lad frowned. We moved closer. With a scowl, Lee tore the feathered headdress from his head and tossed it to the floor.

"Lee..." Nat retrieved the headdress.

"It belongs to a plains tribe."

"Lee..."

He sent his momma a scorching look. "I got two weeks detention."

"Two weeks? Why on earth—?"

"Because I wouldn't wear war paint or carry a tomahawk."

"We'll talk about it later. I'd like for you to meet..." Nat looked in my direction. "I didn't get your name."

"Phoebe..." I nearly slipped and said Crowley. "Phoebe Wynne. I'm pleased to meet you, Lee. My husband is Native."

Though he must have been round ten, he was only a few inches shorter than me. He slanted his right brow. "Phoebe?"

"Ms. Wynne," Nat corrected.

He turned his gaze to the floor. "Forgive me, Ms. Wynne."

His voice was higher pitched than the tenor I had grown to love, but I delighted in meeting him as a lad. "*Netab,*" I said. He regarded me curiously. Deep down, I knew he understood, but 'twould be many years afore his comprehension was unlocked. " 'Tis Algonquian for friend."

Nat smiled, but Lee continued to stare. "*Netab,*" he repeated.

A mist formed. Afore the fog captured me, I said, "Lee, you are Paspahegh." He and Nat faded from my view, and I returned to the *yi-hakan* with the fire crackling in front of me. Why had I been taken to Lee when he was naught but a lad? 'Twas the way of the dreaming. Only time would give me answers.

Exhausted, I curled upon my sleeping platform. At last, I sought my rest.

In the morn, Christopher, William, and I began our journey to the plantation. I assured Wildcat that I would send a message when I discovered the time Wind Talker had been taken to. We traveled for five days on the water. At night, Wind Talker's voice called to me, but I was unable to enter the dreaming to search for him.

Upon our arrival, I greeted my daughters. Little more than a babe, Heather had missed me and needed my attention. In spite of my overwhelming sadness, I rejoiced in being reunited with her. After supper, the family gathered in the parlor. Christopher relayed the tale of our adventure. The grandchildren were in awe, but with the retelling, the more heavyhearted I became. Afore long, Heather squirmed from weariness.

I bid my family goodnight and climbed the stairs to the loft. Though I wished to attempt to reach Wind Talker through the dreaming, I curled up on the feather mattress with Heather in my arms. Having my daughter near brought me comfort, and I soon gave in to my need for sleep.

Phoebe.

I twisted and turned but could not break sleep's hold. A pitiful whine came from aside the bed. I reached out and felt a wet tongue on my hand. "Caleb?"

A dog placed his paws on the edge of the bed and licked my face. 'Twas the red hound that had followed me when I was a lass. As a result, I had been known as Red Dog amongst the Paspahegh.

"Caleb, what are you doing here?" He climbed upon the bed and curled next to me. Momma had always chastised me when I brought him to bed with me. But Momma wasn't here. She had died years ago from the smallpox. I cuddled closer to Caleb. Hadn't he been gone for ages as well? I didn't care. He was with me now, and I felt safer than I had in a long time.

Phoebe.

This time I awoke. 'Twas Wind Talker reaching out to me through the dreaming. Of that, I was certain. Heather, not Caleb, lay next to me. "I'll find him somehow," I vowed to my daughter.

12

Wind Talker

1610

As much as I tried to avoid Phoebe and my younger self, I kept running into them. I wandered along the river bank when a boy and a red dog charged toward me. In the distance a girl chased after them. The boy and dog came to a halt in front of me. I swallowed and knelt down. "Crow in the Woods," I said.

The dog wiggled his tail. My younger self stepped closer. How many times had I read in science fiction that if two selves met, they'd wink each other out of existence? I couldn't risk it, but the boy continued forward. His curious fingers reached out. Frozen in place, I held my breath. When he touched my arm, a shiver went through me. We were both still here. Our gazes met.

"Crow in the Woods!" Out of breath, Phoebe caught up to us.

I stood and she jumped back. "I didn't mean to frighten you, Red Dog," I said.

She stared at me, but quickly lowered her gaze. "You said you speak English?"

"Yes, I speak English," I replied in English.

Her breath quickened. I hadn't meant to scare her, but how could I possibly explain?

"Red Dog!" Her mother's voice came from along the river bank. Phoebe seized Crow in the Woods's hand but kept looking over her shoulder as they followed the path along the river. I made my own retreat in the opposite direction. As I withdrew, I felt penetrating eyes on my back.

I took a quick look. Sure enough, Phoebe's mother and Snow Bird watched me. I sped up and took a deep breath as soon as they were out of sight. My relief was short lived. The following day, Phoebe's mother approached me. I presumed she thought I was some kind of pervert stalking the children. "Why do you call to my daughter in her dreams?" she asked.

"Call to your daughter?"

More comfortable in her native tongue, she lapsed into English. "First she spoke of a man calling to her. She said he used her English name. Yesterday when she saw you, she told me that man was you."

When entering the dreaming I must have been reaching the girl, not my wife thirty-five years in the future. I had no choice but to be honest. As a cunning woman, she might understand. "I've been unintentionally calling to her during the dreaming."

Her eyes widened. "I have been told some of the Paspahegh have visions, but you said 'the dreaming'. 'Tis what I called moving through the realms in Dorset."

"That's because..." I cleared my throat. "Phoebe is the one who showed me the dreaming. I *have* been trying to contact your daughter, but not the ten-year-old girl."

Her mouth dropped open. "We *have* met afore."

"We have—during the dreaming. I'm Crow in the Woods, and Phoebe will become my wife."

"That's why you look like Black Owl." She wobbled on her feet and I thought she might faint. I lent her a steadying hand. "Prove to me you're who you say," she said.

"In 1609, you sailed to Jamestown on the *Blessing*. Your husband was on the *Sea Venture,* and the ship wrecked during a hurricane at sea." I didn't add that he would later return very much alive. "The following February, you ran off with Phoebe. You were afraid that she would starve if you stayed at the fort. You timed your escape when the authorities were burning a man at the stake for having killed and eaten his wife."

"Enough!" Suddenly pale, she swallowed. "I believe you. Why are you here as you are now?"

Since the truth was out, having an ally might be a good thing. "I wish I knew the reason. I've traveled through time before. I hope it's so I can help in some way."

"You said that you and Phoebe are married?" I nodded and she smiled slightly. "Will I have any more grandchildren?"

The knowledge of what Phoebe and I would go through before we married was unimportant right now. "You will. We have a daughter. Her name is Heather."

Her smile widened. "Thank you."

"As you can imagine, I miss both of them."

"Your secret is safe with me. If I can help in any way . . ."

"As a matter of fact you might be able to help. Do you know how I can contact the future Phoebe without the ten-year-old hearing me? It'll be a few years before she enters the dreaming herself, but I need to speak with my wife, not the child."

"There's no doubt the connection is a strong one. Mayhap I can assist you. I can distract Phoebe when you enter the dreaming. I suspect at her age she will only hear your voice if she's asleep."

I refrained from stating the obvious counterpoint, but her suggestion was worth a try. "Thank you, Mother of the—"

"Pray call me by my English name, Elenor."

Phoebe's daughter had been named after her grandmother. There was so much I wanted to tell her, but no good could come from relaying horrific tragedies ahead. And maybe, just maybe, I was here to help avert some grief. "Elenor, I appreciate your help."

"How far have you traveled through time?"

"Thirty-five years."

"And you said this wasn't the first time."

Indirectly, I realized what she was asking. "I think it's best if I don't tell you about the other times. At least, not right now."

"Very well, then I shall keep Phoebe occupied aft the eve's dance. 'Twill be a small window, but you can let me know on the morrow if you are successful."

"Thank you."

She started to turn away but faced me again. "Your name wasn't Wind Talker when we met?"

"No, it was Lee Crowley." Sadness crossed her face. Even without telling her the tragedies straight out, I believe she had guessed. Thankfully she had been in Paspahegh society long enough that she followed protocol and refrained from inquiring further. At least now I might have the opportunity to reach Phoebe.

After the evening dancing had concluded, I retreated to the guest house and sat near the fire. Swimming Beaver had recuperated, but he stayed with my own family where Snow Bird kept watch over him and doted on him. Now, I hoped Elenor was able to keep Phoebe occupied while I entered the dreaming. *Absorb the flame.* The crow flew ahead of me and the wind was at my back. For a change I had a good feeling about being successful. When the mist cleared, a town of mat houses stood before me. It wasn't the Paspahegh town that I currently stayed in, but it looked vaguely familiar—the Sekakawon. Outside one house stood a warrior. "Wildcat?" Thank God he was alive.

Though weak, he intertwined his index finger with mine. "We've been looking for you, brother."

"I've traveled through time again. I've retreated to just before the Paspahegh massacre. I don't know if there's anything I can do to change what happened, but I'll try. Is there any way that you can let Walks Through Mist know where I am?"

"I can send a messenger."

"Thank you, I'd appreciate it."

The wind blew, warning me that we didn't have much time. We intertwined our fingers once more, and before I could say anything else, I stared into the flame. I had returned to the guest house.

On the following morning, I accompanied Silver Eagle and a couple of other men on a hunting trip. At this time of the year, they hunted small game. While I had never become adept at hunting in any form, I was relieved to join them because it kept me away from uncomfortable encounters with Phoebe or my own family.

We set out on foot and followed a trail through the forest. Like so many times in the past, the warriors kept such a brisk pace that I had difficulty keeping up. Although I had improved my stamina since returning to the seventeenth century, I could not maintain the steady rate of those who had lived here all of their lives. In the end, I fell behind with only one of the town's dogs to keep me company. I recognized the dog as the one that usually followed Phoebe. Out of breath, I said to him in English, "I guess it's just you and me."

With the appearance of a cross between a hound and a wolf, the reddish dog pricked his ears in my direction as if he understood me and wagged his tail.

I sat beside him and caught my breath. Unlike most of the town's dogs, he wasn't skittish of people and huddled next to me. "Shouldn't you be on the hunt rather than comforting me?"

He stared at me with mournful eyes, and I patted him on the head. When I was a kid, I'd had a black wolfish looking dog. After his passing, I had always wanted to get another dog, but with the hours I had kept as a cop, I was away from home too much or in apartment life, making the timing never seem quite right.

I reached into my satchel and retrieved a piece of dried venison. I gave it to the dog, and he snarfed it down with relish.

From a few feet away, a man laughed. "Shouldn't a dog work before being fed?"

I looked up at Silver Eagle and stood. "He was keeping me company."

"Red Dog calls him Caleb."

"Caleb." The dog wiggled his tail.

"Wind Talker, you should have told me you weren't ready to participate in a hunt."

In keeping with my story, I made up an excuse. "I thought I was, but I guess the past few weeks have taken more out of me than I realized."

Silver Eagle nodded. "Let's return to town."

To his suggestion, I heartily agreed, and we headed in the direction of town. Before arriving, Caleb's fur bristled and a low rumble came from deep within his throat. We reached for our weapons. Barking and growling, the dog rushed ahead and charged into a cluster of trees. A huffing sound and a clacking of teeth came from the wooded cover. A black bear charged the dog and swatted the ground with its forepaws, swiping cleanly across Caleb's back and shoulders. The dog yowled.

Silver Eagle straightened his shoulders and stood tall. He held his bow in one hand and club in the other to make himself look bigger. Never having encountered a bear in the wild before, I mimicked his lead and raised my hands. The bear clacked its teeth once more, then vanished into the forest. Thankful that our pretense worked, I went over to Caleb and bent down. He had deep gashes on his shoulders and a flap of skin hanging from his back.

"I'll relieve him of his pain," Silver Eagle said, lifting his club.

Recalling a story Phoebe had told me about when she was a child, I raised my arm to stop him. "No! He's Phoebe's dog. She should decide his fate." I pressed some moss to Caleb's gashes to slow the blood flow.

"You called my daughter by her English name. How do you know it?"

I gently picked up the dog and cradled him in my arms. "I'll tell you after we get Caleb back to her."

"Let me take him."

Carefully, I transferred Caleb to Silver Eagle's waiting arms and we resumed our journey to town. Even though he carried an injured animal, he moved swiftly. Before long, we arrived to the edge of town. Phoebe raced toward us upon seeing him, but then she halted. "*Nows*," she said.

"Come quickly," Silver Eagle responded.

With reluctance, she moved forward.

"A bear," Silver Eagle explained. "I shall relieve him from his misery."

"Nay! You mustn't. I can save him."

"You will only prolong his suffering." But Silver Eagle gave Caleb to Phoebe's waiting arms. He howled from the movement.

"Thank you, *Nows*."

Silver Eagle watched as she carried the dog to their house. Outside, Elenor waited beside a boiling pot. After she followed Phoebe inside, Silver Eagle turned to me and asked, "How do you know my daughter's English name?"

I took a deep breath. "Because I know her from a future time, and in that time, she is my wife. I'm Crow in the Woods."

He glanced over his shoulder to the house where my family lived, then returned his gaze to my face and studied it. "I noticed the resemblance when we first met. You could be Black Owl's long lost brother."

"He's my father. I'm Paspahegh." Unlike Elenor, I had no stories that I could share to make him believe my words. The dog moaned from inside, momentarily distracting me. "Caleb will live. With your wife's help, Phoebe will save him."

He eyed me with skepticism. "Then we shall wait to see how the dog fares."

The mat hanging over the doorway was pushed to the side and Elenor stood in the opening. "Silver Eagle, I know not if the hound will survive, but Red Dog is determined to save him. Wind Talker speaks the truth of who he is and where he's from. He told me the same yesterday, and I entered the dreaming last night to verify his words."

Silver Eagle glanced from Elenor to me again. "I didn't reveal the whole story when we met," I said, "because I thought no one would believe the truth. Swimming Beaver and I were held captive like I said, and we did escape. We escaped by traveling through time."

"You have married Red Dog?"

Elenor smiled. "And they have a daughter. Her name is Heather."

"She has no Algonquian name?"

"Snow Bird," I replied.

Silver Eagle's gaze softened. "After your mother. I will honor your secret."

"Thank you. Both of you."

13

Phoebe

1645

With a vow that he would marry Chloe, William returned to the Appamattuck, whilst I stayed behind with my daughter and her family. 'Twas the place that I felt Wind Talker's presence the strongest. During the day, I helped Elenor and Bess with the household chores. I tried to explain to Heather what had happened to her poppa, but she was far too young to comprehend. Whenever I had the opportunity, I entered the dreaming.

Days passed. Wind Talker called to me, but for some reason, I was unable to make the connection. 'Twas like a wall that barricaded me. One eve after Heather had gone to her rest, I followed a path through the mist. The white hound trotted afore me, guiding me. When we emerged into a green forest, I was hopeful. The forest path led me to an area with wooden tables covered by white cloths. Grownups chatted, whilst children laughed and played.

In the twenty-first century, Lee had brought me to a picnic. Without the experience, I would have ne'er recognized the scene. He had explained to me such gatherings were often held outside amongst family. These tables were ladened with hamburgers and hot dogs.

A woman stood. "Phoebe?"

I blinked. "Nat?"

She motioned me o'er to the table. "Come, join us. Did you bring your daughter today?"

"Nay, Heather is with her cousins." I joined them at the table.

Aside Nat sat Lee. "Lee, you remember Ms. Wynne?"

He nodded but made no eye contact.

"Phoebe, please sit down," said Nat, and she made a round of introductions to the rest of the family, consisting of six adults and four other children. Lee's poppa wasn't amongst them. As a police officer, he was on duty. Having been married to Lee when he had been a detective, I understood his absence all too well. We exchanged greetings, then Nat went on to tell the others how we had met at the Thanksgiving play.

Children snickered, and Lee hunched in on himself, not looking in their direction.

"You left suddenly," Nat said, not noticing his discomfort.

"Aye, I needed to return home."

Nat placed a plate in front of me, and the food was passed from person to person. Along with the grilled meat, corn on the cob and watermelon filled our plates, and iced tea our drinking glasses. Except for Lee, the children were boisterous, shouting and jesting. Whilst the grownups talked, he ate his meal in silence. After the apple pie, the children scampered to the woods in a frenzy.

Nat had a pinched smile. "Lee..."

He shook his head that he had no wish to join them.

Nat pointed her finger in the direction of the woods.

Lee got to his feet and trudged after the other children.

"Phoebe, you said your husband is Native. Maybe he can speak to Lee. We try to give him a sense of his heritage, but we seem to be constantly lacking."

"I'll ask him." I stood. "Meanwhile, mayhap there's something I can say."

"Mayhap," she repeated. "You never said where you're originally from. I detect an accent."

"Dorset, England."

"England." She smiled. "That's nice. I thank you for your help."

I hustled towards the woods. Why did the dreaming keep bringing me to the time when Lee was a lad? 'Til I could discover the answer, I would rejoice in seeing this side of him. He had often told me about his troubled youth. Now, I viewed his growing difficulties firsthand. I entered the woods to shrieking children, running hither and thither.

One lad screeched at a lass. "He's going to scalp you!"

She screamed.

The other children danced in a choppy manner, shouting war whoops. Lee continued along the sandy path that led him deeper into the woods. I trailed after him. "Lee..."

He faced me but cast his gaze to the ground. E'en as a lad, he was obviously ashamed that I had seen his tears. His voice wavered when he spoke. "You said I was Paspahegh. How is that possible? They're gone."

"How can they be gone if you are still here?"

He appeared to mull o'er my words. "The other kids call me a savage. Many Indians died because they were savages."

"Nay, don't believe such cruel words. Indians aren't savages, e'en if history paints them that way. Tell your momma and poppa what the others say."

He shook his head. "I can't."

E'en at this young age, I spied the hint of a warrior in his eyes. "They only want what's best for you."

He started walking in the direction of the other children. Relief spread through me, for no doubt existed in my mind, he would grow into the noble man I loved. For a short distance, I followed him, but my white hound stood afore me.

"Momma?"

I blinked. Elenor stood afore me.

"Momma, I'm sorry. I didn't realize you had entered the dreaming."

" 'Tis all right. I saw him as a lad."

"Wind Talker?"

"Aye. I only wish I could understand the meaning. Why do I keep seeing him as a lad?"

Elenor embraced me. "You'll find the answer in time."

She was right, and I would continue to contemplate. "I had better scurry to the loft afore Heather misses me." We said goodnight, and I climbed the stairs. I slipped into bed aside Heather. As I drifted, instead of my daughter, I felt Caleb's presence next to me. When he gasped, I thought of the time he had been attacked by a bear. Silver Eagle had wanted to relieve the hound from his misery, but Momma had shown me how to tend him. He had survived.

When I awoke, I had difficulty believing that he hadn't spent the night with me. After feeding Heather and aiding Elenor with her chores, I held Heather's hand, and we wandered along a familiar trail through the forest. When she could no longer walk, I carried her and made my way to the place where I had often found Wind Talker seeking solitude. As I approached the smaller growth of trees, I imagined his voice singing to the spirits.

The closer we got, the more Heather insisted upon walking on her own. A chill engulfed me and I shuddered, for I, too, had been present when the colonists had attacked the Paspahegh. Musketeers had fired volleys upon us. Momma and I had been separated, and Caleb led me through the smoke. Somewhere near was where I had lost the two-year-old Wind Talker, Crow in the Woods. To no avail, I had gone after him. I, too, had been engulfed in mist, but he had been swallowed by it.

I stepped forward into the zone I had long avoided. Screams echoed in my head, but e'en worse, I spied the bones. A hand, a leg, a grinning skull with a bullet hole—most were partially buried in the sandy soil. Snow Bird had died here and most likely was hastily buried along with the rest. More than three decades had passed since the Paspahegh had been murdered here. Through the long shadows, I viewed the soldiers burning houses. Smoke and screams—I nearly made a panicked retreat.

Hoping my daughter would ne'er witness such carnage, I gripped her hand tighter. Her poppa had come here in an attempt to make peace with the past, and now, he was missing. Mayhap he had rejoined his tribe and his calls came to me from the afterlife.

"Wind Talker, where are you?"

"He has retreated to the time in front of you."

I quickly turned. Afore me stood a warrior attired in a breechclout and buckskin leggings. He was the husband of Wind Talker's sister.

"Swift Deer," I said.

"Wildcat sent me. He has spoken to Wind Talker through what you call the dreaming."

The sensation of feeling closer to Wind Talker at this location, as well as Caleb's presence, finally made sense. Wind Talker had returned to the time when I was a lass. The dreaming had sent me a clue by allowing me to see Lee at the same age as he saw me. Mayhap now that the truth had been revealed, I would be able to reach him. "Come, Swift Deer. You must be weary from your journey. We'll give you sustenance and a place to rest. Pray tell me all that you have learned."

"Thank you, Walks Through Mist. Your hospitality is most welcome."

I picked up Heather and introduced her to her uncle. At least now, I had an inkling on how to direct my search for Wind Talker.

Long after the others had gone to their rest, I scurried from the loft to the outdoors. E'en with a candle in hand, I dared not risk the treacherous path to the resting place of the Paspahegh bones. Instead, I made my way to the dock. 'Twas peaceful with gentle waves and filtered moonlight. "Wind Talker, you share the same ground with me, but in a different realm. Hear my voice."

Mist surrounded me. My hound failed to appear, and I wandered blindly. I collided with a tree branch and nearly fell. On shaky feet, I stumbled forward. I felt Wind Talker's presence nearby and called his name.

A figure stood afore me, but 'twas much too short for Wind Talker. "Phoebe." The woman called me once more and stepped from the shadows.

"Momma?" She came closer. Her hair had flecks of gray, and she looked the same as when I last saw her afore she had died from the smallpox. "Momma!" I threw my arms round her and hugged her in viselike grip.

"Phoebe..."

I stepped back. Tears clouded both of our eyes. "I've missed you," I said.

"And I, you. Phoebe, there's not much time. I'm here to beg you not to contact Wind Talker."

"Not contact Wind Talker? Swift Deer made the long journey to inform me where I'd find him."

"Aye, I know." She grasped my hands. " 'Tis not that simple. Wind Talker is gone from your current realm and will not return."

My throat constricted. "Will not... Momma, I don't understand. If he's gone, why should I not contact him?"

She clutched me tighter. "He has a mission to fulfill. 'Til he completes it, he cannot join you."

"Momma, are you saying—?"

"Nay, Phoebe. He lives, but 'tis important that he completes the journey. His thoughts are with you and Heather, but he must focus on what lies ahead. If you contact him, he will work harder to return to a life that isn't meant to be."

"Momma, I can't lose—"

She pressed her fingers to my lips. "You won't lose him. His heart will always remain with you."

With her words, she vanished. Waves lapped against the dock where I had entered the dreaming, and the candle flickered in my hand. "Momma?" How could I refrain from contacting Wind Talker? "Momma?"

When a scream came forth, I didn't e'en realize 'twas my own. The candle flew into water, dousing the flames. My knees wobbled, and I sank to the wood surface of the dock. "Wind Talker... come to me. I cannot live without you." I placed my hands to my head and wept.

14

Wind Talker

1610

As I had predicted, Phoebe's dog lived. With Caleb's survival, Silver Eagle's doubt about my story of traveling through time faded. He and Phoebe's mother became my steadfast allies. As the days passed, I spent much of my time with Silver Eagle. We hunted, fished, mended nets, and made arrowheads. Sometimes Swimming Beaver joined us. There was no hiding the fact that he was more adept at making tools than I was.

After a few weeks, I had no difficulty encountering Black Owl. In fact, I grew comforted by his presence and talking with him, even if he had no idea who I was. My mother was a different matter. Her gaze would lock onto mine as if down deep, she knew who I was. Unless I could find some way of changing what the future held, I resisted all temptation of telling her.

As for Crow in the Woods, I kept my distance. No one questioned a warrior not interacting with a young child, but anytime I saw him, I froze. Occasionally, I'd wonder if he felt the strange sensation too, but he was likely too young to comprehend. In any case, because of his age, he'd have no memory of our meetings. On the other hand, Phoebe proved to be another story. Unless I had Elenor's help to distract her daughter, I had to refrain from entering the dreaming. Still, I tried with no success.

One evening Elenor invited me over to their outside cook fire and handed me a bowl of stew. Conscious of Phoebe staring at me, I was thankful that Silver Eagle kept the conversation going about an upcoming fishing trip. The stew hit the spot and Elenor ladled out more.

"I'll take it to him, Momma."

Out of the corner of my eye, I saw Phoebe approach me.

She held out the gourd bowl and cleared her throat. "Lee . . ."

My brows shot up. "Lee? How could you have known?"

Startled by my response, she dropped the bowl. Phoebe's mother escorted the girl to the house. Silver Eagle looked at me but said nothing. I could only imagine what must have been going through his mind. "My name among the English before I became Wind Talker was Lee," I said. "I have no idea how she found out."

A long while passed before he spoke. "There is no doubt the bond between the two of you is a strong one."

"But she can't know who I am—not the way I am now."

"She can." Elenor had returned, and I glanced to the mat door to see if Phoebe might be following her. "She's resting. She told me of a dream she had where a carriage existed without horses pulling it, and a house filled with glass windows. She saw herself as a woman, and the man looked like you—only with short hair. He went by the name of Lee, and there was a babe by the name of Heather."

The child Phoebe had undoubtedly envisioned our lives as adults, but my wife had never mentioned such a dream. Was it possible that my presence had changed time? I returned to the matter at hand. "I don't know what to say. I'll try and keep my distance so as not to upset her further."

Elenor rested a hand on my arm. "You are a man of honor. I know you would not hurt her."

"My presence hurts her."

"Nay." She lowered her arm. "She's confused. Your presence frightens her, yet lulls her. When she becomes a woman, she will understand that she has been entering other realms."

"So what do we do in the meantime?"

"Go forward as naturally as possible."

"Easier said than done."

Circle in Time

"Aye, but you're amongst family and friends."

Silver Eagle, who had kept silent throughout our conversation, nodded. "Thank you," I said. "Both of you. I don't know what I would have done without your help."

"You're welcome," Silver Eagle replied.

With that, I wished them goodnight. I headed to the guest house where I had been staying. Once inside, I sat by the fire. More than anything, I wanted to enter the dreaming, but afraid that the child Phoebe would hear my calls, I decided against it. The massacre was near. I could feel it in my bones. I had to find a way to warn the tribe before it was too late.

The heat and humidity climbed, and over the next few days, I managed to keep my distance from Phoebe. Right now, I had more important things to worry about. Silver Eagle agreed to accompany me to meet with *weroance* Wowinchapuncke. We were escorted to a longhouse and shown the way inside. The chief sat on a wood frame, and his advisors, which included a *kwiocos* or a spiritual leader, sat next to him. The *kwiocos* had his head shaved on the sides, and his black hair stood upright in the center. I approached with my head lowered and waited until Wowinchapuncke requested for me to speak. "You wished to see me, Wind Talker?" he asked.

"I do." I had rehearsed in my mind what I had come to say, but now that the moment was upon me, words escaped me. Straightforward was probably best. "The *tassantassas* plan to attack."

"How do you know this?"

I couldn't easily come out and say I had already lived through it. "I had a vision."

Wowinchapuncke nodded. "Go on."

"It will come on August 9." He frowned. How could I translate a date? My tribe measured time by the moon cycles, and I still had difficulty comprehending in such a realm. "What phase is the moon in now?" I asked.

"In four days time, it will be the new moon," said the *kwiocos*.

New moon? Of July or August? "What is the next moon cycle?"

"The corn moon," the *kwiocos* replied.

I swallowed. August had already arrived. Hoping my calculations were correct, I said, "The attack will likely be coming in the next few days."

"You're certain?" Wowinchapuncke asked.

"No, I'm not certain of the date. It's near as I can guess, but it will happen—at dawn. Since I speak their language, I would like to try and help avert it in some way."

"Tensions already run high, Wind Talker. I, too, have been held captive after we refused to trade with the *tassantassas*. Like you, I was able to escape. Why would you risk recapture?"

"Because I believe the Paspahegh's very existence is at stake."

He shook his head. "The *tassantassas* have already cut off a warrior's hand and sent it to the paramount chief in warning. I can't allow you to risk yourself in such a way. In fact, with your warning we shall be waiting for them, and your presence will be more valuable to our defense."

My heart sank, but I was dismissed. Once outside the longhouse, Silver Eagle turned to me. "Tell me what happens."

"Many of the warriors go on a hunting trip, and the English attack while they're away, leaving elderly warriors and women to defend the town."

He smiled. "Then you have succeeded. The warriors will not leave the town defenseless."

The only thing I had likely succeeded in doing was having some die who wouldn't have otherwise, but I didn't voice my thoughts aloud.

"Wind Talker, are you not willing to sacrifice yourself so others may live?" he asked.

"I am," I agreed.

"More women and children will survive if the warriors are ready and waiting for the *tassantassas*."

I only hoped that he was right.

Though there was little time to prepare, Wowinchapuncke managed to get some of the women and children to safety among other tribes. Each morning, the warriors waited for an attack. As each day passed, I detected more tension and impatience. By the fourth day, the day of the new moon, many doubted my words. Wowinchapuncke reminded the warriors that they needed to be certain the attack wouldn't come before abandoning their readiness.

Dawn broke on the fifth morning to the sound of a drum. The beat signaled a peaceful greeting. Silver Eagle nodded in my direction that he was ready. Even though I was not the most skillful bowman, I waited with them. When the remaining women peered out of the houses, the warriors signaled for them to be ready to seek shelter.

Four warriors stepped toward the drummer as a line of English formed next to him. The drummer and his men moved forward to greet the warriors. "Ready! Aim!" Muskets raised.

Before the command to fire could be given, a round of arrows sailed at the greeters. The first line of soldiers, along with the drummer, fell, but more soldiers rushed toward us. The soldiers fired, and more arrows flew in their direction. Women and children bolted in panicked flight. Determined not to let the soldiers reach them, the warriors held their line.

Another line of soldiers set longhouses and cornfields on fire. Smoke furled. Arrows continued to fly as armored soldiers aimed matchlock muskets. I spotted a soldier waving a sword at a woman and her child. A warrior charged him. Before the soldier could bring his sword down on the warrior, I caught the soldier's wrist and struggled against his grip. The blade inched toward me, when he fell to the ground with a scream. A tomahawk protruded from his neck.

I picked up the sword. While the armor covered the soldiers' chests, I aimed for the less protected areas: necks, arms, and legs. Screams surrounded me, and the smoke from the fires nearly smothered me. I kept going. If I couldn't change history, I would die among my people. More soldiers rushed toward me. I brought one down after another, but they kept coming.

As a muzzle flash went off in the distance, someone shoved me from behind. A sharp stinging and burning sensation spread through my upper right arm. The sword fell from my hand, and the warmth of blood filled my shirtsleeve. A red stain spread throughout. I couldn't tell how bad the wound was, but my arm went limp.

"Wind Talker!" Swimming Beaver staggered out of the smoke and guided me away from the fighting. Many warriors had already fallen. The soldiers shot at anything that moved and torched the remaining houses. Feeling lightheaded, I swayed. Swimming Beaver drew my good arm over his shoulder and led the way.

I thought of Phoebe—not the girl, but the woman. I felt her presence and imagined her beside me as we walked along a strip mall. The sun on the pavement made the day seem hotter. I stared at the gas station and supermarket and told Phoebe that at one time there had been hiking trails. When I was a kid, my adoptive parents had brought me to this place. But why was I thinking of the twenty-first century? Had I managed to change time?

"Wind Talker," Swimming Beaver gasped, returning me to the present. He pressed a hand to his chest.

Only then did I realize that he'd been wounded too. Blood trickled between his fingers. I recalled Black Owl's words before entering this time realm. *"Some will live, others shall die. Your decision will not alter the outcome."* Did that mean Swimming Beaver would have died along with me if I had not left the island? I gasped. *The circle will repeat.* This place was where my two-year-old self would walk through the mist and end up four hundred years in the future. I needed to concentrate, or Black Owl's warning might mean both of us would wind up dead.

We leaned on each other for support. Gunfire came less and less often, and we made our way through the fire and smoke.

"Wind Talker, I haven't gone through the *huskanaw*."

"Neither did I."

"Yet you were given an honorable name. Do you suppose I might be granted the same in the afterlife?"

"You're not going to—"

"Wind Talker, I feel it. My time is near."

Swimming Beaver swayed. I caught him in my good arm before he hit the ground. "Swimming Beaver, don't give up."

"I won't." He groaned, then went limp. I lost my grip and he fell. Bending down, I checked his pulse and breathing. He smiled. "I thought I had passed through to the afterlife."

"You're still here, and we will reach safety." I gritted my teeth and helped Swimming Beaver up. "We need to keep moving." As we made our way through the carnage, we sidestepped the bodies. One woman looked familiar. *Snow Bird.* My presence here had changed nothing. "*Nek,*" I whispered. What if Black Owl and Silver Eagle were among the casualties?

Swimming Beaver glanced at me as if understanding. "You did all that you could to save them."

"It wasn't enough." I glanced around but didn't see my younger self anywhere nearby.

"Wind Talker, don't give up."

My own words had come back to haunt me. I closed my eyes and pushed on. I'd grieve later. Swimming Beaver needed my help now. All around us, I heard people crying and dying shouts. As soon as I got Swimming Beaver to safety, I'd return and see who else I might be able to help. After traveling a few hundred yards, Swimming Beaver collapsed. I couldn't keep my grip and he fell flat on his chest.

Carefully, I rolled him over and hugged him as if the gesture could keep him from dying. A contented smile appeared on the boy's face. "I know who you are, Wind Talker. Snow Bird told me."

"I am Crow in the Woods," I admitted.

His smile widened. "You couldn't have changed the way things were meant to be." His head fell back and his breathing became irregular. He choked and gurgled, and his legs and arms spasmed until he lay still.

"Swimming Beaver." I shook him by the shoulders. "Swimming Beaver! Wake up!"

Numb from the loss all around me, I struggled to my feet, holding my wounded arm next to me. I had to clear my head and think. *If only...* I sank to my knees. Others survived. Once again, I got to my feet and traveled away from the massacre. Body after body. I checked each one to see if anyone was alive.

Most were dead, but a few survived. I spoke words of comfort and saw several more to the afterlife. I continued on. I had no idea how long I had been walking through the smoke. As nightfall neared, the shooting muskets and dying screams came less often.

A dog barked, and for some reason, I moved toward the sound. A red-haired girl huddled with a toddler in her arms. "Phoebe?"

With a tear-streaked face, she looked in my direction. "Wind Talker."

"Don't worry. You'll be safe." Exhausted, I moved closer and sat beside her. I instantly froze. The toddler in her arms was Crow in the Woods. Our gazes met and my heart beat in an odd rhythm.

"You're hurt," she said.

Phoebe's voice drew me back to the situation at hand. "It's nothing serious."

Even at ten, she was precocious. She put Crow in the Woods down and inspected my wound. She placed her index finger in my hand. "Can you grip my finger?"

Because of all that had happened I had blocked out the pain in my arm. A burning sensation shot through it, but my fingers were numb. I couldn't grasp her finger. "No."

She packed my arm with moss to slow the bleeding. "Momma or Snow Bird will see to it when we find them."

I didn't have the heart to tell her that my mother was dead. She would find out soon enough. Darkness spread, and she huddled with Crow in the Woods in her arms and her dog nearby. Caleb would warn us if anyone approached. I gave in to my own exhaustion and dozed. Soft cries woke me. *Crow in the Woods.* My younger self had wandered off. Wondering if I could change the outcome, I followed the sound.

"I'm coming, lad," came Phoebe's voice from behind me.

A pale moonlight shone an array of shadows.

"Where are you, Crow in the Woods?" Phoebe called.

I staggered through the darkness and was engulfed by mist. Overhead a crow cawed. Like a beacon, the bird guided the way. While Phoebe continued to call for my younger self, his cries came from within. The mist thickened, but Crow in the Woods got closer. I could feel his presence. Suddenly, as if stepping through a door, Phoebe's calls vanished. In this place, my arm no longer hurt and seemed completely functional. Meg had followed Phoebe into the seventeenth century. Like her, I had stepped into the portal and trailed after Crow in the Woods. I would reappear in the twentieth century. All of the people I knew in that realm would be children. How would I cope? "Crow in the Woods."

His wails came from all around me. The crow cawed. I must believe that Crow would guide me.

A woman stepped out of the mist. The skin on the left side of her face was bright red burns. "Crow in the Woods."

I looked for the child, but she had called to me. "I'm Wind Talker now, *Nek*."

Sadness crossed my mother's face. "I'm sorry I will not be there for you. I've failed you yet again."

"You didn't fail. As you can see, I survived. So did a few of the others."

"But you're caught in an endless circle."

"Not endless." I told her how my younger self would travel through time and grow up in the future. Eventually, the child she knew as Red Dog would follow me after she became a woman. We would marry and have a daughter of our own. As I spoke, her burns vanished.

Even after hearing my story, she frowned. "How will you break the cycle?"

"I don't know yet, but I'll find a way."

With my promise, she vanished and a gentle breeze blew. The crow cawed and once again, I followed him. Along with Crow, the wind showed me the way. "Crow in the Woods." I marched on and on but found no traces of my younger self. "Crow in the Woods," I called again.

Up ahead a light appeared and Phoebe stood before me; not the child but the woman I loved. She wore a long green skirt, a laced top with metal eyelets, and a linen cap. She was dressed the way I had envisioned her during my first experience with the dreaming.

She stretched her fingers toward me. "Come with me for the circle to repeat."

I attempted to raise my right arm to touch her but my arm no longer functioned. I was near the end of the portal and feared she'd vanish before my eyes. I lifted my left arm and grasped her fingers. The crow cawed a warning, but I had Phoebe's hand in my grip. I refused to let go. *Phoebe*.

15

Phoebe

1646

As I gathered herbs, Wind Talker called my name. I looked round but no one was there, except for Bess and Heather. "Did you hear that?" I asked.

Bess shook her head. "Hear what?"

"Wind Talker."

"Hasn't it been months since you last heard his voice?"

Six moons, to be exact. I often felt his presence, but 'twas fleeting. Had I really heard him? I had abided Momma's wishes and not tried to contact him. Yet, he hailed me. Unconvinced that 'twas naught more than my imagination, I moved towards the dock. "Pray keep watch o'er Heather for me." Bess agreed, and I gazed upon the James River. Not a boat lingered. I glanced downriver. Naught.

A gentle breeze stroked my cheek, and I wandered along the forest edge. With the onset of spring, shrubs with delicate white tendrils bloomed. Sweetspire had no medicinal value, so I gave it little more notice. Fire pink had brilliant scarlet-looking star-like flowers. 'Twas toxic and often confused with pink root which was used to rid a body of worms. But I wasn't looking for medicinals now and meandered inland away from the river.

Checking e'ery nook and cranny, I roamed the land surrounding the plantation. A black woodpecker, with a red crest and loud call that sounded almost like someone laughing, flew overhead. I neared the area where I hadn't traveled since Swift Deer had brought me the news of Wind Talker. As I approached the smaller growth of trees, the warm day suddenly felt cold. Arrowheads lingered in abundance as well as clay pot pieces. 'Twas here where Momma and I had fled on that fateful night.

In fear of unsettling the spirits, I dared not venture any closer. *Wind Talker, Momma told me not to contact you.* He was near. Of that I was certain for I could feel his proximity. A zephyr sighed like it had whispered my name. "Wind Talker?"

I spied my white hound and he barked a frenzy for me to follow him. The mist embraced me. At first, I feared I was breaking Momma's wishes, but when the fog cleared, cars honked and people hurried to and fro on the walkway. I recognized a flower shop, a restaurant, a bank, and a jewelry store. 'Twas the spot where I had arrived in the twenty-first century. Only I had arrived at night and the lights had blinded me.

Follow the light.

"Ms. Wynne?"

I turned to the man, standing behind me. E'en though he had short hair like I remembered when he was a detective, he dressed in a T-shirt and jeans, not a business suit. "Wind Talker?"

"Lee Crowley, ma'am. I haven't seen you in years."

Years? Though he was definitely not a lad anymore, his countenance was thinner and there was no hint of lines. I guessed him to be in his mid-twenties, rather than his thirties. "Lee?"

"Lee Crowley. Why don't we go over to the restaurant? My treat, and we can talk. I've been curious about some of the things you told me when I was ten."

"I'd like that." We stepped into the street to cross, and I halted, half expecting a car to come out of nowhere to strike me. I trembled.

"Are you all right, Ms. Wynne?"

Follow the light.

'Twas his voice, leading me to this place and time.

He gently grasped my arm and aided me across the street. "Are you all right?" he repeated.

No car sped towards me, but the piercing sound of a horn and screeching brakes inundated me. Recalling the pain, I closed my eyes. *Soon my beloved, I will join you.*

"Ms. Wynne? Are you in need of a doctor?"

I opened my eyes to discover I was safely on the other side of the street. 'Twas here that Wind Talker had called to me, and I had told him that I would join him. Now, he stood afore me. "Nay, I was in a car accident once. Sometimes, I continue to get chills, but I'm fine now."

He nodded in understanding. "Then, let's go inside."

"Aye."

He held the door open for me. A woman at a counter greeted us and showed us to a booth where we made ourselves comfortable.

I regarded him from across the table, and my heart fluttered. "You're a detective now."

"I've been a detective for about a year. How did you know?" A waitress handed us menus and asked us what we'd like to drink. I ordered water and Lee said, "Coffee."

I bit my lip to keep from giggling. He had given up coffee when we had returned to the seventeenth century.

"Ms. Wynne—"

"Pray call me Phoebe."

"Phoebe..." When he met my gaze, I was certain that he detected the connection. He swallowed. "I hear an accent. Where are you from?"

"Dorset."

He cleared his throat. "England?"

"Aye."

The waitress returned with our drinks and took our order. When she left, he said, "I have this feeling we've met before, and I don't mean the couple of times when I was ten."

Only if I continued to meet him in this manner would I reveal the ways of the dreaming. For now, 'twas best if I remained silent. "Nay, we have not met, except for when you were a lad."

Skepticism crossed his countenance as he sipped his coffee. "When you first met me, you said *netab* and that it means friend. The language sounds familiar."

" 'Tis Algonquian."

He shook his head. "None of this makes sense. You also said I was Paspahegh. That's not possible. The Paspahegh were annihilated in the seventeenth century."

"Not all were."

He blew out a breath in frustration. "I'm not ten anymore—"

The waitress interrupted by placing our sandwiches in front of us. When she left, I reached across and grasped Lee's hand. "In time, you shall understand."

He glanced at my hand upon his, then at me. "Everything inside me says there's no evidence for what you say, but for some reason, I believe you're telling the truth."

"Am I interrupting?"

I withdrew my hand from Lee's, and he jumped to his feet, motioning for the woman to have a seat. "Shae, this is Phoebe Wynne. Phoebe, my wife, Shae."

Shae, in time, we too would become friends, but she would divorce Lee afore that happened. Instead of shoulder-length blonde hair, it reached her waist, and she was much trimmer than when I had known her. "I presume the two of you are working on a case," she said.

"Not exactly." Lee explained how he had met me when he was ten. I smiled as he relayed the story. He was becoming the man I loved.

Mist surrounded me. Though I was unable to see clearly, I spied clay pot pieces and bones. Wind Talker's presence lingered near me. He was close. "Wind Talker?"

I buried my fear and stepped forward. My dress caught on a bush. I swallowed and kept going. A body stretched afore me. Not bones, but a body. He wore a wool shirt and a breechclout. My heart skipped a beat, and I inched towards the prone warrior. Somehow, he had broken through the barrier and made contact, but he looked dead. Was this the mission Momma had spoken of? "Wind Talker?" As I bent down, I fought the urge to scream.

Afore I could touch him, the fog cleared. Only bones surrounded me. I could no longer keep my tears at bay.

16

Wind Talker

Drifting in and out of a feverish daze, I floated in a hazy dream. Phoebe was near. Her close presence made me smile. I longed to touch her, but a gunshot at the back of my mind reminded me of where I was. Waking with a start, I seized the arm of an assailant. With a scream, he fell to his knees. I blinked. *Her* knees.

Her blue-green eyes—wide with terror—stared at me. "Wind Talker?"

"Phoebe?" No longer a child, she looked vulnerable with her straying hair. I let go of her arm. "I hope I haven't hurt you. I didn't know it was you." I sat up and she regained her feet.

Phoebe dusted herself off. "I'm uninjured."

For some reason, my right arm hurt like hell. Half closing my eyes, I hugged it next to my body.

"Let me see." She inspected my arm. " 'Twas made by a matchlock—in the same spot I had dressed a wound during the attack. How can that be?" Before I could respond, she gathered some moss and packed the wound.

"What year is it?" I asked.

"What year? 'Tis 1626."

1626? I wasn't home. While Phoebe was no longer a young girl, she wasn't my wife either. I attempted to stand but swayed.

"We can talk later. Let me help you." She pulled my good arm around her shoulder and helped me to my feet.

My arm burned. I continued hugging it and drew away from Phoebe. "I'm okay."

"Okay?" she asked in confusion.

"I'm all right."

Apparently not believing me, she guided me along the trail. In my foggy mind, I lagged. She lent her support by wrapping her arm around my waist. As we continued on, she trembled.

I came to a halt and glanced around. On the ground, a skull grinned at me. "My God, this is where it happened." I sank to my knees. Bowing my head, I closed my eyes.

" 'Twas more than a decade ago."

I pounded my fist to the ground. "My presence didn't change a thing. The goddamn bastards murdered innocent women and children." I lowered my head and wept.

A gentle hand touched my shoulder. "You fought with the warriors and we survived."

I wiped away the tears with the side of my hand and looked up at her. I shook my head. "It wasn't enough. I've lived through it twice now."

"Twice?"

Feeling lightheaded, I clutched my arm.

Phoebe bent down to help. "Ne'er mind explaining now. I need to get you to the house in order to tend you." Once again, she drew my arm over her shoulder and helped me to my feet. I wobbled. "One step at a time," she said. "You may have lost a lot of blood."

I laughed—weakly. "Maybe I'll be the one to receive a transfusion, instead of being the donor for a change."

"Transfusion?"

"Never mind."

She assisted me through the place of the massacre. Occasionally, I needed rest, but we walked several miles to a familiar pitched-roof house—only it was wood, rather than the brick I remembered.

"Bess!" When the servant failed to appear, Phoebe called again.

A brown-haired guard with a grim face opened the palisade gate and aimed a musket at me.

Phoebe raised her hand. "Wind Talker won't hurt anyone. He's a friend of my father's."

The guard eyed me but lowered the weapon.

"Bess!" A white servant, clutching a young girl's hand, came instead. "Jennet," Phoebe said, "I'll need some water and cloth, then fetch Bess. I'll need her assistance. Pray watch Elenor for me 'til I've seen to Wind Talker."

The young girl was Phoebe's daughter. I had only known Elenor as an adult. The servant scurried off, and we entered the house.

Phoebe aided me to the bed. "Now let me see your arm." She lit a candle and examined the wound more closely. My muscles tensed when she touched my arm. "I know it hurts." Bess entered the room, and Phoebe said to her servant, "This is Wind Talker."

"Bess," I said before the introduction could be reciprocated.

"Have we met afore?" the servant asked.

"In another time."

Bess merely nodded. "I'll fetch some tea."

As Bess left the room, Phoebe helped me remove my shirt. She inspected the wound in my arm. " 'Tis fairly clean and not gaping, which should aid in healing."

Jennet joined us, carrying a glass pitcher. She paled upon seeing my arm.

"Go watch Elenor," Phoebe said.

Pain shot through my arm as she set about to cleaning the wound. I gritted my teeth to keep the swear words from flowing. When she finished, she placed a bandage around my arm to halt the bleeding. Soon, I breathed in the scent of herbal tea.

Phoebe placed a cup to my lips. "Here, drink this."

With a sip, I grimaced and choked back a cough. "What is it?"

" 'Tis bangue. It shall help the pain. You need to drink all of it."

I forced a smile. "Bangue. I know it well. They call it pot where I'm from."

"Then you know 'twill help the pain."

"Indeed I do."

She returned the cup to my lips, and I sipped the drink. After I finished, she left the room, saying that she would be back shortly. Bess entered the room before Phoebe. Thankfully, drowsiness had set in as she set out heavy metal forceps, some kind of needle, and thread. No doubt, these were the tools they were going to use on my arm. I shivered.

Phoebe returned to my side and grasped the forceps. " 'Twill hurt, but I must remove anything unnatural in the wound."

Taking a deep breath, I nodded for her to continue.

When she unwrapped the bandage, blood flowed. With a linen cloth Bess dabbed my arm to wipe the blood away. Phoebe probed with the forceps, and I closed my eyes. She went deeper. More than anything, I wanted to scream. I held it in. Bess's hands pressed a bandage to my arm to slow the bleeding.

Phoebe poked into my arm again with the forceps. I groaned. " 'Twill be o'er soon," she said. Metal clinked in a pan. "I got the musket ball."

Bess mopped the blood away, while Phoebe washed the wound. Phoebe threaded a needle. I had no desire to watch her sew me up like some garment and turned my head away. The needle entered my arm, and I gasped, wondering how much more torture I could take.

The pain lessened. " 'Tis o'er," Phoebe said. "No bones were broken, and the ball didn't hit anything vital. You should be fine."

Exhausted from the ordeal, I drifted. "Thank you."

Her touch was gentle. She dabbed a cool cloth to my forehead. The refreshing feeling spread from my neck to my chest. "Phoebe..."

"Hush now. You've taken on a fever. Save your strength. I'm here."

Thank God, I had found her again. I was home. Her touch returned. The cloth cooled my neck and shoulders. With her tender strokes, the pain faded. She helped me sit up and massaged my back in long, comforting caresses. Once flat on my back again, she loosened the leather strip of my loincloth. Her soothing touches reached my groin. In fond remembrance, I smiled. How much time had passed since we had last made love?

She tossed a wool blanket over me, immediately extinguishing my flames, and I fell into a deep sleep. Stabbing pain woke me. With a groan, I clutched my arm against my body and clamped my eyes shut.

"I shall make some tea."

"Phoebe?"

"I'm here." The only light was from the embers in the fireplace and a candle. Phoebe stirred the fire and placed a kettle over the growing flames. When she returned, she placed a cup to my lips. "Here, drink some tea."

With her help, I drank the entire cupful. "Thanks." I hugged my arm next to me. "I never thought I'd happily be accepting as much bangue as I can get."

"Why? 'Tis a useful herb, naught more."

"You'll understand in time."

She checked my forehead. "You're still feverish, but not as warm as afore."

"Phoebe..." A sharp pain stabbed me, and I couldn't think straight.

"Lee..."

I *was* home—in the twenty-first century. My thoughts clouded. "Phoebe, I missed you."

A warm body joined me beneath the blanket. My body molded to hers as she drew me near. With a tremble, I clung to her until drowsiness overwhelmed me. To the steady beat of her heart, I could rest peacefully. I dreamed of the time when we had lived together, and she had called me Lee.

17

Phoebe

1646

M EG AND CHARGING BEAR OFTEN VISITED THE PLANTATION WHEN my brother traded for supplies with Christopher. Though nervous but happy, my friend was with child again. I made her some tea from the reddish-brown bark of blackhaw to prevent miscarriage. "Your knowledge of remedies is incredible," Meg said, sipping her tea. She placed her cup on the table. "Phoebe, I can see your sadness. Why don't you come back with us to the Appamattuck? I miss you, and we can—"

"Nay." I shook my head. "I can't. 'Tis this place where I hear his voice."

"But you told me that you no longer try to contact him."

Earlier I had told Meg about my encounter with Momma. "As Wind Talker, but I've seen Lee."

"Lee? Wow, I wonder what that could mean."

"I know not. At least, not yet."

She smiled slightly. "I wouldn't mind seeing Lee. How about if we contact him together?"

For the week that my friend remained at the plantation, we entered the dreaming e'ery night. Together we walked paths, reliving our past, but not when Lee was present. After she returned to the

Appamattuck, I traveled the route to the Paspahegh remains at least twice a week. For a moment, I regretted my decision of not returning to the Appamattuck with Meg and Charging Bear. Heather would have had the chance to come to know her people.

As I turned away from the bones, my hound appeared afore me. My heart fluttered for he would take me to Lee. Of that I was certain. I followed him through the mist 'til reaching a familiar walkway. 'Twas crowded with people. 'Twas daylight, but I felt his presence in my bones. Afraid to cross the road, I froze. Carefully, I checked the traffic afore stepping into the road. My breath quickened and my knees quaked, but I safely made it to the other side.

"Phoebe?" Lee stepped out from the throng of people.

Though he seemed happy to see me, I detected sorrow in his eyes. "I was looking for you," I said.

He motioned to the restaurant as a suggestion.

"Nay, I'd like to go to the park that has the heron, foxes, and bison."

He nodded. "All right. I can bring the car around."

"I'll accompany you."

A hint of a smile crossed his countenance, and he showed the way to a parking lot, half a block away. 'Twasn't the T-Bird he had when we were first married, and I knew not the make. He opened the door for me, then went round to the other side and started the car. Once on the freeway, I absorbed the views I hadn't seen in some while. High-rise buildings loomed in the distance. On my first trip, I could have ne'er imagined such towers, nor the many forests having been chopped down to make way for a multitude of houses and buildings.

Lee exited the freeway onto a side road. After a few minutes, he brought the car to a halt in a parking lot. I recalled the place well for he had brought me here when he had been trying to discover if I was indeed a cunning woman from the seventeenth century. We strolled along a hilly path. Again, I spied grief, not merely in his eyes, but in his being as well.

"What's wrong?" I asked.

"Wrong?" He shrugged. "There's nothing—"

"You cannot hide such a thing from me."

We halted in front of a net aviary. A heron stalked along the marshy grass. "How can you know so much about me?" he asked.

"Because I'm a cunning woman from the seventeenth century."

He laughed. "Dare I ask what a cunning woman is?"

"A healer. You may unburden yourself."

"Now you sound like Shae." With the utterance of Shae's name, his eyes grew dark with pain.

The reason for his grief dawned on me. The dreaming must have sent me to the time of his divorce. He had told me how he had struggled through the days thereafter, by consuming ale and being drunken more often than not.

"What can I do to help?" I asked.

"Continue our tour."

We journeyed up another hill to the next enclosure. A bear sat on its haunches, watching the people as curiously as we observed the bruin. Many laughed, but Lee remained silent. We continued on, seeing a gray fox. In silence, we traversed more hills in order to see the bison and otters.

Soon after, we entered a Japanese garden. In Lee's company, I delighted in viewing the stone lanterns, arched bridges, and water lilies. I only wished I could remove his heartache, but e'en if I revealed the future, he would not likely believe me. "I can show you the dreaming," I finally said.

"The dreaming?"

"The dreaming will help you through your difficulties by giving answers to your questions."

He halted and faced me. "I still don't understand. What is the dreaming?"

" 'Tis best to show rather than explain."

"Then show me."

I glanced round at the other people lingering near us. "We must have privacy for me to show you."

He checked his watch and blew out a breath. "Phoebe, I have the distinct feeling you've guessed what's happened. I admit that I'm attracted to you, but I'm really not ready for another relationship."

His dark brown eyes reflected sincerity. I would bide my time, for his heartache kept him from sensing the connection betwixt us.

"I merely want to show you the dreaming. Naught more."

He nodded. "It seems strange, but why do you seem to show up when I think of you?"

" 'Tis an answer for the dreaming."

"All right. You've convinced me." He led the way to his car.

After a thirty-minute drive round the city, we arrived at his apartment. 'Twas the same one he had brought me to after my arrival in the twenty-first century. Like the time afore, clothes were tossed across the sofa and floor. Ale cans filled the bin. I kept my eyes away from the door leading to the bedroom, where we had made love. A dreamcatcher hung on the sliding door. On my first visit, I hadn't known what it was. I pointed to the colored beads grouped in fours. "White, red, yellow, and black represent the four winds amongst the Paspahegh."

"The four winds?"

Having stirred his curiosity, I smiled. "Each morn I face the sun and give thanks to Ahone. I hope that he is nearby, but he has other tribes to attend to. I must face in each direction so that he hears my prayers."

"Ahone, the Great Spirit?"

"Aye." We stood across from one another. So close—what I wouldn't give to be taken in his arms, but I resisted the temptation to touch him.

"Phoebe..." He cleared his throat. "Let's get back to what we came here for. You said you'd show me the dreaming."

In spite of his sorrow, he *did* feel our connection. "If you can fetch a candle..."

"I will." He went into the kitchen and retrieved a candle and holder. "I can't believe I've agreed to this," he muttered under his breath. "Whatever *this* is."

As I sat on the floor near the coffee table, I giggled and cleared away a clutter of papers. " 'Twouldn't be good to start a fire on the table. Now, pray light the candle."

Lee set the candle on the table afore me and lit the wick with a match. "Why do we need to stare at a candle?"

"The candle should help you focus."

His gaze met mine, then his eyes followed the length of my body. He let out a slow breath. "I'm focused all right, but it's not on any candle."

Later, my love. I motioned for him to sit across from me. "I agreed to show you the dreaming."

He laughed and sat on the floor. "Thank you, Phoebe."

"For what? I have done naught."

"But you have. Somehow you seem to know that Shae and I have split, yet you didn't pry. At the same time, you reminded me that there's still good in the world."

If I went to him now, we could retreat to the bedroom. Or make love here. I longed to feel his touches and kisses o'er my body.

"Phoebe? I hope I haven't embarrassed you."

"Nay, but we must concentrate, if you are going to learn the dreaming." I held out my hands for him to grasp. His gaze fastened onto the webbing betwixt the third and fourth fingers of my left hand. Unlike England during the time when I had been birthed, I knew he would not believe the fold of skin to be a witch's mark. He gripped my hands. " 'Twas considered a sign of luck amongst the Paspahegh," I said.

"You keep mentioning the Paspahegh. I fail to understand—"

"The answers you seek can be found in the dreaming. Look into the flame. My guardian spirit is a white hound. In time, you shall discover your own. 'Til then, follow mine."

As his stare fixated on the candle, his handhold grew tighter on mine. His breath quickened.

"Absorb the flame. Let it become part of you." Only on a couple of other occasions had I entered the dreaming whilst already in it. But if I could teach Lee the dreaming now, he would have answers to his many questions afore I physically arrived in the twenty-first century. We might change our destiny of living apart.

After a long while, his grip loosened on my hand. "Nothing."

"Pray don't give up."

"Phoebe, I appreciate what you're trying to do, but—"

"Absorb the flame," I repeated. "Feel its heat."

"The only heat I feel..." He squirmed. E'en from across the table, I could sense his arousal. I snickered at his discomfort. "You think it's funny?"

I clenched his hand once more. "Nay, but if you don't concentrate, you will not enter the dreaming."

"Of all the asinine," he muttered.

"Seek my hound. He will show you the way."

Lee drew a frustrated breath but stared into the flame. I no longer held his hands, but 'twas like we were touching all the same. When his gaze met mine, the mist drew us in. My body shaped to his, holding him in my arms. He shivered in a feverish frenzy, but I kept gripping him, whispering to him that he'd be all right.

He wore a breechclout and had long hair. "Wind Talker?"

"Phoebe?"

The fog surrounded me. When it cleared, I stood near the bones of all those who had died. Both Lee and Wind Talker had vanished.

18

Wind Talker

May 1626

A CROW FLEW OVERHEAD. All sensation in my right hand was gone. Through my clouded mind, I drifted and thought of Phoebe. Her voice whispered on the wind, and she called my name. "Lee..."

Lee? That was my other life, but it was where I had met Phoebe as an adult. Night after night, she tended me. Her touch was gentle and I smiled. She placed a cloth on my forehead, and the invigorating coolness spread throughout my body. But the pain... I sucked in my breath.

"Drink this."

Phoebe's voice was soothing as she put a cup to my lips. Bitter liquid—I nearly gagged. "More bangue?"

"Aye."

I managed to finish the tea without choking. Me, the former cop, indulging in pot. If my arm didn't hurt so much, I would have snorted a laugh. Weariness and worry registered in Phoebe's blue-green eyes. Pain kept resurfacing, and I couldn't think straight. I clenched my teeth and closed my eyes.

Water dripped in a pan, and Phoebe's touch returned. I thought about the first time I had made love to Phoebe, and my body reacted. She had grasped my hand and asked, "Can you not feel it?"

From the beginning, I had been afraid to love her, but I had all the same. After kissing her in a burning hunger, I carried her to the bedroom. We helped each other undress. Serpent tattoos coiled around her breasts and thighs. Throughout the night we satisfied our passion. Only then did I sleep.

When I woke, she was sound asleep beside me with her arms around my neck. Although my right arm was numb, I recalled the night with fondness. I reached out with my left hand to Phoebe's reddish-blonde hair.

She yawned and opened her eyes.

As my hand stroked her hair, I breathed in her herbal scent and whispered her name. My hand slid down until coming to rest on her breast. Never questioning myself as to why she was fully dressed, I briefly caressed it through the fabric, then continued my journey downward. When I reached under her skirt, my hand froze. The Phoebe beside me was in her mid-twenties, not her thirties. I had been dreaming. Suddenly embarrassed, I looked away. "Forgive me."

Phoebe exited the bed in a hurry and straightened her dress with her back to me.

"Phoebe, I'm sorry. I thought you were someone else."

She faced me, but I couldn't look at her. If I did, my arousal would renew. "Nay," she said. "You called my name. 'Tis the same connection I felt when we met afore. You remained distant then because I was a lass, but I'm not a lass anymore. Tell me why I have always felt that I know you."

"I'll tell you everything you want to know." Pain radiated down my arm, and I hugged it next to me.

Phoebe was instantly by my side. "I should have been tending you properly. Let me see."

When she rolled up my shirtsleeve, I realized I was no longer wearing the wool shirt I had arrived in, but a linen shirt instead. " 'Tis looking good. The wound wasn't serious, but you had a fever. I'll fetch some porridge to break your fast, and you'll regain your strength quickly."

As she turned away, Phoebe's servant and daughter descended the ladder from the loft. I had known Elenor closer to the age that

Phoebe was now. The women exchanged their morning greetings, and Phoebe hugged her daughter. Bess entered the house. More greetings circled the room. Uncertain whether I had been flat on my back for days or weeks, I sat up. No dizziness or nausea. At least that much was good. Ever so slowly I placed my feet over the side of the bed and stood.

Although weak, I was thankful to be on my feet again. I stretched my left arm. Only then did I realize Bess stood beside me, ready to help me if I needed any assistance. "I'm fine," I said.

With a growing smile, she nodded. "We have met afore."

Her comment had been a statement, not a question. "I'll tell you and Phoebe at the same time."

Another nod. "If you're feeling strong enough, I'll serve the porridge in the kitchen, and Mistress Wynne will see to Elenor."

"I think I can manage."

She held out a hand and guided me toward the door. Outside an African man greeted me. Like me, he wore a linen shirt, but instead of a loincloth, he had breeches. Unlike many black men of the twenty-first century, his hair coiled in tight spirals about his head. "James?"

"Have we met?" he asked in a musical but broken accent.

"No." I glanced at Bess's advanced state of pregnancy and withheld the fact that I had met their son, who would be named after him.

Bess touched her belly and smiled. "Will my babe be fit?"

"He'll make you proud."

I hadn't meant to give the baby's gender away, but Bess's smile widened to a grin. She placed James's hand on her abdomen. I looked away to give them a moment of privacy. Before long, Bess's hand once again guided me to the kitchen. The wood shack was a couple of hundred feet from the main house. I had been in the seventeenth century long enough to know that land-owning colonials often had the kitchen in a separate building to reduce the risk of potential fires as well as overheating the main house during hot weather.

A couple of small tables lined the walls of the kitchen. I sat in a chair near one of the tables, and Bess brought me a bowl of piping hot porridge that had been simmering over a fire. Although awkward, I picked up the spoon in my left hand. Uncertain what to expect, I blew on the food to help cool it, then took a bite. Instead of being bland, the porridge was nicely seasoned with herbs and spices, and sweetened with honey.

I had no idea the last time I had consumed a decent meal and devoured the porridge as if I hadn't eaten in weeks. Bess brought me another bowl of porridge as well as some corn pone. The cornbread had been baked without milk or eggs and tasted much like what I had experienced in the Paspahegh town.

Instead of being revived after eating, I was hit by a wave of exhaustion. Yet, the pain in my arm remained intense. Bess placed a mug before me with some bangue-infused tea, which I gratefully accepted, then she wrapped a cloth around my arm to make a sling. "Now that you're up and about, 'tis best to rest your arm."

I spent most of the day resting on a straw mattress in the kitchen. Phoebe or Jennet would occasionally pop in, but the women kept busy with their chores. Around nightfall, Bess and I returned to the main house after Phoebe had put Elenor to bed. "I finally have a chance for our talk. How are you feeling?" she asked.

"Thanks to Bess, I'm much better."

"Good. Then, pray tell us how you came to be here and our connection."

"I will, but first, can you tell me how long I've been here?"

"Four days."

Four days? Except for waking to Phoebe beside me, those days were mostly a blur. Suddenly feeling awkward, I couldn't meet her gaze. I took a deep breath and began my story. I told the women how my younger self Crow in the Woods had traveled to the twentieth century during the massacre. I was adopted by a white couple and called Lee.

Phoebe's eyes widened. "In the twentieth century, do they have carriages that need no horses nor oxen to pull them?"

"They do. They're called cars."

Her face went pale. "Then I shall travel there too?"

I didn't explain that she would actually travel to the twenty-first century but nodded. "You will become my wife."

"I saw it in a dream. We'll have a daughter and her name will be Heather."

"And me?" Bess asked. "How do we meet?"

I went on to tell them how I had returned to the 1640s, where I met Bess, the grown Elenor, Phoebe's brother, and my father. I fell silent.

"Wind Talker?"

I looked over at Phoebe. "It may have been over a decade for you, but for me, it's been a few days."

She squeezed my good arm. "E'en so, I oft relive it."

"Did your father?"

"He survived."

That much was good. "And Black Owl?"

She shook her head. "I know not his fate."

If I was in this period for any length of time, I vowed to myself that I would discover what had happened to Black Owl. I swallowed, then continued with the story they had wanted to hear. After making my transition to Wind Talker, Phoebe had rejoined me in the 1640s. I told them how I had been captured by the English and sent to Western Island. As I lay dying, I traveled through time to when Phoebe was a young girl. During the massacre, I had gone after Crow in the Woods and was captured by the mist yet again, but for some reason came to this time rather than being sent to the twentieth century.

Both women pondered my story. "When I was a lass I heard your voice in my dreams," Phoebe said.

"It's when I tried to contact you in the future through the dreaming."

She nodded. "I understand."

When she smiled, I looked away. No matter how I tried otherwise, I kept seeing the Phoebe I loved. She was married to Henry Wynne now, who was currently away at sea. In time, even he would become my friend. I got to my feet and headed for the door. "I'll sleep in the barn tonight."

"Lee..."

As I turned to face her once more, Bess quietly exited the house. "Phoebe, I can't stay here. The time isn't right."

"Aye, I know." She stepped closer and stood directly in front of me. "I'll send a messenger to Silver Eagle and Momma."

My gaze locked with hers, and I nearly caressed her cheek. More than anything, I wanted to pick her up and carry her over to the bed. Thankfully my injured arm prevented me from making a fool of myself. "I'll see you in the morning, Phoebe."

"You know my other name."

"Walks Through Mist," I said in Algonquian.

"On the morrow, Kesutanouwas Wesin."

When I turned away, I hoped Silver Eagle and Phoebe's mother received the message soon. I had no idea how long I could be around Phoebe without acting on my impulses. In this time, such intimacies would likely be rejected and break my heart. As I stepped outside, I briefly thought of trying to contact Phoebe in the future. I shook my head. The present Phoebe would hear my voice, and unlike before the massacre, I wouldn't have her mother to help me to distract her.

Over the next couple of days, in spite of sleeping very little, I regained some of my strength. Bess recommended that I keep my arm in the sling for the time being. The arm remained quite painful, and I heeded her advice. In the evenings after the chores for the day had been completed, the family gathered in the parlor to tell stories. Bess and James told tales from Africa and how they had come to Virginia. More the nervous sort, Jennet said very little. And then, when Phoebe spoke, I lingered on every word. The way she smiled and tilted her head made my heart pound. I chastised myself for acting like a lovestruck schoolboy and looked away.

Before my turn came to speak, I excused myself and went outside. The May evening was clear and warm. The moon had passed the first quarter and in less than a week would be full. I silently laughed to myself. In the twenty-first century, I knew nothing about moon phases much less had any ability to track them.

"Lee..."

In this time period, Phoebe frequently used my English name. Both were part of me. I accepted that fact and turned to her. "I'm not a very good warrior when I don't hear someone approaching me from behind."

"I suspect your thoughts were elsewhere."

"That doesn't excuse letting my guard down."

She stepped closer but kept a respectable distance between us. "Inside the palisade there's little need to worry about intruders. 'Sides few visit except for Momma and Silver Eagle."

In the distance an owl hooted. "I'll be glad to see them again."

"They shall be pleased to see you too."

Small talk—was that all we could share in this time? I cleared my throat. "Phoebe, I'm finding this awkward."

She laughed slightly. "Aye, 'tis for me too."

Unable to resist any longer, I drew her closer and kissed her on the mouth. Instead of pulling away, she reciprocated. Her body molded to mine.

"Mistress Wynne!"

I let go of Phoebe and stepped away from her as James and Bess approached us. "The baby's comin'," James said.

Leaning on James for support, Bess held a hand to her belly. " 'Tis time."

"But I've ne'er birthed a babe as the sole midwife afore," Phoebe replied.

"You'll do fine," I said. Both women looked in my direction. "Trust me."

"Thank you." Phoebe escorted Bess into the house and closed the door behind them.

This was an era when men were unwelcome in the birthing room. In time-honored tradition, James did what most men had in the past. He paced.

I sat on the steps. "You might as well get comfortable. It's likely to be awhile. They'll send news when your son is born."

He grinned with pride. "A son. Aft bein' beaten and abducted to this land, I could ne'er have imagined happiness again."

From inside the house, I heard crying and sniffling. Although I didn't think it was Bess, James moved toward the sound. I drew him back. "They'll let you know if you're needed."

Once more James paced. A woman moaned, and more weeping followed. Thankfully, James paced far enough away from the house to not overhear. Then, came a shriek. The door flew open and Jennet galloped down the steps like a spooked horse. James furrowed his brow, and his eyes widened.

I stood. "Let me check for you."

Inside the door, Phoebe helped Bess walk about the room. "Lee, can you see to Elenor 'til Jennet gathers her wits?"

"I'll be happy to. Is everything all right?"

"Aye. Tell James the babe will be here soon."

When I called Elenor, she came right to me. Even though I had known her only as an adult, a kinship remained between us. She was like a daughter. Holding her hand, I escorted her outside. James looked at me hopefully. "She's fine," I said. "The baby will be here soon. Phoebe wanted me to watch Elenor until Jennet recovers."

Minutes passed, then an hour. As the night grew darker, I made a bed of straw for Elenor. She curled up and fell asleep. By early morning light James continued to stride across the yard. If Bess's labor went on for much longer, he'd wear a noticeable rut into the ground. Finally, Jennet returned. Although she clenched her hands, she appeared calmer. "I'll see if I'm needed inside afore taking Elenor off your hands," she said.

"She hasn't been any trouble," I replied, "but I'm sure she'll be wanting breakfast soon."

Jennet went up the stairs and vanished inside. We continued to wait. After a few minutes, a young man, probably in his late teens, in a floppy hat, linen shirt, and breeches, approached us. He stared at me and halted.

"He's friendly, lad," James said.

He moved toward James but kept staring at me. I resisted temptation to say something that I'd likely regret later. He handed James a paper. " 'Tis from England," he said.

A baby cried from inside the house as James knocked on the door. "Mistress Wynne, Mistress Wynne."

Phoebe called out. "Bess and the lad are fine, James."

He continued his frantic rapping. "Mistress Wynne, word from England."

Jennet cracked the door open. "The mistress will speak to you when she can. You have a fine son." She closed the door again.

A letter from England? It must have been from Henry. At least half an hour passed before Phoebe opened the door. "Bess and the lad are in fine health."

With the news, James grinned.

"Now, what is it that you wanted to tell me?"

He gave Phoebe the paper. "A missive from England, Mistress Wynne."

"From Henry." She opened the letter. "Go see Bess."

I watched her struggle to sound out the letters to read the paper. Before I could offer to help, her face paled. "Is everything all right?"

She looked up at me in confusion. " 'Tis Henry. He has the smallpox and may ne'er return."

When I approached her, she sobbed on my shoulder. I stepped back and dried her tears with my good hand. "Henry will survive and return to Virginia."

"You know what happened?"

"Henry showed me the events through the dreaming. He will barely survive and it'll take him two or three years to return."

"Pray tell me all that you know."

I shook my head. "That wouldn't be wise."

"Then why did you share with me about Henry?"

"To spare you some grief."

"Thank you."

Her blue-green eyes had always mesmerized me. I longed to hold my wife and daughter. Would I ever see them again?

19

Phoebe

1647

M<small>EG HAD RETURNED TO THE PLANTATION</small> to birth. "Phoebe, I'm scared."

I pressed my hand to her belly and felt a wriggle neath my fingertips. "This one is very much alive." I continued to feel her belly. The babe was head down in the womb. "Your babe is ready for birthing, Meg. This won't be like the last time."

My friend grinned, but a pain caught her unawares. She groaned. When she caught her breath again, she said, "The *kwiocos* has said she'll be a girl. Don't tell Charging Bear, but I've already decided to call her Falling Rain."

Bess brought o'er some tea. "What is it?" Meg asked, sniffing the tea.

"Snakeroot tea. 'Twill help with your birthing pains."

Meg swallowed the tea, then I held her arm whilst we paced the floor. When she rested, I faced the four winds. Meg laughed. "I still don't know how much I believe."

"It doesn't matter, Meg. I can pray to your god as well."

"Phoebe . . ." Meg held her belly. "I think my water broke."

Water flowed down the length of her legs. "Aye. Your birthing time is near." I helped her to the birthing chair.

Bess spread straw neath the chair. I fetched more tea, which Meg gulped down. Whilst I rubbed Meg's back, Bess pressed on her belly, trying to force the babe out. Meg gritted her teeth and closed her eyes. Blood trickled down her legs, and we urged her on. Afore long, blood gushed. Elenor hurried o'er and mopped up the mess.

I knelt afore Meg and spread her legs wide. After a few more spasms, the babe's head appeared betwixt Meg's legs. "She's almost here, Meg," I assured my friend.

Meg uttered another groan, and I caught a blood-covered babe in my arms. Definitely a lass, and with a lung-filled squall, Falling Rain was raring to meet the world. She was a rich russet color with black hair. "Like the *kwiocos* predicted, she's a lass."

"I'll wait for the caul," Bess said, pushing on Meg's belly.

After a few more spasms, the caul came forth. Bess cut the navel cord with scissors, and I brought the babe to a basin to scrub her clean. Once finished, I handed Falling Rain to Meg's waiting arms. With a pride-filled smile, my friend placed her new daughter to her breast. "Thank you, Phoebe." She glanced at Bess. "And you, Bess."

"You did most of the work," I said.

"Still, I was so scared after losing my boy. You showed me how to collect blackhaw to prevent miscarriage and make the tea."

" 'Tis a simple remedy. If I hadn't shown you, one of the Appamattuck women would have. Let me fetch Charging Bear. I'm certain he would love to meet his daughter." I left Meg with Bess and Elenor and went outside, where my brother waited. "You're the father of a fine lass. Go in and see Meg."

He picked up Tiffany to take inside to meet her new sister. In the excitement, she dropped her corn-husk doll. Heather raised her arms for me to do the same. I obliged and gathered her in my arms. She carried a doll I had made from cloth. I grew vexed. Had I been depriving my daughter from knowing her people? Nay, on the plantation she had become friends with her grown sister, Elenor, as well as her cousins.

O'er the next couple of weeks, Meg regained her strength. She and my brother had decided to return to the Appamattuck the following morn. "You can come with us, Phoebe," Meg said.

I shook my head. "I can't."

"Because of Wind Talker?"

I smiled but said naught.

"You haven't said anything about him since I've been here."

" 'Twouldn't have been right. You were birthing and now have a family to care for."

She snuggled Falling Rain, who slept soundly in her arms. "Have you forgotten who you're talking to? Phoebe, I came with you to this time. I know what he means to you. Tell me what you know."

I shrugged. "There's naught to tell. He survived the massacre and has traveled in time again, but I know not when he's been taken to. Like afore, I occasionally hear his voice, but I remember my vow not to reach out to him."

"He's been gone nearly two years."

Two years? In the beginning, I had counted the days that passed. Then, after Momma had contacted me through the dreaming, I lost track. Each day was a struggle to carry on, not knowing what the morrow would bring. "I can't let him go, Meg."

"No one expects you to. Didn't you say that your English husband took three years to return?"

I should have known that I could count on Meg to support my decision not to leave the plantation 'til I discovered Wind Talker's fate, but circumstances differed. I had not shared all I knew. "Aye, when Henry had the smallpox. I received a missive from England when he usually arrived in the spring that he had contracted the disease and would not be returning then. Meg, this differs than when I awaited Henry."

"How so?"

"Momma..." Nearly choking, I caught my breath. "Momma ne'er said when I will rejoin him. Only that I shall. What if she meant that we'd meet again in the afterlife?"

Meg's countenance took on a stricken look. She hugged me close. Without saying a word, we shared our tears.

A good cry with a friend, who understood my pain, revived me. Momma's message had come so long ago. I wondered now if merely contacting him one time would bring harm.

"You're having second thoughts," Meg said.

'Twasn't unusual for Meg to know what I was thinking. "I wish to contact him."

"Then do so. I'll watch the girls."

"Thank you, Meg." I gave her and Falling Rain a hug. Where should I enter the dreaming? I would try to reach him from this place. I concentrated on traveling to the next realm but heard the lasses giggling, which distracted me. I got to my feet and hiked to the spot where I had heard Wind Talker's voice in the past.

Out of breath by the time I arrived near the bones, I waited 'til I recovered. As I entered the dreaming, mist captured me. Up ahead, I spied my hound. "Take me to Wind Talker," I said.

The hound loped away from me, and the fog totally engulfed him. I could not find my way. I spread my hands afore me, but the haze was so thick, I stumbled along.

Out of the mist stepped Momma. "Phoebe, I beg of you. Pray don't contact Wind Talker."

"But Momma, I hear his voice. He calls to me."

"Aye, he misses you, but his mission is not complete. You will know when the time is right. Afore then, many lives are at stake."

"Lives?"

She nodded. "Now vow to me that you won't contact him."

A vow to not contact Wind Talker? Momma would ne'er make such a request 'less circumstances were dire. My heart shattered into a million of pieces. "I . . . I vow."

Momma drew me close, squeezing me tight, then she faded into the mist. My hound trotted afore me and whined. Wobbly on my legs, I latched onto his collar. When the mist faded, I stood at the end of a twenty-first century shopping center. 'Twasn't the same spot as to where I had traveled afore, but the stores looked familiar. Momma had said not to contact Wind Talker, but naught about Lee. Half-expecting to see him, I turned round. He wasn't standing behind me.

I ambled along the sidewalk. Few people lingered. In the parking lot, a T-Bird pulled into a space. I waved. After Lee parked, I joined him aside the car.

"I had a feeling that you'd be here this morning," he said. For a moment, I thought he might take me in his arms, but his countenance etched with grief. "I haven't been here in years—not since I was a kid."

Sorrow—we shared it. We could comfort each other. I looked round the shopping area and recalled my familiarity. Lee had brought me here. If he hadn't told me this place was where he had been found wandering in the forest as a lad, I would have ne'er recognized it. Had they discovered the bones of the Paspahegh when clearing the trees? "Tell me."

He shrugged. "There's not much to tell. My biological parents abandoned me here when I was two. Me, the detective, and I haven't the faintest idea why."

He had taken on a reserved stance that I knew all too well. "Your answers are in the dreaming."

"The dreaming again? I haven't had much luck so far."

"Then I shall offer my guidance again."

He gazed about the shops. "It was a forest when my parents ditched me."

"Aye, I know what happened, but 'twas beyond your parents' control." I held out my hand.

Perplexed, he stared at my outstretched hand. "Why do I always have the feeling I know you from somewhere else?"

"We have met afore. The dreaming will tell you how and when."

He grasped my hand, and we returned to the T-Bird. How much I had changed since my arrival in the century. Because I had been struck by a car, I had initially feared them. Though I had maintained some hesitation, I had overcome my fright and e'en learned to drive. Now, I was with Lee and let him guide the horseless carriage throughout the streets.

When we arrived at his apartment, my heart soared by his proximity. We went up the steps and inside. Like afore, clothes were in disarray. "I'll get the candle," he said.

I sat on the floor aside the table near the sofa, and Lee lit the candle when he returned. He seated himself opposite to me. "Are you certain you wish to proceed?" I asked.

He gazed upon me, and my heart pounded with desire. "If it'll give me answers, yes," he said, slowly.

I grasped his hands. His grip was strong and firm. As he looked into the flame, I did the same. Afore long, my hound appeared afore us. With the hound leading the way, mist swirled round us.

Circle in Time

Up ahead, I saw Wind Talker. I moved closer. He wasn't Wind Talker. His black hair was cropped short. Neither time nor space could break the connection.

I threw my arms round his neck, and our mouths met in feverish kisses. Whilst I unzipped his trousers, he pushed up my skirt. My legs went round him. We were not naked, but I didn't care. His hips pressed against mine, and the man I loved penetrated me. Faster and faster, I came down upon him again and again 'til he spilled his seed inside me. I continued my motion and seeing my need, he continued to thrust. Once more, I cried out and felt a gentle warmth spread throughout me. Bathed in soft radiance, I leaned against his chest.

He gently pushed my stray locks aside and kissed me. "Phoebe..."

Once again, I saw Wind Talker. I blinked, and he was Lee. My legs remained wrapped round him. But this was the dreaming. "I'm not part of this time."

Our bodies were still locked as one. When he rocked his hips, I groaned. "Then how did this happen?" he asked.

"I don't care to explain it. I only know that *nouwmais*."

He mouthed the word, as if translating in his head. "I love you too."

Not only were we joined in each other's bodies, but our spirits as well.

20

Wind Talker

1626

THROUGHOUT THE NIGHT, I had dreams of making love to Phoebe on a cot in the kitchen until our energy was spent. A warm body snuggled next to me.

"Good morn," Phoebe whispered.

I smiled and drifted. Her hand wandered the length of my side until reaching my groin. Had I become feverish again? No, she was really beside me. Her fingertips fondled me until I nearly howled with foolish pleasure. Suddenly wide awake, I stared into her eyes. Our naked bodies pressed against each other. It hadn't been a dream. I traced around the serpent tattoos on her breast. When I kissed her there, my hand slid downward. I caressed her between the legs. In invitation, she opened her legs for me to enter her, but I continued to stroke her.

A stab of pain shot through my arm. Not wanting to spoil the mood, I said nothing. As if reading my thoughts, Phoebe placed her legs on each side of me. She climbed atop me and shimmied her hips until she encircled me. When she rocked her hips against me, the mist formed before my eyes. A crow cawed. Was I Wind Talker or Lee? Phoebe had shown me that I was both. I would meet her again in the twenty-first century. Yet, the chain had been broken.

She cried out and gently fell to my chest in exhaustion. "*Nouwmais, Kesutanouwas Wesin.*"

"I love you too." I held her and we fell asleep. When I woke again, light streamed through the window.

"I need to see to my chores," Phoebe said. She hurriedly grasped her clothes and dressed. Before leaving, she kissed me. "Come to the house later, and I'll check your arm." She rushed from the kitchen.

For nearly a week, Phoebe and I spent blissful nights together. During that time, my arm got a little stronger. One afternoon Silver Eagle and Elenor arrived with a couple of warriors in tow for added protection while traveling. I recognized Little Falcon because I had viewed this time period through his eyes during the dreaming when I was in the twenty-first century. Phoebe had turned to him in a time of grief when she thought Henry was dead. Privately, I hoped my interference had changed that scenario, but I kept my thoughts to myself and greeted him as I would any other warrior for the first time.

Elenor and Phoebe exchanged excited mother/daughter greetings before Elenor turned to me. As she hugged me, tears entered her eyes. "We thought you had died."

Silver Eagle intertwined his index finger with mine, then he pulled me close and embraced me. "How did you survive the attack?" he asked, taking a step back.

"It's a rather long and complicated story. We might want to talk inside."

Before Phoebe led the way, she looked at me in despair. I felt it too for I had no desire to leave her side. Once inside, Jennet and Phoebe went to the kitchen to prepare a meal for her mom and stepfather, while I relayed the story of how I had arrived in this time. I spoke in Algonquian for Silver Eagle's sake.

"That explains why you haven't aged a day since we saw you," Elenor said, choking slightly. She closed her eyes. " 'Twas nearly sixteen years ago. We all lost so many loved ones."

"I had hoped my presence meant that somehow I could save my people. That's why I tried to warn Wowinchapuncke."

"Like many others, he and his family perished," Silver Eagle said.

I clenched my right hand. "I had hoped more would survive with the warriors not being away on a hunting trip."

Tears entered Elenor's eyes. " 'Tis not your fault. The blame rests with the soldiers firing the guns."

Deep down, I knew she was right, but kind words didn't help me shed my feeling of guilt. Silver Eagle's solemn gaze alerted me that he understood. "If I'm in this time for a while," I finally said, "I hope I can discover if Black Owl survived. In the original time, he sought refuge with the Sekakawon."

"When you're stronger, I'll take you there," Silver Eagle said.

Grateful for his help, I nodded. In this time period, a few Paspahegh remained alive. The fact that I wasn't the only one brought me some comfort. Phoebe and Jennet returned carrying clay pots and iron kettles. Elenor stepped in to help, while Silver Eagle and I were told to have a seat at the table. Silver Eagle sat in the chair at the head of the table, and I got comfortable on the bench at the side.

The women served a creamy asparagus soup and chicken meat pie. When Jennet went to feed the warriors waiting outside, Phoebe and Elenor joined us at the table. Phoebe sat next to me. All too aware of her presence, I rejoiced in having her nearby. When I stole a glance in her direction, she smiled. I had no doubt the others caught our looks of longing.

After the meal, Silver Eagle and I retreated outdoors with the other warriors and passed a pipe. They told us about their trip downriver to Henry's homestead. Suddenly I felt shame. In another time, Henry and I would become friends. How had I repaid him? By sleeping with his wife. But she was my wife too, and Phoebe's marriage with Henry had been a forced one. For some reason, that didn't seem like an acceptable excuse.

"You appear sad," Silver Eagle said.

"I don't want to leave here," I admitted.

"Do as your heart tells you, and you will place her life in danger."

His words were honest and to the point. "Why is it that no time seems to be the right one?"

"There is a right time. If not this one, then another, but I don't think you would wish to jeopardize her life. I wish she could live with us, but her father has made certain she remains here. The guards won't let her daughter pass through the gate of the palisade."

How could I have forgotten? I had witnessed the events through the dreaming. Even though Phoebe was allowed to roam at will, her daughter was kept locked inside the palisade as a hostage. "I would never do anything that would knowingly hurt her."

"I trust your word as a warrior."

I only hoped I could live up to his trust. Soon after the warriors retired for the night, I went out to the James River. The moon cast a glow, reflecting off the water. I had no idea how long I stood there when a soft tread of footsteps came from behind. I turned to Phoebe.

" 'Tis the first I was able to get away."

I drew her close and kissed her on the mouth. How could I leave her? Yet I must. "Come with me."

She stepped out of our embrace. "I cannot."

"We can find a way to bring Elenor with us."

"Nay. My English father would hunt me down. He would make certain that I ne'er see my daughter again."

I couldn't ask her to make such a sacrifice. "Then what? We're in the same time period, but we must live apart?"

"You can visit."

Visit—I guessed that would have to suffice. I caressed her cheek, and her arms went around my waist. For the longest time, I was content just holding her, then I felt her shaking. She clasped me tighter, and I knew she was crying. "We can contact each other through the dreaming," I suggested.

Without breaking our embrace, she looked up at me. "Aye, but what if . . . ?"

With my thumb, I brushed away the tear streaking her cheek. "You can say it. Ask."

"What if you vanish from this time period as well?"

Soon after meeting Phoebe in the twenty-first century I had asked her a similar question. "We never know what tomorrow will bring. The circle can't be complete without traveling the path."

A hint of a smile appeared on her face. Unable to hold back any longer, my mouth met hers in a burning hunger. I had to believe my own words. For now, I was with her and would make the most of it.

Gunshots and screams surrounded me. Swimming Beaver staggered out of the smoke and guided me away from the fighting. I woke with my heart racing. A hint of pink shimmered in the morning sky.

Phoebe stroked my chin. "It's all right," she murmured.

Glancing out at the James River, I calmed. *Nothing more than a nightmare.* Phoebe was in my arms. My pounding heart settled, and I huddled next to her with my head coming to rest on her breasts. Her fingers traced through my hair. I took a deep breath and closed my eyes.

Throughout the night, we had declared our love and comforted each other. I didn't want to leave. I needed to gather my courage together. I could never forgive myself if anything happened to her because of my presence. I flipped her reddish-blonde hair off her shoulders, revealing her pale, white breasts. Unlike some women I had known, she showed no shyness. Her hands went through my hair as she whispered my name. I kissed her, first on the mouth, then I traveled the length of her body.

Footsteps. At first, I was so caught up in the moment that the sound didn't register. Out of the corner of my eye, I spotted a figure and reached for my weapons' belt. When Bess gave a startled cry, I dropped the knife I had retrieved, and she averted her gaze away from our naked bodies.

"I had come looking for Mistress Wynne. It seems I have found her."

Phoebe had a hint of a smile. She pulled up her dress to cover her bare form. "What was it you wanted, Bess?"

"The others will be rising to break their fast soon. I thought you might wish to be present when they do."

"Aye. I'll be there right away, Bess."

Bess scurried in the direction of the palisade as if she couldn't return to the house fast enough.

"She had already surmised the nature of our bond," Phoebe said.

"I'm not ashamed."

"Neither am I." With a squeeze of my hand, she kissed me, then began to dress.

I watched while she did so. The contentment of the night gave way to harsh reality. In this time period, I was regarded as nothing more than a heathen savage, and I suddenly longed for the twenty-first century. With a sigh, I gathered my clothing and dressed.

As Phoebe braided her hair, she turned away. "Bess and I will make certain that you have enough supplies for your trip."

When I touched her shoulders, she tightened her muscles. I kissed her bare neck.

She faced me and, with a quaver in her voice, said, "Come back to me."

"You know I will."

"You will let me check your arm afore you leave?"

"It's doing much better, but I will."

She laughed slightly. "I had noticed last night."

I shrugged. "What can I say? You possess my heart and soul."

She threw her arms around my neck, and we shared a long, intimate kiss. I never wanted to let go, but I stepped back. "We should be getting up to the house before someone besides Bess comes searching for you. If you want to go ahead of me, I can wait here for a few minutes."

"Aye, I'll go ahead."

I watched her as she headed toward the palisade, then waited. By the time I reached the house, the family was stirring. Phoebe went to see to her daughter, while Bess and Jennet brought in breakfast. Silver Eagle and Elenor joined us, and we shared a meal of pottage. In the time that I had been in the seventeenth century, I had learned the dish could be a soup or stew. This time, it definitely tasted like thick oatmeal with eggs and spices.

Phoebe sat next to me. I was grateful for the extra few minutes. As I ate, I detected her watching me. I stole a glance and she forced a smile. I quickly looked away and found myself no longer hungry. I played with the food a bit before giving up. When the meal came to an end, the others gathered supplies together and left Phoebe and me alone for a few minutes.

"I guess it's time," I said with some awkwardness.

"Aye."

I drew her to me. Reaffirming our love, we shared a final kiss, then walked outside where the others waited. When we waved goodbye, tears streaked Phoebe's cheeks. Nothing I could say would ease either of our minds, so I remained stoically silent. The gates of the palisade opened, and she ran after me. One last hug, and I walked through the gate to join the others. I dared not look at her for a final glance, or I might weaken and turn around.

Silver Eagle led us away from the river to a forest trail. No one spoke, and once again, I was relieved that the custom among Natives was one of not forcing small talk. Each step was agonizing, taking me further from Phoebe. Like the first time I had traveled from Henry's house, a flock of green birds with yellow heads chattered from nearby trees. In the century in which I'd grown up in, the Carolina parakeet was extinct. In this one, they thrived. Their story was much like that of my own tribe.

The warriors kept a brisk pace. More fit than I had been on my first journey, I was able to keep stride with them, and Elenor remained beside me. "The first time I walked this path was with Charging Bear," I said.

"Who is Charging Bear?"

Only with her question did I realize that in this time her son hadn't gone through the *huskanaw* yet to obtain his adult name. "Sly Fox."

She sent me a pride-filled smile and we continued on. After several miles, the trail returned to the river. Near the bank, the warriors brought us to a dugout. Elenor got in, and the rest of us shoved the canoe into the water. We paddled upriver. No matter how many times I traveled by boat, I would never get used to the energy required. My muscles ached, and at sunset, when we landed for the night, I was all too ready to collapse.

We built a fire while Little Falcon and the other warrior caught some fish. After cooking the fish over the fire, we added parched cornmeal to complete the meal. As we ate, the men traded stories. Shortly after eating, I fell asleep in exhaustion. In the morning, we set out at dawn. The Arrohateck lived near the waterfalls and rapids, which were west of Richmond in the twenty-first century. Once, we came ashore to avoid a colonial ship, and I noted how they seemed fewer than when I had traveled the same route later in the century.

Three days passed before we arrived at the town of the Arrohateck. Familiar arched houses with covered mats came into view. I was concerned that I might have to prove myself yet again in this society, but I needn't have worried. The chief introduced himself and considered me a guest of Silver Eagle and Elenor's. The townspeople greeted me, and there was an evening of feasting and dancing. Instead of staying in the guest house, I remained with my friends, where I met Phoebe's adolescent brother Sly Fox. Soon, he would endure the *huskanaw,* where he would be isolated in the woods with other initiates for several months, and become the man I knew, Charging Bear.

After the others had retired, I sat along the bank of the river, thinking of Phoebe. Should I try to contact her through the dreaming? In my mind's eye, I spotted the flame, and a gentle breeze blew in my ear. Good, the wind was with me. The mist formed. *Phoebe.*

21

Phoebe

1648

Upon hearing my name being called in the night, I spied a light. A man stood at the center. He wore a wool shirt and breechclout. I ran towards him, but the wind kept me from reaching his side. "Wind Talker—"

"Phoebe?"

After nearly three years absence, my husband stood afore me. "Wind Talker, what time have you been taken to?"

"1626."

The wind faded slightly, and I moved closer but still could not touch him. "I was married to Henry then."

He nodded. "Your mother and Silver Eagle have brought me to the Arrohateck."

"That much is good." I reached out. Our fingertips nearly touched, then he was gone. I sat up in bed. After all this time, Wind Talker had finally contacted me. Heather squirmed on the bed aside me. I drew her into my arms and she settled. "I saw him, Heather," I whispered. "I saw your poppa."

I laid down but rolled on my side, then back again. Fortunately, my movements did not awaken my daughter. After much restlessness, I got to my feet and dressed. Bess lay in the opposite bed and would see to Heather if she required assistance. In the dark I held the rail to guide me down the stairs. Upon reaching the first floor, I tiptoed to the door so as not to wake the rest of my family. Once outside, I ventured to the bank of the James River and watched the waves ripple softly neath the moonlight.

"Wind Talker, I heard your voice. Now, I know when to reach you."

As soon as I uttered the words, I heard Momma's voice ring through my head in a dire warning, reminding me of my vow. *Wind Talker.* Lives were at stake, and I would honor my word. Instead, I would seek Lee. I concentrated. Afore long I walked through the mist. When I emerged, I was surrounded by smoke and neon lights. The smoke was not a fire, but cigarettes from the inside of a tavern.

A man with a rotund belly and an ale in his hand approached me. "Are you busy tonight, say at 2 a.m.?"

Confused by the man's question, I knew not how to answer.

"She's busy." Sending the man a glare, Lee stepped betwixt us.

The man bowed and backed away.

"I thought I might have scared you off." Lee motioned for me to have a seat at an empty booth.

"You could ne'er do that." I seated myself in the spot he had indicated, and he sat across from me. Since he was attired in a business suit, I presupposed he had recently got off duty from his detective work.

"Then why haven't I heard from you? It's been three weeks, since we..."

Since we had made love. For him, the passage of time had been weeks. For me, it had been months. "I will inform you what I can, but not here. 'Tis too noisy and crowded."

Ready to escort me from the establishment, Lee stood, when a man with puffy brows and a cleft chin joined us. "Lee!" he said in an overly loud voice. I recognized Lee's partner, Ed. He had a kind, smiling face. "Aren't you going to introduce me to the lovely lady?"

After a quick introduction, Lee said, "We were about to leave, Ed."

Ed's eyes twinkled as he waved us away. "Then off with you two. We'll visit another time."

Lee escorted me to the T-Bird. "I don't wish to presume. Where shall we go to talk?"

"Your apartment will be fine."

He nodded and started the car. Once inside the door to his apartment, he faced me. "I don't understand how you can just come and go. I thought we shared more than a one-night stand."

"A one-night stand?"

"Don't pretend to look so innocent."

"But I don't understand your words."

He stared at me in confusion. "They really don't use that phrase in England?"

"Lee, I come to you through the dreaming. I do not control when I'm here. If I did, I would be with you always."

"Always?"

I grasped his hand. For a moment, I thought he might draw away. "Can you not feel it? What we share is not a 'one-night stand,' but timelessness."

"Phoebe . . ." His voice had gone soft, and he swallowed noticeably. He withdrew his hand from my grip. "You said we'd talk."

"We shall, but later, my love."

His dark eyes gazed intently into my own. "What if you vanish again before we have the chance?"

"Then we shall talk another time. The circle cannot be complete without traveling the path."

"The circle . . ." He nodded that he understood. "I was certain that I had met you before."

His mouth met mine in a raging hunger. My arms went round his neck, and he carried me o'er to the divan. When we joined, time drifted afore my eyes. The planes intersected, yet constantly shifted. I finally comprehended the meaning.

Tears streaked my cheeks as I slumped against him. He held my head and kissed me. Past, present, and future—all existed in unison for the circle in time to be complete.

After spending much of the eve making love, I wrapped my naked body in Lee's bathrobe and sifted through his collection of artifacts.

His adoptive parents had tried to give him a sense of heritage, but had no concept of how to go about such a quest. I pushed aside a medicine staff, a flute, and a tomahawk.

"Are you looking for something in particular?"

"Aye."

"If you tell me what it is, maybe I can help."

I reached the arrowheads. Some were made of stone, others bone. I carefully inspected each one, 'til I uncovered one made from a deer antler. "This one." I placed the arrowhead that Black Owl had made into his hand. "Keep it with you always. 'Twas made by a brave warrior."

He fingered the contours. "And you're not going to tell me anything about it?"

"Not yet."

"What will you tell me?"

"That I'm a cunning woman from the seventeenth century."

"That's why we can only meet through the dreaming because you're from the seventeenth century."

I detected sarcasm in his voice and wondered how forthright I should be for the present. "For now. I wish for you to continue to learn the dreaming."

He hugged me close. "Phoebe, more than anything I want to believe you, but the seventeenth century? I understand now why you said that I'm Paspahegh—"

"We shall be married and have a daughter. Her name will be Heather."

He withdrew from our embrace. "When I was ten, you told my mom that you had a Native husband."

"He is you in a future time." *Or past.* "Now you see why I can't help but love you."

"And the dreaming can prove that all of this is true?"

"Aye."

"I'll get the candle." He went into the kitchen. When he returned, he carried a candle. He set it on the coffee table and lit it. As he stared into the flame, my mind cried out for him to absorb it. He shook his head. "Nothing."

"Try again."

He nodded, and I spied my white hound. 'Twas working. Lee had made the connection. I stepped outside the plantation house. At first, I thought the dreaming had returned me to my time, but the heat was stifling and the house, much newer with a palisade encircling it. "Wind Talker?"

"Mistress Wynne! Mistress Wynne!" I hadn't seen my servant Jennet since I had gone to the twenty-first century. She placed a hand to her chest and gasped, "Indians coming."

"Indians?"

She took another deep breath. "Your momma, poppa, and Wind Talker."

'Twas the time Momma had warned me to avoid. I hadn't meant to travel here. For some reason, Lee had brought me. In the fading daylight, I craned my neck to peer o'er Jennet's shoulder but saw naught. A guard readied his musket, and I raced to the palisade gate. "Lower your weapon. 'Tis my momma."

Obeying my order, he lowered the musket and opened the gate. Momma, Silver Eagle, and my brother Sly Fox accompanied Wind Talker. I greeted all of them with a kiss on their cheeks and a hug. Wind Talker pulled me close and reciprocated with a kiss to my mouth. I tingled from his closeness.

"Phoebe, how have you been?" Momma asked.

I stared upon their countenances with such delight that I knew not what to say.

"Silver Eagle, Sly Fox, and Wind Talker," Momma said, "are going to the Sekakawon to see if Black Owl has survived the massacre. I thought I'd stay with you 'til they return."

Stay with me? "That would be lovely, Momma." We went into the house, which was made of wood, not brick. A ladder, not a staircase, led to the loft, verifying that I had traveled to 1626.

Momma greeted my daughter Elenor, who was a young lass, rather than a grown woman. Delighted to see her myself, I squeezed her close. Bess and Jennet called me to the kitchen. I excused myself to go outside once more. I was home, really home. Inside the kitchen, my servants had already cut a chicken into slices. As Bess fried them in butter, Jennet added sweet herbs and nutmeg. Chicken fricassee—I knew the recipe. Due to the special occasion, I used white wine instead of broth. Eager to see my family once again, I returned to the house.

Sly Fox complained that he was starving.

" 'Tis not good for a warrior to whine," I reminded him.

As e'eryone laughed, except for my brother, I felt Wind Talker watching me. When Bess and Jennet brought in the meal, we gathered round the table. Silver Eagle sat at the head of the table with Momma at the opposite end. Wind Talker sat aside me. Once, because of my left handedness, we bumped elbows. A grin spread across his countenance.

I blinked. 'Twas Lee, not Wind Talker. "I don't understand," he said. "It was me, but I was different. They called me Wind Talker."

" 'Tis the way of the dreaming."

"Phoebe..." He reached out to caress my cheek, and he too vanished. Under the soft glow of moonlight, I stood along the bank of the James River.

22

Wind Talker

1626

During the previous night's meal after our arrival at the homestead, I had the distinct feeling of being reunited with Phoebe, my wife. Then afterward when I met her outside, the feeling had vanished. Nothing could restrain my desire from seeing her again, but I was perplexed by what had happened. I worried that my confusion might make me seem distant for I had no wish to hurt Phoebe of any time period.

After breakfast the following morning, Phoebe's mom herded everyone out the door, and I found myself alone with Phoebe. "There's not much time," I said.

She came over to me and hugged me. I gave her a kiss, after which we stood holding each other. Finally, I stepped back. No words were necessary. We should see one another in a couple of months. I stepped through the door.

Ready to leave, Silver Eagle and Sly Fox waited outside. I joined them. When we reached the gate, I waved. Phoebe kept a brave front and returned my wave. The gate closed behind us, and we started our journey to the Sekakawon. Our first stop was at the mass grave. When I saw the bones, I closed my eyes and fought the tears. To Silver Eagle, the massacre had taken place over a decade ago, but for me, the wounds remained fresh. All the same, no length of time could ever allow me to forget. Silver Eagle placed his hand on my shoulder like a father would his son. "My mother is buried here," I said.

"I know. She died bravely, protecting her own."

I stood there, thinking about her sacrifice. After a long while, I nodded that I was fine and took a deep breath. We returned to our trip.

The first time that I had traveled to the Sekakawon, my father and brothers had accompanied me. The event had also taken place nearly twenty years in the future. After much of the day had passed, we traveled from the territory the English had claimed as their own, since most of their settlements remained along the James River. That was a stark contrast from my first trip because they had spread to the York River as well. Like that trip, we were loaded with supplies.

Late in the afternoon, we met our first traveler, a Chiskiack warrior. Thankful for a rest break, I relished the time to catch my breath and stop and chat. As was the custom, we passed a pipe and shared the latest news and foodstuff. The main town of the Chiskiack lay up ahead, and we were welcomed to spend the night.

By the time we arrived in the Chiskiack town, dusk had fallen. Instead of the common greeting a guest normally received, no one met us. No drums sounded, and no people danced. A small circle of houses showed us that we had entered the town, but the lack of activity seemed out of character. Finally, a man with two warriors beside him approached us. He greeted us and introduced himself as *weroance* Ottahotin. He led us to the *yi-hakan,* the only longhouse left standing. Even though the tribe had little to give, they served us corn and venison. In order to help them, we shared some of our supplies as well.

After the meal, we learned that few were left in the town as it was in the process of moving west. The colonists had retaliated against them after Opechancanough's organized attack in 1622. I closed my eyes. During the dreaming I had seen the attack through Phoebe's first husband, Lightning Storm. Innocent women and children had been killed—a type of warfare that was totally new to Natives. The

English had called the onslaught a massacre, but the annihilation of my own people was considered a justified attack. The *weroance* went on to tell us that he had drunk poisoned wine during a so-called peace meeting and barely survived.

So much grief. When I relived the nightmares, I longed for the era that I had grown up in. Silver Eagle relayed our experiences as Paspahegh to the group. Ottahotin nodded in sympathy. Few could understand the heartache, but I believed he certainly did. He struggled to move his people due to English encroachment, and for what reason? The Chiskiack wouldn't survive to the twenty-first century anymore than the Paspahegh. On that point, I kept silent. For now, he had hope.

The warriors accompanying Ottahotin escorted us to the guest house. Because all of the women had already left the town, we weren't offered female companionship. Neither Silver Eagle nor I minded, but I got the feeling that Sly Fox felt otherwise. Kids—so eager to make their first score. If only I could tell him that after the death of his first wife, he'd marry Phoebe's best friend, Meg.

The house itself was falling in disrepair. Mats, used for the walls, frayed. I had looked forward to a platform to avoid sleeping on the ground. No such luck. The only platform available was three legged and tilted at an uninviting angle. I sighed. At least we had a roof over our heads. As the others settled down for the night, I struggled to stay awake to contact Phoebe through the dreaming. I failed. Unable to keep my eyes open, I fell asleep before I could reach the misty realm.

The following morning, a couple of warriors escorted us across the York River in a dugout. We wished each other well and continued our journey. During the day, we met two travelers. Like the first time I had made the trip, I envisioned arriving at our destination a week or two later. I needn't have worried. Another day and a half passed and we reached the Rappahannock River and the home of the Opiscopank tribe. Here, we had more comfort and were honored with the townspeople greeting us and a feast. The evening included dancing. This time we were offered female companionship, but Silver Fox and I declined, much to Sly Fox's disappointment,.

The sleeping platforms were a godsend. Again, I was too exhausted to contact Phoebe through the dreaming, but I dreamed about her the old-fashioned way instead. What I wouldn't give to live with her. I didn't care which century as long as we could be together with Heather.

In the morning before we set out, we cleansed ourselves and gave thanks in the Rappahannock. While doing so, I spotted a crow on a nearby branch. Taking the journey had been the right decision. I breathed easier. Like the Chiskiack, the Opiscopank helped us navigate the major river. Upon reaching the opposite bank, the major bodies of water were behind us, and we set out on the last leg of our trip to the Sekakwon.

This region was where I had originally met William Carter. At eighteen, he had been a runaway indentured servant from an abusive master. In this time period, he would have just been born somewhere in England. Funny, but I had never learned what county he was from. A smile came to my face, thinking of our friendship.

On this portion of the trip, we only crossed paths with three travelers from two different tribes. Two days later, we neared the Sekakawon. Crows greeted me more often, and I hoped that was a good sign. Finally, arched houses with woven mats appeared on the horizon. When we reached the outskirts of the town, people greeted us. I looked at each face, hoping that I'd see Black Owl among them. I spotted no familiar faces, but with everyone twenty years younger, I wondered if I'd recognize anyone I had met before. The *weroansqua,* or female chief, welcomed us with a speech. We were informed that some of the warriors were out hunting, but would return before nightfall. She introduced us to the line of people. Then, I spotted him. His gaze met mine and a smile spread across his face. "Wind Talker?" He glanced beside me. "Silver Eagle. I never expected to see either of you again."

I reached out to shake Black Owl's hand. Catching myself in time, I lowered my hand and interlocked index fingers with him. He turned to Silver Eagle and did the same.

"Singing Voice, my wife," he said, introducing us to the woman standing next to him.

My mother. I blinked. Though her resemblance to Snow Bird was uncanny, she wasn't my mother. Next to her stood a young boy around five years old. Undoubtedly he was my half-brother, Wildcat. At this age though, he would have a child's name. As if reading my mind, she said, "Our son, Restless Mouse."

Singing Voice was noticeably pregnant as if she might give birth any day now. I suspected she carried my sister New Moon. Only then, did I observe that Black Owl hadn't moved his left arm. As if embarrassed by my discovery, he shifted uneasily on his feet. "We'll talk later."

Indeed we would. This time I planned on telling him who I was. The *weroansqua* distracted us and proceeded down the line of people. After the usual speeches and a feast, I discovered how Singing Voice had gotten her name. Her voice was mesmerizing, almost hypnotic, when she sang. As soon as the evening's activities had ended, we met with Black Owl in private. Silver Eagle told how his family had managed to survive the massacre, then silence surrounded us.

"I tried to save my wife and son," Black Owl said. "But to no avail." I stayed silent and let him continue before I revealed who I was. "I briefly saw Wind Talker. You fought to help our people. A *tassantassas* aimed his musket at you. I threw my tomahawk. Before going down, he shifted his aim, and the bullet went straight through my arm. I believe it missed you."

Not only had Black Owl saved my life, his action was most likely why my wound was less severe.

"I'm indebted to you," I said.

"You're not. You tried to save my family." He turned to Silver Eagle. "I'm pleased that your family survived."

I removed the leather cord from around my neck and handed the arrowhead to Black Owl. "There's a reason why we look like brothers."

He studied the arrowhead, then looked at me in confusion.

"You made it for me when I was a boy. I was Crow in the Woods."

"How can that be?"

I told him the story of how I had traveled through time after the massacre and grown up in the twentieth century before returning to the seventeenth. Silver Eagle added his voice that I spoke the truth. Unlike the last time I had told Black Owl my story, I was older than him by a couple of years.

He clenched the arrowhead, then raised his eyes. I spotted a hint of a tear. "I thought you had died."

"I know. I tried to prevent what happened, but it was beyond what I could do to help."

Black Owl nodded. He went on to tell us that after the death of my mother, he wanted to get as far away from the area as possible. His left arm was of little use. He showed us that he could flex his hand slightly, but not make a fist. As a result, he felt useless as a warrior, but he had found refuge among the Sekakawon, where he had met Singing Voice. We spoke long into the night, even after Silver Eagle and Sly Fox had bedded down.

After Black Owl retired for the night, I sought Phoebe through the dreaming. Crow and the wind were with me. *Good.*

23

Phoebe

1653

Upon hearing Wind Talker call me, I felt my heart pound. My hands trembled. How long had it been since I had last heard his voice? Five long years. Occasionally, I'd contact Lee through the dreaming. I loved him in any time, so e'en that small measure helped me face each day, but to hear my husband again brought a surge of elation.

"Momma, was I wrong?"

His voice was no longer there, and I blinked. My daughter stood afore me, and I held a plant with large leaves and hairy looking, white flowers in my hand. "What was it you said, Heather?"

" 'Tis quinine. The leaves can be used as a poultice on burns, and the flowers are for periodic fevers."

"You're correct." Normally, I smiled with pride on Heather's achievements. At ten, she was well on her way to learning the art of being a cunning woman. As we continued along the trail, I hoped to hear his voice again. On the path's edge, large white flowers bloomed with a bright red center. I pointed to the flower.

" 'Tis swamp rose mallow," Heather said. "The leaves and roots are used for . . ." She scrunched her face.

Like my momma and Wind Talker's momma had taught me, I remained patient, ne'er scolding Heather. "Can you remember how they are used?"

She looked o'er her shoulder, afore shaking her head.

"You're correct that the leaves and roots are used. They soothe severe diarrhea."

A crow cawed, and once again, my heart thumped. A black bird flew from a tree to another. 'Twasn't a spirit, but a bird of the forest. We continued on, but I came to an immediate halt. At the trail's end stood a man in a woolen shirt, breechclout, and moccasins. He held out his hands, then vanished.

"Momma, who was that man?"

I gaped at my daughter. "You saw him?"

"Aye."

I bent down to her level and nearly flooded her with tears. "That was your poppa, Heather. He's reached us through the dreaming."

She hugged me. "Tell me again what happened."

O'er the years I had told her the story often, so she would know her poppa had not intentionally abandoned us. In many ways, she was very much like him—not just physically with her black hair, brown skin, and dark eyes, but her mannerisms as well. She much preferred the bow and arrows that Charging Bear brought to the dolls that I made for her. " 'Tis time, Heather."

"Time?"

"For you to accompany me during the dreaming. In time, you will learn your own way, but I would like to lead you on the initial journey. I have vowed to your grandmother to not seek out your poppa, but we can travel through the realms together."

My daughter beamed. "I'd like that Momma. Where?"

"Right here." I grasped Heather's hand. "Are you ready?"

She hopped up and down.

"You must contain yourself, Heather, or we will not be successful." She stopped jumping, and I gripped both of her hands. "You shall see my guardian spirit and much mist. Don't be afraid. You won't be lost. I'll be aside you the entire time."

Heather nodded that she was ready. I breathed deeply to help broaden my thoughts. A misty tunnel formed afore us. At its center stood my hound. He took off at a trot, guiding the way. The mist thickened and Heather clenched my hand e'en tighter. I reassured her, and we wandered on. My hound slowed his pace, leading us through the fog.

Follow the light.

I sucked in my breath. Up ahead, I spied the city. Lights upon lights. Why here? Why must I continually confront this place where I was struck by the car? I was with Heather now. I needed to make certain she remained safe. I took a deep breath and tread forward.

The fog faded, and the street swarmed with people. Instead of being frightened by the racket, Heather stared at e'erything with wide-eyed amazement. We both wore T-shirts and jeans. "Where are we, Momma?"

I trembled but hoped she didn't feel my hand shaking.

Blinded by the lights, Heather stepped into the road. I yanked on her hand to return her to the sidewalk. Brakes screeched, and an angered driver waved his fist. I placed a hand to my wildly thumping heart. Thankfully, he had missed hitting my daughter.

"We must watch the traffic afore we cross," I said. I showed her that we looked from left to right, then back again.

When 'twas safe, we crossed the road. Afore reaching the other side, I saw him. With a huge grin, Lee waved and moved towards us. "Phoebe, why is it that when I get this feeling you'll be here, you are?"

" 'Tis the connection." We greeted each other with a hug and a kiss. He gazed upon Heather. "This is Heather," I said. "Your daughter."

"My..."

His jaw dropped open, and I snickered. "It might be best if we go where we can talk."

"Umm..." He nodded. "Do you want to go inside and introduce Heather to cheesecake?"

"Aye, I'd like that." We went into the restaurant and made ourselves comfortable in a booth. Heather stared at Lee with adoring eyes, making him squirm in his seat.

After the waitress had served our water and taken our orders for cheesecake, Lee swallowed. "I know that you said we had a daughter, but I expected a little girl, not a preteen."

"Time isn't fluid," I responded. "I birthed Heather when we were married."

"Isn't that sometime in the future?"

"Aye."

"But you said you were living in the seventeenth century."

"Aye, we are." Dumbfounded, he gawked at me, then Heather. I couldn't help but giggle.

"I'm glad you find this amusing. I thought I was finally figuring out the dreaming. Now I have to get my head around time travel too."

Once more I snickered, then the waitress served our cheesecake. After she left our table, I grasped Lee's hand. "The dreaming has allowed you to meet our daughter. For that blessing, I'm fore'er grateful."

He smiled and watched Heather taste cheesecake for the first time. "Me too." She smacked her lips together in delight. His eyes danced. "I think she likes it. Heather, I'm very pleased to meet you."

"Momma is teaching me *wisakon*."

Lee shook his head. "My Algonquian isn't what it should be."

"The art of healing," I replied.

Beaming, he leaned back in the seat. "So you're going to be a cunning woman?"

"Aye."

"If I can get her to concentrate," I said. "She prefers warrior games to learning *wisakon*."

With a little laugh, he shrugged. "Nothing wrong in learning both, is there?"

"Nay, there's not." I detected a gentle breeze and knew our time grew short. As if sensing the same, Lee stood. Heather and I got to our feet, and we all embraced. For a brief instant in time, we were together—as a family. The moment faded all too soon, and we were engulfed in mist. Heather was no longer aside me, and I worried what had happened to my daughter.

"Momma?"

Relieved that she was nearby, I asked, "Where are you, Heather?"

"Momma?"

Her voice came from all round me. I turned in e'ery direction but could not locate her. "Heather!"

"I'm not of this time."

Suddenly panic stricken, I fumbled my way through the fog to locate her. "Heather, you mustn't leave me." I continued calling for her but got no response. She was gone. *Heather.* Why had I shown her the ways of the dreaming? As the mist faded, I lowered myself to the ground and sobbed.

"Momma?"

I brushed my tears away and looked up. Heather stood afore me. I swept her into my arms. "I thought I had lost you."

"Nay, Momma. You'll ne'er lose me."

Closing my eyes, I squeezed her tighter. The dreaming had sent me a message. It's meaning terrified me.

24

Wind Talker

1626

I'M NOT OF THIS TIME.
I woke with a start, wondering who had uttered the words. *A dream, you silly fool.* But I couldn't shake the feeling that Phoebe had attempted to contact me. I glanced around the *yi-hakan*, trying to recall where I was. Embers from the fire were in the center. I had returned to the Sekakawon tribe. Silver Eagle, Sly Fox, and I were lodged in the guest house for the duration of our visit.

As my breathing returned to normal, I went over to the embers and stoked them until a fire resumed. Phoebe's presence remained strong. I would try to contact her through the dreaming. Crow flew overhead, but the wind was missing. Without it, I doubted my success. Then, a gust roared in, nearly knocking Crow out of the sky. Almost bowled over myself, I struggled to stay upright. My shirt flapped against my arms, and I almost felt like a bird. Leaves whirled around me. The swirling cloud shifted direction, and I was sucked inside the torrent. Barely able to breathe, I looked up. A circular opening rotated overhead. Cloud walls revolved and lightning struck in an eerie twisting pattern. Smaller whirlwinds broke free with a loud hissing noise. Before I could make sense of what was happening, I was slapped to the ground and darkness overcame me.

The sound of a crow cawing madly woke me. My head felt like it had been split wide open. Still groggy, I opened bleary eyes. I blinked. The crow was pure white. "I must be dead," I muttered.

"Nay, you're running a fever."

"Phoebe?"

"Aye, I'm here."

Sweat dripped into my eyes, blurring my vision further. Raised bumps covered my body. Each one felt like a shotgun pellet was buried beneath my skin. I wanted to scream, but the blisters filled my mouth as well. I couldn't breathe. *Phoebe.*

She called to me but mist surrounded me. As I stumbled through a forest, I shuddered, telling myself that I wasn't lost. Even though the feeling was nothing more than a childish fear, I had difficulty fighting it. The misty world was the way of the dreaming. I halted and took a deep breath, but could see nothing through the fog. I fought to remain calm and held out my hands. If I could sense the directions, I would face the four winds. Which way was east?

A soft light shone in the distance. *East.* I faced it and gave thanks. I turned to the south. I had failed to change history and save my tribe, but my father and Phoebe's family had survived. I faced the west. Besides Phoebe, my tribe had sought refuge with the Arrohateck and Sekakawon. I might not be able to change history, but I would do whatever I could to aid them in the days ahead. I turned north. I could not fault myself for failing to change history. The blame lay with the colonists, who had fired the guns. Once again, I had made a circle.

The first time I had faced the four winds, I had finally comprehended the sacred circle. Now, I was definitely convinced that time was very much a part of it. Why had I spent well over thirty years in the future, only to keep circling through the seventeenth century?

The light in the east grew larger and formed a tunnel. Moving toward it, I stepped out of the circle when a warm breeze brushed against my cheek. The white crow flew ahead of me. I had no idea what the meaning could be, but I followed the bird. Suddenly, the light brightened, nearly blinding me. I shielded my eyes with my hand. Crow sailed through the light and vanished. The wind caught me and I continued forward.

Up ahead stood Snow Bird and Swimming Beaver. Beside them, my adoptive parents waved at me to join them. "Lee..." My mother smiled. Crow reappeared. The wind captured me, and I floated through the clouds toward the light.

25

Phoebe

1658

IN THE FALL, HEATHER TURNED fifteen. With the swell of her breasts and fullness of her hips, she would reach her moon time soon. In the tradition of the Arrohateck, I had forewarned her of her body's changes and what to expect. When her courses began, Bess and I instructed her in the ways of womanhood. She giggled when we explained how babes were made. "I've heard the grunts and groans of Elenor and Christopher," she said. "They sound like they're in agony. Such pain is really for making babes?"

"Heather..." I held back my own laugh. "I assure you, if you care for someone, the activity can be most pleasurable." When Bess echoed my statement, I had a sense of longing. So many years had passed since last seeing Wind Talker—or even Lee—much less touching him. Similar anguish reflected in Bess's eyes, for she had been a widow e'en longer than I had been apart from Wind Talker.

"Momma..." Heather touched the back of my hand. "I know you miss him."

My throat tightened and I could not speak. I cleared my throat. "On this day, we are here to celebrate your entrance into womanhood, not mourn our losses."

Heather hugged me. "Momma, I love you."

"And I, you," I said, returning my daughter's embrace. "The English have no special ceremony as did the Arrohateck, but we can honor you all the same. If you are like your sister and me, you shall likely enter the dreaming soon."

"Thank you for showing me, so I know what to expect."

"E'en though I have shown you what 'tis like, it can be frightening the first time." I sent her a pride-filled smile. I had reached forty-six winters, and both of my babes were now grown women. Bess, Elenor, and I cooked a feast for Heather. The men were a bit perplexed. 'Twas a secret initiation shared amongst the women. We continued the feasting and teaching for two more days.

On the following morn I found Heather in the kitchen curled on a rug. As I approached her, I had an inkling of what ailed her. I bent down and rubbed her back. "You've had a 'dream.'"

"Aye."

I took her into my arms like I had when she was a lass and held her. "When I first entered the dreaming, I saw the English make war on the Arrohateck."

She smiled slightly. "'Twas naught like that. A black swallowtail butterfly with a blue splotch in the shape of a half moon, and white spots on the edge of its wings guided me to see Poppa."

No doubt the butterfly was her spirit guide. "Poppa?"

"I was naught but a babe. You held onto my finger and Poppa took me into his arms. I was so elated."

Pleased that she had viewed a joyful memory, I hugged her once more. "Was there anything else?"

She shook her head. "Nay. E'erything was peaceful. I felt true happiness that we were a family. Momma, if I continue to explore the dreaming will I have the chance to really know Poppa?"

"'Tis possible. Whilst the dreaming doesn't always show us what we'd like, many times we can focus on them and have them become reality. If you should see Poppa again, pray tell me about it."

Heather tightened our embrace. "I shall."

In parting, I kissed her upon the forehead. "When you're ready, come up to the house. We shall have another day of feasting." As I left the kitchen, Heather laughed. She relished the meals without having to participate in their preparation.

The next afternoon Heather traveled to the site of her ancestors' bones. Their spirits remained unsettled, and I had avoided visiting the spot for years. Yet, I feared for my daughter. When the sun began to set, I traced along the path to fetch her. As I neared the area, I thought I heard Wind Talker's tenor voice, singing to those who had died. I quickened my pace only to discover that he wasn't there. 'Twas only wishful thinking.

Heather stood o'er the graves with her head bent in sorrow. With tears streaking her cheeks she turned to me upon hearing my footsteps. "My grandmother is buried here."

"Aye. Snow Bird. Along with your other grandmother, she taught me the ways of *wisakon*."

She nodded. "Momma, I saw him again."

"Your poppa?"

"I saw him flee this place in a cloud of mist."

More than once, I had told her the story of how her poppa had escaped certain death by vanishing in the mist. "He did. 'Twasn't 'til I went to the twenty-first century myself that I learned how he had done so."

In the fading daylight, she gazed out upon the bones. "I fear I too will vanish in the mist."

Trembling, I grasped her hand, leading her towards the trail to the house. "Is that why you think you've seen Poppa?"

"I don't know."

Darkness had settled by the time we returned to the house. Elenor and Bess had rabbit stewed in wine flavored with nutmeg and lemon waiting for us on the table. We joined the family for the exquisite meal. Throughout, I detected Heather's tension. She pretended to enjoy her food but ate very little. When we settled down for the night in the loft, I continued to worry. 'Twas a long time afore I slept.

In the middle of the night, I awoke with my heart racing. Heather was no longer aside me. I hoped she had slipped from my side in order to use the pisspot. I searched the loft, but she was nowhere to be found. Gripping the handrail, I tiptoed down the stairs. An ebbing light came from the fireplace, and a snore came from the main bed. All were asleep. Afore shuffling out the door, I picked up a candle, dipping it into the fire embers. So as not to wake anyone, I shielded the flame with my hand.

Outside the door, I called for Heather. An owl hooted in response. Unsettled by what might have happened, I searched the farmyard and barn. When a dog yipped, I shuddered. My white hound trotted to my side. Moving forward, he whined. "Take me to Heather."

He loped ahead of me, and I could barely keep up. The path was the same one that we had traveled earlier in the day. When I neared the site of the bones, I called for Heather.

"Momma?"

Her voice had come from a short distance ahead. "Heather, I'm here."

"Momma, I'm frightened."

"There's no need to be. Wait for me."

"I can't. I'm not of this time."

"Nay, Heather. You mustn't leave me!" I spied the black butterfly with the blue splotch, guiding her through the mist. A branch swiped my arm, and I dropped the candle. I stamped the flame out afore the brambles caught afire. Only shadowy moonlight lighted my path. "Heather!"

Brambles caught my skirt as I stumbled along the path. I pressed onwards 'til immersed in the same mist. My hound stood afore me, and I gripped his collar. "Take me to her." Forging ahead, he led me through the fog.

"Momma!"

"I'm here, Heather. Where are you?" E'en with my hound's help, I staggered.

"I was two when I came to this time. I will be two again, but not in this time."

Her voice echoed round me. 'Twas like the time when I had followed Crow in the Woods in the mist. "Fetch her," I said to my hound. He raced off 'til he was naught more than a blurry shape. I waved my arms afore me, staggering through the mist.

"Momma, I see him."

"Poppa?"

"He's waving for me to join him. I belong in his time."

Silence surrounded me. "Heather!" I called again and again but got no response. Unlike when I had gone after Crow in the Woods, the mist failed to vanish.

Follow the light.

'Twas his voice. Mayhap, I would join him too. No longer fearful, I embraced what lay ahead. We would be a family again. Bright light streaked across the heavens. 'Twasn't torches, but city lights. I had reached the twenty-first century. As I stepped out of the fog, I searched the street for Lee. When I found him, I'd be reunited with Heather.

I breathed deeply and checked the traffic afore crossing the street. "Phoebe..."

Thank goodness, I had found him. I rushed into his arms. He held and comforted me. After calming myself, I stepped back without breaking our embrace. "Pray take me to Heather."

"Heather? I haven't seen her since you visited with her."

"You haven't seen...?"

"Let me take you to my apartment where we can talk in private."

Numb, I grasped his hand as he led me to the T-Bird. My mind was in turmoil. I had been rejoined with the man I loved, but our daughter was missing. Lee pulled into a parking space and escorted me to his apartment. I sat on the divan whilst he made some tea. I continued to fret and paced the floor.

"Please sit." Wringing my hands, I did as he asked. He placed a mug of tea on the coffee table and sat aside me. "Now, tell me what's happened." When my words came in a rush, he raised his hand. "Slower."

His calmness, a role I was all too aware he had perfected whilst working as a cop, was what I needed. I sipped the tea and relayed what had happened.

He thought o'er my words afore speaking. "I haven't seen her. You said she was fifteen?"

"Aye." Though I and the other women had remained silent to the other men as to why we had been celebrating, Lee was Heather's poppa and had a right to know. "She had begun her moon time. We were honoring her entrance to womanhood."

"Is there a significance to her age besides becoming a woman?"

" 'Twas the first time she had entered the dreaming on her own. Like my momma and me, we experienced the dreaming at that time."

"Obviously that must run in the family on the women's side."

"It does. My other daughter Elenor was the same. This wasn't the dreaming though. I believe she's traveled through time."

He pointed at himself. "To me?"

"She said you were waving at her for her to join you."

"Then it must be some future time."

E'en with my clouded thoughts I should have seen the truth. I grasped his hand. "Lee, how old are you?"

"How old—"

"How old are you?"

"Thirty-two."

In three more years, my younger self would arrive in the twenty-first century. Heather would not be born 'til almost two years later. Is that what she had meant by being two in another time? I felt aged. "And I've become an old woman."

Gazing into my eyes, Lee stroked my cheek. "You're not old. I see you the same way as when I was ten."

Ten? As he hugged me, mist formed round us. I hadn't traveled to this time, anymore than Heather had. Lee vanished afore my eyes, and I found myself tossing and turning in bed. Sick to my stomach and covered in sweat, I scrambled for the pisspot, barely making it in time to retch. Unable to catch my breath, I retched again. After birthing four babes, I knew the symptoms all too well and caught my breath. But I was much too old. My moon times had ceased o'er two years afore, and I had only shared intimacies whilst in the dreaming.

Heather. On my knees, I pressed a hand to my belly. She was trying to tell me the time she had traveled to. *When are you, Heather?* The fog lifted, and I stared at the bones. *Heather!*

26

Wind Talker

1626

Hearing Phoebe scream, I halted in my tracks.
"Wind Talker?" Silver Eagle asked.

I blinked away the echo. "Phoebe, my wife, not the one of this time, was calling for our daughter."

Though he could never understand the division I lived with, he placed a hand to my shoulder. "You will find out what has happened."

I nodded. "Thank you. Let's resume our journey."

Only a few miles from the plantation, Silver Eagle, Sly Fox, and I continued along the forest path. Over the past few weeks, I had enjoyed getting to know Black Owl in a way I hadn't been able to the time before. Still a relatively young man, he was a family man, and I was able to glimpse what life would have been like had the massacre never taken place. When the weather had grown chillier and fall settled in firmly, I knew Silver Eagle needed to return home. I had debated whether to stay with Black Owl and the Sekakawon or leave with Silver Eagle, but there had been no contest. I wanted to see Phoebe, even if only for a few hours or days. At the same time, I worried what her call from the other time frame could be about.

We reached the mass grave, where I stopped to pay my respects. No matter how I tried to distract myself, I couldn't tune out the dying voices. I should have died here alongside my mother. How did I manage to keep beating the odds and surviving? I moved closer and could clearly see the outline of bones. Because little more than a decade had passed, rather than the thirty years upon me seeing the spot the first time, the soil had yet to cover much of the skeletal remains.

A melodic voice came from beside me. In memoriam Silver Eagle sang in honor of those who had died. I joined him. Alongside me, Sly Fox raised his voice as well. When we finished, we raised our hands to the sky with a silent prayer to Ahone.

I lowered my arms and stood in silence awhile longer. Silver Eagle and I had tears in our eyes. But it was time for the living. I turned toward the house, and we traveled through the forest in silence. The closer we got, the more I longed for Phoebe. When the palisade came into view, my heart beat faster.

Before we reached the fortification, a woman appeared on the path. Her shape was more rounded than Phoebe's. "Jennet?"

She placed two fingers to her lips for us to remain quiet and came closer. "The guards saw Indians coming, and the mistress sent me," she whispered. "Her father is visiting."

Phoebe's father—the bastard who had her whipped for having an affair with an Indian. Future time, I reminded myself. Not only that, time had changed, and *I* was that Indian. I exchanged a glance with Silver Eagle. Knowing that his English was limited, I translated for him. I could only imagine what went through his mind, when he thought of Phoebe as his daughter. We needed to tread carefully to keep from endangering her. "Thanks for the warning," I said. "Should we wait here?"

"Nay, the mistress said to continue."

We moved forward. As we arrived at the gate, the guards made no motion to open it.

"We wish to enter," Jennet said.

"You may," the bearded guard said, "but the heathens remain here."

"The master gave his permission," Jennet reminded him.

With some reluctance, the guard opened the gate. Wondering what sort of reception we'd receive, I stepped through the gate and scanned the grounds for Phoebe. James waved from the drying shed. Then, I spotted him. A man who would have been regarded as heavy-set during the seventeenth century, but not in the twenty-first, strode toward us. His eyes smoldered and his hands curled to fists. *Easy.* He stood across from us when I realized his gaze was directed at Silver Eagle. He examined Silver Eagle from head to toe as if sizing him up. "You're the savage who claims to have married my wife?"

Silver Eagle glanced in my direction. Again, I translated for him. "I am Silver Eagle," he said in English.

"What gives you the right to steal my wife?"

This time, Silver Eagle didn't know enough English words to reply in the language. "She thought you were dead. She and Walks Through Mist were starving. I took them into my home and cared for them. I saw that they were no longer hungry, and they learned the ways of the Paspahegh."

I interpreted his response for Phoebe's father. As if noticing Sly Fox for the first time, his eyes narrowed. "And this is your bastard?"

"Robert!" Elenor and Phoebe moved toward us. "Sly Fox is my son. If you don't approve, then leave."

I resisted every urge to pull Phoebe out of the fray, as I'm sure Silver Eagle did with Elenor. Right now, any action I took would make the situation worse. Between the guards at the gate and Phoebe's father's servants, we were outnumbered.

Phoebe's father grew red-faced as he turned to Elenor. "How could you shame me in this manner?"

"Shame you?"

Their voices grew louder. While the two argued, Phoebe and I exchanged knowing looks. No words were necessary. Jennet slipped her arm through mine, distracting me. Fluttering her eyelashes at me, she gave me a coy smile, then I noticed that Phoebe's father was watching us. She had provided a distraction. I would thank her later.

"Come," Elenor said, taking Silver Eagle's hand. "I'll take my disgraceful hide out of here and leave. You can tell them I died,

Robert. That way no one will ever know that you've been shamed." She motioned for me to accompany them.

Before turning, I sent one last look to Phoebe, and Jennet snuggled closer. Only after we stepped through the gate and were out of sight from the guards did she drop the pretense. When we were out of earshot, I asked, "Now what?"

"We wait 'til Robert leaves," Elenor said. "I told him that we were returning to the Arrohateck. We must make it look like we're doing so. Give Jennet a goodbye kiss, and pray make it convincing. Others may be observing."

"Jennet?"

She motioned for me to kiss Jennet. "I realize the Paspahegh did not kiss afore the English came ashore, but they quickly discovered the pleasure in doing so."

"Huh?" She waved at me to get on with it. As I bent down, Jennet wrapped her arms around my waist. *Pretend she's Phoebe.* I closed my eyes and kissed her on the lips without any intimacy. "Goodbye, Jennet."

With a devilish smile, she winked. "Goodbye, Wind Talker." She scurried along the trail back to the palisade.

Elenor scowled and Silver Eagle chuckled. Finally, she smiled. "I know she's not my daughter, but the deception was necessary for Phoebe's sake. You'll see her aft Robert leaves. Meanwhile, we pretend to travel to the Arrohateck."

As we wound our way along the forest trail near the river, I spotted the Carolina parakeets. Always when I left Henry's house, I saw them. For some reason, I grew homesick for the twenty-first century. Not only did I miss Phoebe, I ached to see Heather.

After several miles, the trail returned to the river bank, where we uncovered the dugout. Like the time before, Elenor got in, then Silver Eagle, Sly Fox, and I shoved the boat into the water before getting in ourselves. This time, we paddled only a couple of miles before bringing the canoe back ashore. Then, we waited.

Another day passed before we followed the same paths back to Henry's house. We timed our arrival with the setting sun and waited a safe distance from the palisade. Elenor had told me that Phoebe would give us a signal if her father had left. I called to her in the voice of the crow. Every few minutes, I tried again. As nighttime fell, a whippoorwill responded. Phoebe's signal. We moved forward.

When we reached the palisade, the guards seemed reluctant, but at Elenor's urging, they opened the gate. We stepped through, and Phoebe ran from the house with her arms spread wide. She came so fast that she nearly bowled me over in her greeting.

We kissed and hugged. For now, no words were necessary. We held each other for a long while. Nothing else mattered. When I stepped back without breaking our embrace, I noticed the others had left us to our privacy. Phoebe smiled shyly and grasped my hand, placing it to her abdomen. "Wind Talker, I'm with child."

I opened my mouth to respond, but nothing came out.

"Say something. Anything. I'm so very frightened."

Could that be why Phoebe of the future had been calling to me? I drew her close. "Could it be Heather?"

She trembled. "Possibly, but I don't know."

"In the twenty-first century when you told me about Heather, I was ecstatic. I want to do the right thing, but what is it in this century? Especially when we don't know if I'm here to stay."

"That no matter what happens you'll love her and care for her."

So she thought the baby might be Heather. "You know I will. What do we do now?"

"Come." She led the way toward the house. "We'll talk more later."

Inside, the rest of the family waited. The women scurried to place a large pie on the table. They motioned for everyone to have a seat. Again, Silver Eagle sat at the head, and the rest of us were arranged on the benches at the side. After everything was served, Phoebe sat beside me. The pie was some sort of meat, which I guessed was beef, with a nice mix of spices, eggs, and raisins.

Conversation brought all of us up to date, but notably absent was any mention of Phoebe's father's visit or her pregnancy. As I ate, I wondered to myself if even I had absorbed the news.

"Wind Talker..."

I blinked. Bess was serving an almond cake for dessert. I had no doubt the nuts were a rare import and only for the special company. After the cake, when Silver Eagle and Sly Fox went outside, I lingered behind. Elenor grasped her granddaughter's hand, and the women made a hasty retreat. Once again, Phoebe was in my arms. If only we could remain like this, but there was an innocent life—a baby—involved. "I was a fool," I said.

Phoebe withdrew slightly. "Nay—"

"I was. You didn't have a baby during this time frame before. Obviously, I wasn't thinking with my head."

She stepped back and snickered. " 'Tis the consequence of loving each other. Naught more."

That was definitely the Arrohateck speaking. The English preferred to shame women. "Need I remind you that we're not married in this time period?"

With a frown, she shook her head. "I wish we were. Momma has agreed to take her. E'en if Henry hadn't been gone so long, he would know she's not his babe."

"Because she's part Indian. Phoebe, I don't think it's a good idea that your mother takes her. I'll bring her to the Sekakawon."

"Your father's family. Why?"

Not ready to talk about my reasoning, I closed my eyes.

"Kesutanouwas Wesin, pray tell me."

I swallowed but still avoided her gaze. "In about three years time, there will be a smallpox outbreak among the Arrohateck. Very few Natives have any immunities to the disease and many will die."

"Immunities?"

Of course she wouldn't understand the term in this time period. "It's a natural resistance that a body has to fighting disease. The colonists have some resistance to smallpox, which is why many survive. My people have little to none, and most die. I thought I might be able to spare Heather the risk."

Phoebe's face wrinkled, thinking over what I had told her. "And you?"

Because I had arrived in the twentieth century after the disease had been eliminated from most of the world, regular vaccination had ceased. "If I remain in this time period until then, I could be equally at risk."

"What about Momma, Silver Eagle, and Sly Fox?"

Should I tell her?

"Nay." She buried her face into her hands.

Obviously my expression answered her question. "Sly Fox will survive. First, he'll become Charging Bear. But there is hope. Bess knows a method that can help many. Maybe she can show it to your mom to save more people. Time can be changed." I touched her abdomen. Though her belly was still flat, a baby grew inside. Our baby. "I just want to help you in any way I can."

She hugged me. We would find answers. Together.

27

Phoebe

1659

O'ER THE next six months, I sought Heather through the dreaming, making e'ery attempt to locate the time she had traveled to. More often than not, my searches brought me to Lee. In the comfort of his arms, I found some solace. As well as relief, he had reawakened a part of me that I thought had been lost along with my moon time. We lay with our naked bodies pressed together under a blanket, each breathing in the other's scent. I longed for the moment to ne'er end, but I knew 'twas not possible. Only time would reveal when I would be able to live the life I yearned for—all of us together. I dared not think 'twould not come to pass for I would lose all hope.

A beam of light passed through the window, and in the distance, my hound barked. " 'Tis time," I said.

When I rose from under the blanket, Lee grasped my hand. "I've tried to reach you through the dreaming, but it only seems to work when you contact me."

"Keep trying. You will succeed."

He let go of my hand and watched me dress. How many more times would I need to pretend my leaving didn't matter? Finished dressing, I turned away, struggling to withhold my tears. Afore long, his hand caressed my cheek. I faced him. He had dressed whilst my back was turned.

"Come back to me," he said.

"I will."

"And I cherish every minute." He pulled me to him and we kissed once more. The mist formed, and I sat near the fireplace in the kitchen.

"Momma..."

For a moment, I thought Heather called me, but 'twas Elenor. I had suffered much the same when she had been left behind in the seventeenth century, but I took comfort that she had a good life and was happily married with children of her own.

"Momma, Meg's here."

"Meg?"

Elenor pointed out the window. Alongside a couple of other warriors, Charging Bear, Meg, and her daughters Tiffany and Falling Rain meandered towards the house. I went outside to greet them. Tiffany had reached twenty winters and was heavy with child. She could barely walk. One of the warriors, who I presumed was the babe's poppa, helped her. Meg and I exchanged hugs. "I wanted my friend to deliver my grandchildren," Meg said. "She's having twins, and I want the best for her."

"I'd be happy to, Meg." I ushered e'eryone inside. After a meal and relaying all that had happened since our last meeting, I checked Tiffany with Bess and Elenor's help. We all agreed with Meg's assessment that her daughter carried twins. She would likely deliver in the coming days or weeks. 'Til then, we could only wait.

O'er the next few days, I rejoiced in my time with Meg. She was a friend who had stayed true to me throughout the years. Along with me, she cried o'er my loss of Heather. "You'll find her. I know you will. Meanwhile, you seem to be able to connect with Lee."

"Aye, but he sees me as I was, not as I am—an old woman."

Meg smiled. "You're not old. It only means the two of you are connected in spirit. That transcends any physical age. From the beginning, I knew he had a thing for older women. Weren't you born in 1600, and he about ten years later?"

Her jest made me laugh. Something I hadn't been able to do in a long while. "Aye, but need I remind you that I was nearly five years younger when we met as adults in the twenty-first century?"

We shared a laugh, then Meg grew serious again. "Phoebe, there's something else I need to tell you."

"What's wrong, Meg?"

"After the babies are born, we'll be moving west."

At the thought of losing my friend and brother too, I swallowed. "West?"

"The English continue to take the land, rob, and... rape."

I gripped Meg's hand.

"We can't risk visiting anymore. They expect us to wear a badge to travel legally."

Afore I could respond, Tiffany joined us with her hands on her enormous belly. "Momma, Phoebe... I think it's time. I'm passing water."

Meg clapped her hands in delight as I went o'er to check on Tiffany. "If your water has come down," I said, "then the time is definitely near. Let's go inside where I can check you more thoroughly."

Inside the house, I told Elenor the news. She brought out the birthing chair, then said, "I'll fetch Bess."

I helped Tiffany to the chair and examined her. "Your babes are breech."

"They can't be," Meg said with wide eyes.

"They still may turn on their own afore they're born."

"And if they don't?"

"Then we shall deliver them breech."

Meg gripped my arm and drew me aside. She whispered so Tiffany would not overhear. "Phoebe, this isn't the twenty-first century. We can't do a C-section."

"Why would we want to?"

"We could lose them—or Tiffany."

"Meg, I know you are vexed aft having lost a babe of your own. I've lost one too, but I have Bess and Elenor's help. There's a risk with any birth. These babes are fully formed and ready to be born."

Unsure whether my words brought Meg any comfort, I returned to Tiffany's side. The day came and went with one of us remaining aside her at all times. E'en then, she had few birthing pains. Meg lingered, holding her daughter's hand, sometimes trembling as she did so. Bess and Elenor traded gazes with me. I nodded and grasped Meg's arm, taking her outside. "Your daughter needs her privacy. Her thoughts are with you and not her task ahead."

"You're asking me to leave?"

"Aye."

"What if—?"

"Tiffany needs all of her strength for birthing the babes." When Meg realized I wasn't going to allow her back inside, she shuffled off. No doubt she was annoyed, but I returned to the one who needed my attention. I'd console Meg after two healthy babes were born.

Soon after Meg's departure, Tiffany was nearly ready to birth. I pressed down on her belly. The babe hadn't shifted position. "The babe remains breech."

"Momma worried about a breech birth. She said 'twould cause serious problems 'less they were turned."

I shook my head. "Your momma learned her medicine in the twenty-first century. A time where they forgot women had been birthing babes from the beginning of time. There should be no need to turn the babe."

Tiffany's countenance etched in terror.

"There's no reason to be affright, Tiffany. You have three cunning women to aid you through the birthing."

When a birthing pain caught her unaware, I whispered words of praise. Because the babe was breech, we had her lie down, rather than using the birthing chair. She bore down with each pain. Within minutes, the babe appeared betwixt her legs.

" 'Tis a lad."

"How can you tell already?" Tiffany asked.

"I see his ballocks."

Tiffany giggled, but another pain gripped her. She bore down once more. His bum appeared. I adjusted his body, so he would birth easier. More pains followed. With one last grunt and groan from Tiffany, the lad's head came out. He cried, and I placed him on Tiffany's chest. She hugged, kissed, and cradled her newborn infant.

Bess picked up the babe, wiped him down, and swaddled him, whilst I massaged Tiffany's belly. Afore long, Bess returned the lad to Tiffany's arms. Nursing would set off the birthing pains for the second babe. Elenor offered Tiffany sips of water, and I continued to massage. Like the first one, the babe was breech.

As Tiffany took shallow pants, Bess cradled the firstborn. 'Twas time to deliver the second babe. Tiffany edged to the end of the bed with her feet propped on the birthing chair. She worked with the pains. A tiny foot emerged betwixt her legs but quickly vanished back inside. Another pain and both feet appeared.

During the birthing, I supported the babe's body as it came forth. As Tiffany closed her eyes, her countenance twisted, and the babe emerged to her waist. " 'Tis a lass." Another pain and the main portion of her body was out of the birth chamber. Her arms fell free. Time was growing short. "Work with the next pain, like you've ne'er worked afore. The lass needs to be born."

Elenor helped Tiffany sit more upright. Tiffany groaned, and the babe was finally born. Her heart was beating, but she wasn't breathing. I massaged her. "Talk to her," Bess said.

Tiffany called to the babe and stroked her. "You're a fine, lass."

At last, she took a deep breath. She gurgled and I placed her in Tiffany's arms. "You have two fine babes." Exhausted, I let Elenor wait for the cauls. "I'll tell Meg and the proud poppa." I went outside. After a quick search, I found Meg and the rest of the group waiting for news in the kitchen.

My friend clutched a mug handle, as if she had been doing naught else since I had sent her away from the birthing room. "Tell me that everything is okay."

I waved at her to calm herself. "You have two fine grandchildren—a lad and a lass. Momma is doing well too."

With tears filling her eyes, she hugged e'eryone in sight. "Thank you, Phoebe. Thank you."

" 'Twas naught. Your daughter did most of the work, and she didn't need a C-section to produce healthy babes."

She embraced me. "That's why I brought her to you."

* * *

That night I had difficulty taking my rest. I checked on Tiffany and the babes. Feeling her age, Bess had retired, but Elenor had stayed with them. "Momma, you need rest."

"I can't rest." I wandered outside to find Meg staring at the full moon.

She turned to me. "Looks like I wasn't the only one who couldn't sleep."

"I'm oft restless."

"It's not fair. Coming to this time has been a godsend for me, but you..." She squeezed me close.

"I shall find the right time. I mustn't give up hope."

Gripping my hands, Meg stepped back. "No, you mustn't. May I accompany you in the dreaming one last time?"

One last time. Her words reminded me that soon she and her family would no longer be nearby. "I've seen Lee."

"I know. I'd like seeing him again."

"Then we shall enter the dreaming together." I led the way to the kitchen. Because of the late hour, no one lingered. Picking up a candle, I lit it from the embers in the fireplace and placed it on a table. We sat on chairs across from one another. Afore long my spirit dog guided us through the mist. When the fog cleared, we stood inside a hallway. The tread of footsteps came from behind us, and I turned to Lee. Attired in a business suit, he had his keys in hand and trudged towards us.

"Phoebe..." He gave me a quick kiss on the lips.

"This is my friend, Meg."

Meg hugged him. "It's good seeing you again."

"Again?" He rubbed bloodshot eyes and went o'er to unlock the door. "Sorry, I don't remember meeting you before, but then, you've caught me at a bad time. Been up all night working on a case."

As we went inside, I chuckled. "In reality, you will meet in a few years time, but for now, it's through the dreaming."

"I see. I don't think I'm ever going to understand the dreaming."

"In time you will." The fog captured us once more, and Lee faded from my view. I turned in e'ery direction looking for Meg. I called for her but could not find her. As I walked through the mist, I felt heavy with child. 'Twas no longer possible, but this was the dreaming. A black butterfly hovered in front of me, and I touched my belly. "Heather?"

A smile spread across my countenance, for I had found her.

28

Wind Talker

1627

OVER TIME, the baby grew inside Phoebe and she became rounder. By wearing a baggy black skirt with a bulky scarf, she attempted to hide her pregnancy, so no one outside the family or friends would be any wiser. No matter what anyone said, I thought she was very sexy, but we were only able to see each other sporadically. For weeks on end, I lived my life as a warrior among the Arrohateck. Time played a cruel twist of fate. In this period, I never questioned who I was or where I had come from, but Lee was a strong part of my psyche. Were Phoebe and I continually destined to be kept apart in some way? Even though I couldn't see how, believing that all would somehow work out in the end helped me face each day.

Then, I thought of Phoebe and the last time I had visited. She had placed my hand on her abdomen. Beneath my fingertips, the baby had squirmed, then came a solid kick. The sensation had made me breathless. Could this baby really be Heather?

For now, I stood along the bank of the James River to moonlight casting a gentle glow. Phoebe was downstream from me. I longed for a time when I could have hopped into the T-bird and taken the freeway to my destination.

Someone approached me from behind, and I turned to Phoebe's mother.

"I didn't mean to intrude," Elenor said.

Even though she was fluent in Algonquian, she almost always used English when speaking to me unless Silver Eagle was present. "You're not intruding. What can I do for you?"

She cleared her throat. "I wondered if you would to speak to Sly Fox?"

"Speak to Sly Fox?"

"He'll be going through the *huskanaw* soon—"

"I never went through the *huskanaw*."

"Aye, but you know what it's like to be a lad betwixt societies. Sly Fox was lucky to grow up amongst the Arrohateck, but he believes his English roots will fail him."

"Sure, I'll speak to him."

Even in the scant lighting, I could see that her hands went to her hips. I imagined her staring at me as well.

"I'm guessing that you want me to speak to him right now."

"If you could."

"I will." Together we headed back to the main section of town. Sly Fox stood near a campfire, listening to the men tell hunting stories. I waited until they finished to speak to Sly Fox. We separated from the group. I never had a child Sly Fox's age and only through my experience as a cop had I ever dealt with teens. Even then, I was uncertain how to open the conversation. Straight forward was probably best. "Your mom says you have some concerns about the *huskanaw*."

"She shames me."

"She doesn't. She thought I might understand because I'm also a product of mixed societies. Sly Fox, you have nothing to worry about."

"Is it true that you have traveled through time?"

"It is."

"Do you know what will happen with certainty?"

"Not with certainty because time can change. In the time line that I'm familiar with, we will become friends. You had your adult name and guided me when I needed it. Your English heritage is a part of you. As a result, you can speak both languages and are an asset to both of our people."

He mulled over my words, then slowly, a smile spread across his face. "An asset? Because I speak both languages?"

"Very much so."

"Then I will become a worthy warrior?"

"You will, but first you need to concentrate on getting through the *huskanaw*. Don't let such knowledge go to your head. As I said, time can change."

He straightened his shoulders and stood taller. "I will make you and my father proud."

"I'm sure you will." We headed back to the main section of the town.

Two nights later, I had the distinct feeling that Phoebe needed me. A shimmering figure stood at the end of my sleeping platform. I squinted for a better look. "Phoebe?"

Like a ghostly image, she moved closer. "Wind Talker, I shall be birthing soon."

With her message delivered, she vanished. Startled awake, I sat up on the platform. *A dream.* But the dream had carried a message. Next morning, I readied to head out to the homestead by a small canoe. Silver Eagle and Elenor were going to be involved with the upcoming *huskanaw,* but I had taken the trip often enough that I felt comfortable journeying without extra help. Even then, as I shoved the boat from the riverbank, the worried look in Elenor's eyes pervaded.

"She'll be fine, Elenor," I said.

"I know, but I worry how taking her babe from her will affect her."

"Me too. I'll let you know what happens as soon as I can." I got in the canoe and began rowing. Downriver was definitely easier, since the current did most of the work. I passed miles and miles of forests. In the coming years plantations would spread, and eventually highways would be built. A dull ache swept through me. I should be rejoicing, I reminded myself. Heather would soon be here, but that thought brought sorrow too. I was traveling to take her to my tribe. If I stayed in this time long enough, I could watch her grow to adulthood. If . . .

Circle in Time

The first day was uneventful. I didn't even spot a colonial boat. When the sun got low in the sky, I came ashore and built a fire. While I had learned how to make a fire in boy scouts, if anyone had told me that I'd be doing such a thing on a regular basis, I would have laughed them silly. My stomach rumbled, reminding me that I hadn't eaten since setting out. Elenor had packed a few supplies of some dried, chewy venison and parched cornmeal. I had consumed worse—in the twenty-first century, no less.

By the time I finished eating, the sun had set, and I listened to the night sounds. Cardinals and mockingbirds made their final calls, then an owl hooted. In my previous life, I would have never known the distinction between the birds and their sounds. Then, I thought of my people and the battle when so many had died. Solitude gave too much time for reflection. Alone in my thoughts, I tossed and turned on the cold, hard earth.

Again, I heard Phoebe's voice, "Wind Talker, the babe is coming."

"I'll be there tomorrow."

"Just in time, my love."

When morning arrived, I dug into more of my supplies for a meal, then set out once more. As I went downriver, I began to see plantations. Most were overgrown and had been abandoned. Once I spotted a colonial boat and went ashore until they sailed past. Toward the end of the day, I brought the canoe up on the riverbank a few miles from the homestead.

Alongside the river, I made my way through the forest trail. Thinking about Phoebe and that I'd be seeing her soon, I walked faster. Out of breath by the time I reached the palisade, I stood outside the gate. The bearded guard, who often greeted me, sent me an annoyed look but opened the gate. I stepped through and when I reached the house, James hurried toward me. "Wind Talker, the babe be here soon."

"I'd like to see Phoebe."

He shook his head. "My Bess won't allow it. Men in the birthing room are bad luck."

I sighed and recalled when Heather was born. Instead of coaching Phoebe, all I could do was pace.

"I was the same when my lad was born," James said.

I had almost forgotten his presence and stopped pacing. He was in a similar situation. Because of his indentured servitude, he was unable to marry Bess at present time.

"Everything will work out for you and Bess," I said.

"Aye, but the master won't be pleased."

"I think he'd be less pleased with my indiscretion than yours."

My remark made James laugh. "Aye, if he finds out, he'll be out for blood."

"No doubt."

"Wind Talker..." Bess appeared in the doorway. "Your son has arrived."

Son? But Heather wasn't a boy. James cuffed me on the back in congratulations.

"Wind Talker?"

"A son?"

Bess grinned. "Aye, and he's raring to greet the world."

As Bess waved the way, I went inside. With her red hair astray, Phoebe lay on the bed with a nursing bundle in her arms. She stroked the still damp hair with a loving smile. "His English name shall be Jaysen."

A lump rose in my throat. All things were connected in this endless circle we called time. I touched the baby's tiny hand while he suckled. "Jaysen?"

"He's a healer and will connect all of us, including Heather."

I sat on the edge of the bed next to her. "I thought he was going to be Heather."

"Whilst birthing, I felt something amiss. He's not Heather. She will wait for that future time."

"Phoebe, we don't have to take him to my father's."

"We must. I can't keep him here."

"Then, come with me. Bring your daughter. Let her know that she is Little Hummingbird."

"I cannot. My father would hunt us down if I run off."

I placed my arms protectively around them. In time, maybe I could change her mind.

29

Phoebe

1665

As near as we could guess, Bess had reached her sixty-fifth year. O'er the past few moons, she had become frail and showed her advanced age. Her condition worsened when influenza struck her. She spent two days alternating betwixt freezing and boiling. I made her some marigold tea to aid in relieving her fever. With no energy, she remained bedridden and refused all meals. At night, I slept aside her and prayed she would pull through. Throughout my vigil, Elenor remained at my side more often than not.

"Phoebe..." Bess gasped for breath.

I took her feeble hand. "I'm here, Bess."

"I had a dream... about Wind Talker."

"Wind Talker?"

"He's alive... and well... in our past."

When he had connected with me, 'twas the same as what I had seen. "Did you see anything else?"

She coughed and wheezed, unable to catch her breath.

"I'll make more tea."

Bess shook her head. She coughed more, then finally managed to take an inhaling breath. "You... and Wind Talker... have a son."

Whilst in the dreaming, I had been heavy with child, but I had also seen Heather's guardian spirit. "A son?"

"Aye... his name... is Jaysen. Now I must... take my rest." Exhausted from the activity, Bess closed her eyes.

I patted her hand. "Sleep well, my friend."

A son. I once had a son with my first husband, Lightning Storm. His name had been Dark Moon. He had died from throat distemper, or as Lee called it, diphtheria. But now, Wind Talker and I had a son. I wondered if I would e'er meet him in my current time frame. "Jaysen," I whispered. Mayhap, he could lead me to Heather.

O'er the next two weeks, I had little time for the dreaming. Caring for Bess filled most of my hours. When her fever finally gave way, she still had difficulty breathing and coughed. She insisted upon returning to her chores. Unconvinced she was well, I watched her e'ery move. She waved me on, insisting I acted like an overprotective momma bear.

After a couple more days passed, I relaxed my scrutiny, but her cough returned with a vengeance. That night she was unable to sleep because she couldn't lie down. "Feels like..." She gasped. "One of the horses... sat on my chest."

She had all the symptoms of pneumonia. If I were in the twenty-first century, I would have taken Bess to the emergency room. Instead, I made a root tea from goldenseal and remained by her side.

"He calls for you..."

I had no doubt she referred to Wind Talker and grasped her hand. "Rest, Bess. I want you to get well. We can talk later."

"He says he'll take... Jaysen to the Sekakawon."

Many with pneumonia went into a frenzy, but Bess seemed to be making a connection with Wind Talker. "Why would he take Jaysen to his father's people?"

"To avoid the smallpox."

My English poppa had died during the outbreak. Watching him bleed to death was the only time I had felt sorry for him. Most Indians had fewer immunities to the disease. Wind Talker and our babe would unlikely be exceptions. He was right in taking our son to the Sekakawon. "Pray, rest Bess."

With glazed eyes, Bess sat up and coughed. I patted her back 'til she caught her breath. "You didn't want him to leave. You couldn't face losing another babe... but the master would know Jaysen wasn't his son when he returned."

I often regretted making the vow to Momma, but now I began to comprehend which lives might be at stake. "Bess, you must rest."

She shook her head. "To hide the truth from the master... I offered to say Jaysen was my babe."

I squeezed Bess's hand. She had always been a devoted servant, but o'er time, we had also become friends. I e'en recalled when she referred to me as Mistress Wynne. "Thank you, Bess."

"Jennet thought she... should fill the role."

"Jennet?" I hadn't thought of Jennet in years. Because of her skittish nature, the idea she would make such a suggestion took me by surprise.

"She thought my skin..." Bess held up her arm. "...was too dark for others to believe... Jaysen was mine. He looked more like Elenor. She pretended to be... his momma, so he wouldn't need to leave." She finally laid back and rested.

How could it be? A son I didn't e'en know. The one person I could connect with was Lee. Should I tell him? Nay, naught would be gained 'til I could verify that Bess wasn't delirious. And where was Bess's son? I had sent word to James that she was gravely ill, but he had married and moved north. He might not learn the news 'til 'twas too late.

I stretched myself aside Bess and fell asleep. In the morn, I could not wake her. Her hands and feet were puffy. Occasionally, she murmured, but I could not make out what she was trying to say. As the day progressed, the swelling spread to her arms and legs. Her breathing grew fitful. 'Twas naught left for me to do, except see her through to the afterlife.

Afore long her trunk had swollen. Again, she muttered. I bent nearer to hear her better. "See... James."

Had she meant her husband or son? Her husband had died long ago. I grew vexed. Her chatter changed to her native African tongue. Death was near. I had no doubt she was going home to the place she thought she'd ne'er see again. Her breathing became more and more irregular, 'til finally it halted. She was gone.

With tears filling my eyes, I bowed my head. I clasped her hand. "Momma..."

Not hearing Elenor enter the hovel, I turned and hugged her close. We cried on each others' shoulders. Throughout the day and into the night, we stayed aside Bess 'til her body grew cold. On the following morn, we washed her swollen body and prepared her for burial. As I ran a linen rag o'er her countenance, I admired her prominent cheekbones adorned with tribal scars. "James and Bess were the first Africans I had e'er seen," I said to Elenor.

She smiled wistfully. "She has always been here. I can't imagine my household without her round."

For the rest of the day, we shared stories about Bess. The next day we laid her to rest aside her husband. Afterwards, I wandered the land 'til arriving at the spot near the bones. I thought o'er Bess's dying words. "Wind Talker, I don't know how much more I can endure. If 'tweren't for Elenor and her family, I don't think I could go on."

No response returned to me. Had I been expecting one? I stared at the bones. A mist formed afore my eyes, and my hound trotted towards me. He whined, then wagged his tail. As he led me through the fog, a light pierced through forming a passageway. At the end stood a human figure. "Lee?" I hurried towards him, but slowed my pace. The shape belonged to a woman.

"Momma?" she said.

"Heather?" I raced ahead to embrace my daughter. I stepped back to admire her. No longer an adolescent, she appeared to be well into her twenties and wore trousers. "You've gone to the twenty-first century, haven't you?"

"I can't tell you right now, but I'm happy, Momma."

"And your brother?"

She blinked. "Did you meet Jaysen through the dreaming?"

"Bess told me about him afore she went to the afterlife."

A frown crossed her face. "I recall Bess. She was always so kind and gentle. She taught me much about herbs and healing." She waited a moment afore speaking again, "Momma, I'm here because I wanted you to know that I'm fine. I know you've been worried, so concentrate on your needs right now. Seek out Poppa."

Struggling to keep my tears at bay, I hugged her once more. "I've made your grandmother a vow to refrain."

"No, you've been connecting with him all along."

Did she mean Lee? "I've relished those times, but I wish to speak to Wind Talker, my husband, not Lee."

She sent me a knowing smile. "He is both." A butterfly fluttered afore us, and the mist spread, separating us. " 'Tis time for me to go. I love you, Momma."

I vowed my love for her, but she had already vanished. When Lee had taken the name Wind Talker, I had reminded him to keep both names, so he could walk in both worlds. My link with Lee would eventually take me to Wind Talker. Already my daughter possessed much wisdom.

30

Wind Talker

1629

I VISITED PHOEBE and Jaysen as often as I could—every two to three months. I cherished the time of watching our son grow from a baby to a toddler, but those precious moments were all too short. As time for Henry's return grew nearer, I knew that I must break our connection—at least for now.

Phoebe awoke in my arms and stretched. "Good morn." A smile crossed her face but quickly vanished. "What's wrong?"

With a heavy heart, I said, "It's best that I don't visit anymore."

"Henry's not due to return for another two months."

"Maybe not, but your father will. If he finds me here, he'll punish you."

She sat up with the blanket falling, revealing her naked form. Normally not shy, she quickly covered herself. "Punish me?"

I touched my temple, hoping that I remembered the details in the correct order. "He'll whip you. It'll begin a chain of events that I don't wish for you live through again."

Her hand went to my arm. "Tell me."

I shook my head. "It's better that you don't know."

"Wind Talker, if I know what lies ahead, mayhap I can avoid it."

Her eyes pleaded with me. *Should I tell her?* I cleared my throat. "In the initial time frame, your father discovered that you were having an affair with an Indian. His men tied you to a whipping post, and he threatened to return you to England. In this time frame, that Indian is me, and I can't be the cause. As it is, I worry that he'll discover you're Jaysen's real mother, not Jennet, and history will repeat itself."

"Nay, we'll succeed. Was my father successful in returning me to England?"

"No, Henry will return before he has the chance, but something else happens. And this is where I need Bess's help before we leave. When smallpox breaks out among the Arrohateck, your mother will plead with you for medicine. You'll give away what you need for your own family."

"How can Bess help with the smallpox?"

"She knows of a way to inoculate people to help their chance for survival."

"Inoculate?"

"A method of taking taking the smallpox virus from one person to another, which hopefully gives them a less severe form of the disease."

She shook her head. "Some of your words are strange, but I think I understand the meaning. In the time you know, who did she inoculate?"

"All of you here. Everyone survives, except for your father. He was the original donor. The Arrohateck aren't as lucky and most will die. Henry took you to them, and you helped as much as you could, but it'll be too late for Bess's method. That's why it's important she shows your mother what needs to be done before we leave."

"She'll show Momma."

"Good." I held back from telling Phoebe about the witchcraft trial. Little point would be served in telling her everything, and with luck, we had changed the course of time enough that she wouldn't have to relive those events. But would it also keep her from traveling to the twenty-first century? I couldn't think about such a consequence because I no longer lived in that century either. Our time—

if we were to have one—was here in the seventeenth. Beside the bed, Jaysen gurgled from the trundle bed, then gave a shrill cry that he was hungry. I hurried to my feet and quickly adjusted my breechclout before picking him up. He settled in my arms and I savored the moment. *My son.*

He started squealing his annoyance, and I handed him to Phoebe. As she placed him to her breast, muttering came from the loft. The rest of the family was waking. Deciding to save everyone from the awkwardness of finding me here, I finished dressing and sent Phoebe a parting smile. I stepped outside.

Bess and Phoebe's mom walked toward the house. Both greeted me good morning. I reciprocated. I'd speak to Bess later about showing Elenor the smallpox inoculation. I wandered to a secluded pool along the James River. After removing my shirt and breechclout, I plunged into the pool for my daily bath. Even though it was spring, the water was cold and sent chills to my bones. No matter how long I remained in the seventeenth century, I doubted I'd ever get used to the lack of accessibility to warm water unless it was heated by a fire.

Afterward, I joined the others for breakfast. Anytime I left, solemn faces surrounded me. This time even more so, since I had no idea when or if I'd see Phoebe and Jaysen again.

"Bess says she'll show Momma how to inoc... inoculate," Phoebe said. "She'd like for you to be present too."

Not being a medicine man, I had no idea how I could be of help, but I nodded that I would comply. The rest of the meal was eaten in uncomfortable silence. I stole a few looks in Phoebe's direction, but my heart was breaking. If it were just Henry, I'd confront him, but Phoebe's father cast a dark shadow that I could not ignore.

As soon as breakfast was finished, Bess poised with a sharp knife. "Here's what must be done. Aft the first person gets the pox, you make a small cut in one of the pustules, like thus." She sliced a slab of raw, red meat and it bled. She ran a piece of thread through the slit, and a crow cawed in the distance. I looked around. The white crow that I had envisioned two years before appeared.

"Bandage the wound, then make a similar cut on the person who hasn't had the pox."

Bess's words were drowned out by the crow's cries. All around me lay people covered in bloody blisters.

Once again, Bess ran the thread through the cut in the meat. "This action infects the other person. Place lint and a rag o'er the cut, afore bandaging, and they too will get the pox—usually a milder form."

I blinked back the vision of dying people. "Usually?"

"Aye. With this procedure, you will give hope to those who may have had none afore. Some may still perish though."

Some. Better than nothing—especially since most of the Arrohateck would die otherwise. Even Elenor, she might have a chance as well. She nodded that she understood, and Bess had her go through the motions on her own. This time, I studied each step without distraction. When the time came, if Elenor needed help, I'd be able to give some input.

The time finally came for us to say goodbye. Elenor and Bess left us to ourselves, and I cradled Jaysen in my arms. "Come with me, Phoebe."

"You said my poppa will die from the smallpox. When he's gone, I shall join you. I don't think Henry will wish to keep me here any longer."

For once, there was hope. Bess had given us the means for many to survive, and soon, I would have the chance to be reunited with Phoebe.

31

Phoebe

Dreaming: Present Day

Because of heather, I sought Lee through the dreaming. He had made progress whilst in the dreaming by himself. Sometimes, he e'en sought me out in the seventeenth century. Our connection became stronger, and I was certain I would eventually discover my answers. I watched him as he set a candle on the coffee table. He lit it, then sat across from me. "Will I ever get to the point where I can enter the dreaming without using a candle?"

"Aye."

"And that's all you'll say about it?"

"Aye. You will discover your answers in your time, as I shall mine."

He smiled slightly. "I've never known anyone who speaks in such a cryptic manner."

I recalled him often saying such a thing when we had first met in the other time line. We grasped hands. "Now, look into the flame. We ne'er know how much time I have here."

He stared at the flame. Afore long, he shook his head. "It's not working. Phoebe, when you're near, I have difficulty thinking of anything but you."

Though pleased he found me enchanting, I refused to show my approval. "Absorb the flame."

"The only flame I have right now—"

I sent him a scorching look.

"Right, ma'am. Back to the task at hand." His dark eyes gazed upon the candle.

Concentrate. His grip tightened on my hand, and I saw my hound up ahead. On a nearby tree, a crow cawed. Good, he was breaking through the realms.

"I see a crow," he said.

In the future, he would learn the crow was his spirit guide. "Follow it," I said.

When the mist gave way, Lee was no longer aside me.

"Do not fear it. You will be reunited with what once was."

Upon hearing his voice, I turned in e'ery direction. "Lee?" No answer. "Kesutanowas Wesin, where are you?"

"Walks Through Mist..."

I blinked only to see my brother Charging Bear holding my daughter Elenor. She was naught more than a lass. Aside me stood a small lad. *Jaysen?* Bess had said Wind Talker and I had a son.

"Wind Talker isn't here," Charging Bear said.

"Not here? He entered the dreaming with me."

A gentle wind rustled nearby leaves. *Forward.*

'Twas the time when I had gone to the twenty-first century, only it differed from the way it had happened. The dreaming had sent me here for a reason. I picked up Jaysen. "This way," I said and stepped into the stream. Near the middle, water churned about my waist. I feared I'd lose Jaysen to the rapids afore I could reach the other side. Once on the far bank, I was lost.

Trees were e'erywhere. We tripped o'er the gigantic roots. "Are you certain this is the way?" Charging Bear asked.

I halted. "Where my love? Where are we to go?"

Shouts raged from the opposite bank, and torches formed bright flames. Henry would be amongst the mob. Lee was the one who had lead me to safety. I listened for his voice.

"Walks Through Mist," he said, "follow my voice."

"This way," I said to Charging Bear.

We trod through the forest 'til my hound stood afore me. A thick mist swallowed Jaysen and me. "Charging Bear!" No matter where

I looked, I could not find my brother and daughter. 'Tis the dreaming, I reminded myself. I would go forward as I had originally. I gripped my hound's collar.

A crow cawed, floating on the currents ahead of me. I held Jaysen tighter as I stumbled through the fog. A ship swayed neath my feet, and a wave of nausea overcame me. The hound failed to break stride.

The mist grew thinner. "Follow the light," Lee whispered.

Up ahead, I viewed the lights. As I stepped out of the fog to the sound of cars rushing to and fro, the hound and crow vanished. The sidewalks swarmed with people. Jaysen cried from the clattering racket. Not wishing to relive my experience of being struck by the car, I remained firmly on the sidewalk. I stood consoling Jaysen 'til he quieted. He insisted on being put down, but I clenched his hand.

Tires screeched, and Jaysen broke from my grip, darting into the road in front of an oncoming car. I went after him. More lights chased our way, blinding me, but I managed to latch on to my son. Brakes squealed. The earth trembled, and I went flying afore striking the pavement. Not moving, Jaysen lay aside me.

I reached out. He no longer breathed. "Jaysen!" I blinked and sat in Lee's apartment with him across from me. "That's not the way it happened. What could it mean?"

He moved next to me and drew me into his arms. After a long while, my shaking subsided.

"I saw what happened," he said. "I kept telling you to follow the light. It doesn't make any sense to me."

I withdrew from his embrace and began to tell him how I had arrived in the twenty-first century. Once again, my daughter had been left behind, and this time, my son had died. I gazed across at Lee. *Our son.*

"A son," he said with his voice trembling. "I was just getting used to the idea of a daughter, and now you're telling me that he's . . . dead?"

Still shaken myself, I placed my hand on his arm. "The dreaming doesn't always happen in the way it shows. Mayhap, 'tis a warning."

"How so?"

"When my younger self arrives in your time, she will likely bring Jaysen with her. With the dreaming's warning, mayhap we can avoid the tragedy."

"How?"

"One of us will contact her through the dreaming to inform her."

"I'm barely able to contact you."

Fully comprehending his frustration, I touched his cheek. "But you will make contact. 'Twas your voice calling to me. It always has been." Behind me, my hound barked. Though I wished I could stay and console him longer, the dreaming wasn't going to allow it. " 'Tis time, Lee."

He gripped my hand.

"I shall see you again—hopefully soon." We kissed. Instead of finding myself back at the plantation where I had entered the dreaming, I wandered through the mist. My hound guided the way, and when the fog faded, I stood on the grounds. Only the house was wood, rather than brick, and a palisade encircled the buildings. My breasts were full.

I hadn't had such a sensation since Heather was a babe. From inside the house, a child cried. After viewing my arrival in the twenty-first century, I understood why I viewed this realm. I was present to aid my younger self. I moved towards the sound. Aside the bed, a young lad wailed. I stepped o'er to the trundle bed. "Jaysen," I whispered. I picked him up and placed him to my breast. Though I sensed he'd be weaned soon, he quieted with contented gurgles.

"Missus," Bess said. "I'll see to Jaysen." She grasped him away from me.

Bess. Seeing my servant again, I nearly reached out. E'en though she hadn't called me "missus" in years, she was alive.

"Phoebe."

The stern voice of my poppa coming from behind me made my legs quiver. I faced him and curtsied. More gray covered his head than blondish-red. He had wrinkles on his forehead and round his mouth. I recalled the day of his arrival all too well. Only in this time frame, he'd accuse me of more than fornicating with an Indian. I'd had Wind Talker's son.

"You have deceived me. You said Jennet was the mother of Jaysen. Who is the father?"

I swallowed hard. "Wind Talker."

"You have fornicated with a savage, birthed his child, then lied to me in an attempt to save yourself."

"The Indians are not savages—"

Narrowing his eyes, he held up a hand for me to remain silent. "You shall be punished." He waved to the guard. The guard seized my arm and half dragged me outside. I struggled against his grip, but others joined him. They pulled me to the nearest tree and lashed me to an overhanging branch, whilst nearly wrenching my shoulders from their sockets. With my arms stretched out, my toes barely reached the ground. I struggled against the ropes, when Poppa stood afore me and said a prayer.

I screamed.

"Phoebe...?"

I blinked away the misty realm. Once again, I was in Lee's apartment.

He held me in his arms. "What just happened?"

I trembled. "I saw my younger self again. He whipped me."

"Who whipped you?"

"My poppa."

He gently traced his hand o'er my back. "That's what the scars are from?"

"Aye."

"Your own father..." He clenched his right hand to a fist.

I snuggled into his arms, and his anger faded. Through the dreaming, I had been sent to Lee's time for a reason. Though much work lay ahead, for now, I would accept it.

32

Wind Talker

1629

Painful searing spread across my back. My wrists burned and I fought against invisible bindings. *Wind Talker.* In the original scenario, Phoebe's lover Little Falcon had barely escaped with his life, and Phoebe was punished by her father. In the twenty-first century, I learned of the incident through the dreaming and managed to call her back from the other realm. I had held her and comforted her. Since *I* was her lover in this time frame, I had thought my not being present would spare her. Nothing had changed. Her father had whipped her, and she was on a collision course for being tried as a witch. I resisted the urge to go to her. Nothing would be gained by making a rash decision.

"Wind Talker..." Silver Eagle placed a hand on my shoulder.

"Time remains the same," I said.

"In what way?"

I explained to him what had happened. The muscles tensed in his arms when I told him about the whipping. "I can gather several warriors—"

"No, we wouldn't have enough men to fight them. We need to remain calm." I didn't know whether Elenor had told him about the smallpox epidemic that loomed in the coming months. "Besides, there will be a grave concern that we will need to worry about here."

"The white man's sickness."

I nodded.

He continued, "Because of your intervention, we have ways to combat it."

I only hoped his faith in Elenor and me was true. Throughout the day, I attempted to contact Phoebe through the dreaming. I would continue to try until I reached her. When the evening dancing began, instead of participating, I found a spot near the river. A crow cawed. Since it was nighttime, the bird was definitely a spirit. *Good.* A light appeared at the end of a misty tunnel. I moved toward it. As I walked the path, a chill overcame me. "Phoebe?" Mist engulfed me until only a pinpoint of light remained. I focused on it. Closer and closer, but as I reached it, the light vanished. The cold intensified, sending shivers up my arms.

The mist rolled around me, gradually clearing. A flock of crows screamed a warning. The birds clustered in a nearby tree, shrieking a horrendous racket. At the center perched a pure white crow. The black birds quieted and gathered around.

The white crow flew to a closer branch and spoke in a series of clicks and rattles. *Wind Talker.*

The voice in my head was distinctly female. In spite of the chill, sweat beaded my brow, and my legs felt shaky. "I've seen you before," I said weakly.

The crow clicked. *I'm here in warning.*

"Warning?"

You will be tested beyond anything you've experienced before.

Closing my eyes, I nearly screamed. The death of my people wasn't enough of a test? "How?"

The disease.

"Smallpox?"

Yes.

With the epidemic months away, I failed to understand why her warning came now. "Bess has shown us a way to combat it."

You will require the knowledge.

"Why are you here now?"

You will soon understand. You may now see the one you seek.

The crows took flight and the rest of the mist faded. "Phoebe?" I half-expected the wind to buffet the birds, but they sailed smoothly overhead. I followed a trail through the forest until coming to the plantation, except the house was brick, not wood. After all this time, I had reached my wife, not the younger Phoebe. But where was she now? "Phoebe?"

The door opened, and she stood in the entryway. Her red hair had streaks of gray running through it. "Wind Talker?"

Both of us ran forward, until we nearly collided. When I swept her off her feet, her laughter filled the air. I set her down and kissed her. "I wasn't certain I would see you again," I said.

"You've been seeing me all along."

I stepped out of our embrace. Even though I had been intimate with her younger self, guilt filled me like I'd had an affair. "You know what's happened?"

"Some. Time has changed, my love."

"For the better?"

She shook her head. "I can't answer, for I do not know. I felt being lashed by my father, but 'twas my younger self, not me in this realm."

I hugged her once more, and she took a deep breath. "How can I prevent what's about to happen?"

"Some things are meant to remain the same."

I withdrew from our embrace and gripped her hands. "Phoebe, we have a son. His name is Jaysen."

"I met him recently."

Unable to tell whether she was upset or not, I said, "I'd like to see Heather."

"She's not here. She will become a woman—in another realm."

Aware my people believed that if a child died they would grow to an adult in the afterlife, I presumed the worst. My throat constricted. "Phoebe . . . is she—"

"Nay, she lives, but not in this realm."

I took a moment to catch my breath. At least Heather was alive. "Why can't I reach her through the dreaming?"

"I know not. I suspect 'tis like our own separation. We must learn from the other realms in order for us to meet." Phoebe's face grew pensive. "You have a mission to fulfill."

"A mission?" As I met her gaze, I knew she would be unable to answer my question. Crow had warned that I would be tested. Were the test and my mission one and the same? Crow cawed that our time together would be ending soon. A breeze came between us, and I drew Phoebe into my arms. My wife. If only I held her tight enough... The wind gusted, and I gave Phoebe a kiss. Then, she vanished. I sat near the river in the same place as I had when first entering the dreaming.

Behind me I heard whoops, and I returned to the gathering. By the time I got there, everything was calm again, but I easily discovered the source of the cries. Five colonial men had entered the town. Their weapons were lowered, and they spoke to the chief. Charging Bear was the interpreter.

As I made my way over to offer my assistance, a crow cawed. The white crow flew to a nearby branch. The sign was clear to me now. In the coming months, these men would bring smallpox.

33

Phoebe

1667

AFTER SEEING WIND TALKER AGAIN, my mind reeled. How much of our past would remain the same? He did have a mission. Of that, I had no doubt. As did I. Whilst in the dreaming, I walked in a familiar hall where others hurried hither and thither. 'Twas where Lee worked as a detective. I turned the corner and entered a door. He hunched o'er a desk and did not see me 'til I was aside him.

"Phoebe." He stood. "I didn't expect to see you here."

He seemed distressed, and I peeked at the case he worked on. A murder case—of a five-year-old lass. "Can you spare a few minutes?" I asked.

"For you, I can always spare a few minutes. The case has gone cold anyway. I was just checking to see if there was something we've overlooked."

"Have you inquired through the dreaming?"

"Why would I enter the dreaming for a case?"

"Mayhap, you can contact the lass."

His countenance became thoughtful, but he shook his head. "The problem is there's no body. We've found traces of her blood at the suspect's cottage, and tiny bone fragments in his wood burning stove. Unfortunately, they were too small to extract any DNA. Without evidence, we can't get a conviction on the bastard."

"The lass may still give you answers. Isn't it worth a try?"

"You didn't come here to help me with my case. What is it that you wanted?"

Though he presented a stoic visage, I detected fear in his heart. "Lee, any time I spend with you is cherished. Our realms have been brought together for a reason. I'm honored to help in any way that I can."

He smiled slightly. "Then, I'll accept it, but I didn't bring a candle to work."

I gripped his hand and lightly caressed it. "If we can find a quiet place, you don't need a candle. You're ready for the next level of the dreaming."

"I'll find a quiet room."

As he led me through the cluster of detectives and other masses, Lee's partner approached us. Ed stared at me with a smile. "Good to see you again, Ms. Wynne."

"Phoebe's here to help me with the Doyle case," Lee said.

Ed motioned for us to proceed. When Lee and I entered an empty room, he closed the door behind us. His gaze met mine and our lips met. Though I could relish being in his arms fore'er, I withdrew from his embrace. "For now, we must concentrate on the dreaming."

Disappointment and frustration crossed his countenance. "Right. The dreaming."

"Lee, we will be together for real, but I know not when it shall be."

He nodded. "Then, let's concentrate on the dreaming. How do I focus without a candle?"

" 'Tis easy. I think you know the answer yourself. Think of the candle in your mind." We joined hands. "Close your eyes to envision it."

He shut his eyes.

"Do you see it?"

He shook his head.

"Concentrate. The candle's flame is the entrance to the dreaming."

He reopened his eyes and gazed into mine. 'Twas a spellbound stare. "Phoebe, I see a crow. Why do I always see one when I enter the dreaming?"

" 'Tis your guardian spirit. Follow it."
"The bird isn't moving."
"What's it doing?" I asked.
"Preening."
"Tell the crow you wish to meet with the young lass." Fog surrounded me, and I held Lee's hand as we walked through the mist. A crow flew o'erhead. A light shone and the haze gradually lifted.

A young lass jumped up and down upon seeing us. "Poppa!"

Mystified, Lee stared at her. "Heather?"

"Aye." Overjoyed at seeing her again no matter her age, I picked her up and hugged her, afore handing her to Lee.

She grinned, but he held her awkwardly. "I'm not sure I understand. How can seeing our future daughter help me with my case?"

"She's about the same age as the lass in your case. Think like a poppa."

His countenance wrinkled in anguish. "The hardest job I have is telling someone that a loved one has died. It's worse when that loved one is a child."

The thought of Wind Talker delivering the news to me that Henry had died came to the forefront of my mind. Though he had tried to hide his torment, I always saw neath the surface of what was in his heart. "You can give resolution to a grieved family."

He embraced Heather and set her down, keeping a tight grip on her hand. When we moved forward, Heather broke free of his grasp and raced ahead. She vanished, then another figure stood within the mist. Heather, now about the same age as her poppa, stepped towards us. "Mom!" We hugged each other. She turned to Lee and kissed him upon his cheek. "Dad, I know you haven't met me yet, except through the dreaming, but you will in a few years."

Her dialect was the same as Lee's. At long last, I knew the century she had traveled to. Lee cleared his throat. "Heather..."

She smiled but grew earnest once again. "There's not much time. Amy spoke to me." At first I wondered who Amy was, but then I recalled that she was the lass in Lee's case. Heather continued, "Your fear was correct. The perp burned pieces of her, but he buried the rest of her body." As she proceeded to tell Lee the details, I noted that she spoke like a cop. My daughter, a detective? I could ne'er have fathomed her in such a role. She had broken the long line of cunning women. Whilst the thought brought some sadness, I held a sense of pride, for in the twenty-first century, women had many more opportunities than I had when coming of age.

My white hound appeared afore me. For now, my time here had ended. For whate'er reason, I had been meant to bring poppa and daughter together. I followed my hound through the mist 'til seeing the light. Again, I felt Wind Talker's presence, but my hound shifted course. When the fog faded, I was once again standing afore the plantation house, but like afore 'twas wood, not brick.

In my hands, I held a hoe. I recognized the garden I had tended many years afore. In the beginning I had difficulty adapting to planting in rows like the English, instead of the mounds like the Arrohateck. A figure walked towards the house. I blinked. *Henry.* With his dark brown hair, he looked the same as when we had first married. I dropped the hoe and took a hesitant step in his direction. He saw me and quickened his pace.

"Henry..."

His arms stretched towards me. Upon reaching me, he embraced me with a kiss. I gritted my teeth when he unintentionally pressed against the healing wounds upon my back. *I had been transported to the time after my lashing, and this moment was Henry's homecoming.*

With a huge grin, Henry stepped back. "I missed you." He studied me. "My God, Phoebe, what has happened to you?"

I blinked. "I'm not certain what you mean."

"You've become so thin—and pale. Have you been ill too? I'm so long in returning because I had the smallpox."

"I've not been ill. Henry, come inside. Pray tell me all that has happened."

When his grin reappeared and became sly, I grew vexed by what had entered his mind. I feared that he would insist upon his marital rights. He placed a hand to my back to escort me inside and I winced. "Phoebe?"

" 'Tis naught."

"But it is. You're in pain." He drew me inside and insisted to see my back.

" 'Tis naught," I repeated.

He motioned for me to disrobe.

He is my husband. I removed my skirt and bodice. Only my shift remained.

E'en without me undressing completely, he studied my back. "What has happened?"

I faced him and his brow furrowed. "I've been flogged."

"For what?"

I had no doubt that e'en my younger self would reveal the truth. "For birthing a son," I said.

A smile spread across his face. "Why would you be flogged...?" His smile vanished and rage entered his eyes. "Tell me about the lad."

"His name is Jaysen and he's two years old."

His green eyes simmered. "And his poppa?"

"Wind Talker."

No longer simmering, Henry's eyes blazed. Like a madman, he punched a fist into the wall. Uttering blasphemies in pain, he cradled his bleeding hand.

I grabbed a cloth and began wrapping his hand. "I ne'er meant to shame you, Henry."

"You thought I was dead?"

A look of hope appeared on his countenance, but I couldn't e'en give him that small measure of comfort. And with only brief glimpses of how time had changed, I was unable to provide a full explanation. "Pray sit and allow me to tend your hand."

He sat at the table, and I washed his hand. "You love him?"

Without answering, I wrapped his hand.

"Well..."

In any time realm, I couldn't deny the truth. "Aye."

He clenched his hand.

Though I had ne'er loved Henry, I hadn't meant to hurt him. "I'm sorry," I whispered.

He laughed to cover his anguish. "This wasn't the homecoming I had expected."

"I'm sorry," I repeated. Suddenly cold, I crossed my arms. "Give me whate'er punishment you feel I deserve."

"I'm not like your father," he said, raising his voice.

I grasped his hand. "I don't blame you if you scorn me."

"Scorn you? Phoebe, I could ne'er scorn you, for I have always loved you."

His words made my pain worse, for I had only married him because Poppa had vowed my hand to him.

"What do we do to make things right?" he asked. When I failed to answer, he shook free of my grip and pointed to the door. "Then go to him. Leave."

"Poppa would hold my children hostage."

His brow wrinkled and his eyes narrowed. "I am the master here, but aye, the children shall stay."

"You haven't e'en met Jaysen."

"Does it matter? By law, the children are mine."

"And I could ne'er leave them."

"If you stay, I expect you to behave as my wife." I could do naught but obey. "I also want to meet with Wind Talker."

" 'Tis not safe for him to come here."

He met my gaze with an intensity I had ne'er seen the likes of afore. "I said I'm the master. I give you my assurance he will not be harmed."

No matter what had happened, I trusted Henry. He was a man of his word. I wished my younger self strength in accepting the challenge.

34

Wind Talker

1629

Although the messenger had no details, he insisted that my presence was urgent. Elenor warned me that Phoebe's father likely planned an ambush. Unsure of the exact timing of the smallpox outbreak, I was fairly certain the epidemic was at least several months away. That gave me the necessary time to discover what the crisis was and return beforehand. Even though Henry was likely home now, I couldn't chance not going. Phoebe or Jaysen might need my help.

"Then allow me to come with you," Elenor insisted.

"That's not a good idea. Phoebe's father could come after you as well as me. I think it's best that I go alone."

She gripped my hand. "Pray be careful. I want to see you become a member of my family."

I nodded that I would follow her advice. The trip downriver was uneventful. As I approached the palisade gate, I wondered what kind of reception I would receive. The guards eyed me but opened the gate. Phoebe's father, Robert Knowles, along with a couple of guards raced toward me. The guards carried flintlocks. Knowles grasped one of the muskets and aimed in my direction. "Go ahead, savage. Give me a reason to fire."

"Halt!"

The shout had come from somewhere near the house. A man moved closer. He seized the flintlock from Knowles and aimed it at the ground. *Henry.* His hair was dark brown, rather than the gray I remembered, and he had no wrinkles. I had to remind myself he wasn't the same Henry that I had known and called a friend.

"Wind Talker," he said.

"I won't fight you, Henry." I held out my hands with my palms up. "Do what you will with me."

His face remained harsh. "First, we'll talk." He shot a glare over his shoulder at Knowles, then led the way to the kitchen.

"Why are you helping me?"

"You said my name as if you know me, and I feel as if we've met afore."

I couldn't come out and say that we were friends in a future time, nor that we had met before then, during the dreaming. "I don't think we've met."

Mouth-watering smells drifted through the window, reminding me that I hadn't eaten since the previous evening. We entered the kitchen, where Jennet prepared the morning meal.

"That smells good, Jennet," I said.

"I'll get an extra bowl," she replied.

Henry motioned for me to be seated, then pulled up a chair across from me. "You haven't asked about her."

"I didn't think you'd appreciate me doing so."

"She is my wife."

And mine, but I didn't voice my thoughts aloud. "What do you want, Henry? You must have requested my presence for a reason."

"Aye, I wanted to meet the man who claims her love. I have vowed to her that you will not be harmed. Yet, I'm having difficulty restraining myself from challenging you to a duel."

"I've already said that I won't fight you. If you want me dead, you're going to have to do it yourself or break your promise."

He studied me a moment. "You're not afraid. Why?"

"Because you're not like her father. I know you're angry. You have every right to be, but you want what's best for her."

"And if our roles were reversed?"

"I'd step aside."

He clenched his hand. " 'Tis easy for you to make such an assertion."

"Easy? It's anything but easy. We've been living apart because you and her father have decided to hold her daughter hostage. I presume you're doing the same with *my* son." When his eyes narrowed, I realized I had said too much. "I'm sorry, Henry. I shouldn't have said that."

He waved at me to get out. "Take your son."

"I can't because of what it would do to Phoebe."

His gaze softened slightly. "Then what are we to do?"

"Let her and the children go. She identifies with the Arrohateck."

A distinct harshness returned to his eyes. "Get out of here, Wind Talker. If I e'er see you round here again, I shall break my vow and kill you myself."

I got to my feet and headed for the door.

Once outside the kitchen, Henry's voice came from behind me. "Wait."

Without turning around, I halted.

"Wind Talker, I know we've met afore."

I slowly turned to face Henry. With straight shoulders, he approached me. I supposed now was just as good as any other time to come clean. "We met during the dreaming."

He eyed me, then spat on the ground. "The dreaming is naught more than Indian blasphemy."

"It's not Indian. Phoebe learned the dreaming from her mother when she was a girl, and Elenor was taught in Dorset by her mother."

"Aye, I see. 'Tis a cunning woman's rite—she would have been regarded as a witch in Dorset."

I kept quiet about the witch trial Phoebe would be involved in, if time remained static. "You wanted to know where we've met before. Whether you like it or not, I've provided you with the information."

He mulled over my answer and finally took a deep breath. "I once saw Phoebe in a state. I can only describe it as she seemed lost in her mind. She tried to tell me about the dreaming, but I forbade her of e'er performing such a ritual again. No matter whether 'twas Indian or a cunning woman rite, I thought 'twas sacrilege. Now, you're telling me this is where we met?"

"I am. Phoebe taught me the dreaming long ago."

"How long ago?"

"Years."

"How many?"

I finally saw his veiled question for what it was. He wanted to know if I had met Phoebe before they were married. I *had* known her when I was Crow in the Woods and Lee before I had taken the name Wind Talker. "Around six or seven years ago." Because of my previous training as a cop, I could normally guess what a person was thinking or how they might react. With Henry, his expression was totally unreadable. "Well?"

Henry met my gaze. "I believe you. Upon first laying my eyes upon you, I knew we had met afore."

"So what do we do now?"

He shook his head. "There's naught we can do."

"If you won't let her and the children leave, at least give us the chance to say goodbye."

Ever so briefly, his eyes smoldered. "Aye, I'll let you see her and the lad, but you must vow to ne'er return. I will order the guards to shoot you on sight."

Never return? I reminded myself our friendship was from a future time. One that he hadn't lived through, but my heart was breaking. Could I really blame him? "You have my word."

He motioned for me to return to the kitchen. "Wait there."

Henry went inside the house. I returned to the kitchen, and before long, Phoebe entered. Her arms went around my neck. "Wind Talker, I feared I'd ne'er see you again."

In her arms, I could easily let go, but I had no doubt that sentries or Henry himself were posted outside the door. I forced myself to break the embrace. "Phoebe, I must say goodbye."

"Goodbye?" A soft choking sound came from the back of her throat.

"It's the only way you and the children will remain safe. I couldn't forgive myself if anything happened to you because of something I had done. We've already risked too much."

She turned slightly and brushed away the tears. "You asked me to come with you afore. Why not now?"

"The time's not right."

Her arms went around my waist, and I closed my eyes. "We can find a way to make it right."

Reopening my eyes, I resisted touching her. "I promised Henry that I would say goodbye and never return."

"A vow made in haste."

Swallowing hard, I nearly broke down. I could only prove my love in one way. "Phoebe, the only way Henry will let us walk out of here together is without the children. I wouldn't ask you to make such a sacrifice."

"You didn't ask."

My resistance weakened, but I caught myself and stepped away from her. "We will make it work, but in a future time. If you don't mind, I'd like to say goodbye to Jaysen."

"Then what?"

"Cherish our memories until the time is right."

Her face grew solemn. "What if—?"

I shook my head. "There will be a right time for us. We have to believe it in our hearts."

She grasped my hand and kissed my fingers. "Wind Talker..." She turned, but I spotted tears in her eyes. "I'll fetch Jaysen."

After she stepped out of the kitchen, Henry returned. "I want to hate you, but for some reason, I can't."

When I had first viewed the world through Henry during the dreaming, I had a similar feeling. Over time, both of us had shown the other that neither of us were savages. "Thank you, Henry."

"I meant what I said. If I e'er see you here again, I will break my vow and kill you."

"I have no doubt, but I think you also know that we *will* meet again under a different set of circumstances."

He gave no further response, and after a short while, Phoebe entered with Jaysen. He clutched Phoebe's fingers. When he shrieked with excitement upon seeing me, I spotted the hurt in Henry's eyes. But soon, our roles would be reversed, and Jaysen would see Henry as his father. *Don't think about that now.* We were together for a few minutes longer. I picked Jaysen up. Already an active boy, he squirmed until I returned him to his feet.

Henry motioned that I should leave. My throat constricted, and I choked out my goodbyes. As I headed for the door, tears streaked Phoebe's face. When I stepped outside, I couldn't think straight. Phoebe's father strode toward me with a flintlock on his shoulder. I continued toward the gate, and he aimed. "Halt!"

"Let him go," came Henry's voice from behind me. "He's vowed to ne'er return."

Knowles muttered something about me being a "savage" but lowered the weapon. Funny, how those who proclaimed the Indians were savages described themselves. I reached the gate, and the guards seemed only too happy to open it. I fought the urge to turn around for one last look. I had to believe my own words about another time being the right one for us.

Without a glance over my shoulder, I went through the gate. It closed behind me like the door of a tomb. "Goodbye, Phoebe," I whispered under my breath. "Goodbye, Jaysen."

35

Phoebe

Dreaming: Present Day

At a smoke-filled tavern, Lee celebrated his thirty-fifth birthday. E'en after having lived in the twenty-first century, smoking confused me. The Paspahegh and Arrohateck used tobacco for ritual purposes, not e'eryday usage. Here, youth and elder, men and women inhaled cigarettes.

Ed toasted him with a raised glass of ale. The other detectives joined in wishing him well. He sipped the ale, yet his countenance remained downcast.

Ed lifted his glass once more. "Not only is today his birthday, Lee cracked another cold case—a homicide that took place eight years ago."

This bit of news brought a hint of a smile, and he gazed at me in a thank you. The dreaming had shown him ways of solving cases that he could have ne'er imagined. "I've been asked to join the cold case team," he said.

The detectives sent up a round of cheers, and Ed thumped him on the shoulder in congratulations. After each had praised him individually, the group retreated to other areas of the tavern, except for Ed. He seated himself in a chair across from me. "I'm going to miss you, partner."

"I haven't said I'm taking the job yet," Lee replied. "It's not like there's a pay raise involved, nor much overtime."

Ed chuckled. "Whatever you decide, you know I'll support you." Lee muttered his thanks, and Ed continued, "It's your birthday. I'll leave the two of you to celebrate it together." He got to his feet and grasped my hand. "Good seeing you again, Phoebe."

We wished each other "goodnight," and I turned to Lee. He had grown sullen again. "What ails you?" I asked.

"Today isn't really my birthday. It's the date my adoptive parents gave me because I was found wandering alone in the woods. Through the dreaming, I've learned why, but I still have no idea when I was really born."

Should I tell him? "You were born during the first moon of *cohonks*."

"*Cohonks*?"

"Canada geese. The moons of *cohonks* mark the season of their return from the north lands—winter."

A smile crept across his countenance. "I guess my parents were off by a few months. Do you think I should inform my mother?"

"Nay, she did the best she could."

"I know." When he gripped my hand, I frowned. "What's wrong, Phoebe?"

"E'en though 'tis not really your birthday, it has made me aware of our age difference in this realm."

"It doesn't matter to me. Besides, I keep telling you that I see you as I did when I was ten."

Was he trying to indulge me? "Lee, there is more than a twenty year difference in this realm."

He sent me a wily grin. "Don't you know that women are like a fine wine? Besides, older women have more experience."

I giggled. "Sometimes, I have difficulty keeping pace with your passions."

His grin widened. "I thought it was the other way around. Your energy seems boundless."

I withdrew my hand from his grip.

"Phoebe, I love you. I don't care what realm we're in." He motioned to the metal box playing music so loud 'twas painful to my ears. "Should we go somewhere that's a little quieter? If you just want to talk, I swear that's all we'll do."

"Aye, I'd like that."

He escorted me to the T-Bird, and we returned to his apartment. Once there, I wanted more than to merely talk. His calmness gave way to his pressing desire. It mattered not that I was in the dreaming realm. The man in my arms was all that mattered. Past, present, future—time had no meaning. The planes intersected as much as our intertwined bodies. The circle in time would eventually sort out, but for the moment, we were together.

When I roused, I was alone in my bed at the plantation. After Bess's passing, I had taken my place in the hovel that she had once shared with her husband. Here, after aiding my daughter, Elenor, with the household chores throughout the day, I could retreat in solitude to engage in the dreaming. On this morn, I felt lonely. I touched the empty side of the bed. What I wouldn't give to awaken aside the man I loved. 'Twasn't meant to be.

Melancholy overwhelmed me more than usual, and I struggled to rise. I drew my green skirt o'er my head, then put on my bodice. I much preferred the loose clothing of the Arrohateck. E'en in the twenty-first century, I had the choice for what I wished to wear, and not to be confined to skirts and stays. After I finished lacing my bodice and covering my hair, I went to the main house to greet Elenor and Christopher. The children had come of age long ago, but I missed them almost as much as Heather. I trudged through the day.

At the day's end, I returned to the hut and continued my usual quest of entering the dreaming. My white hound guided me through the mist. As he led me along the path, I felt something amiss, but then a tall figure stood in the light at the center. I rushed towards him. "Lee!"

A young man in his late twenties or early thirties stepped into the open, and the haze faded. Like Lee, he had short black hair and brown skin. "I'm Jaysen," he said.

My son. Hadn't I seen him die? He was here now, and I hugged him. "Jaysen..."

"Mom, I think I can help."

"Help?"

"I'm a doctor. If I can break through the realms, I believe I can help Wind Talker."

I noted that he had called me "Mom," and Wind Talker by his name. What was I missing? None of that mattered now. "In what way?"

"I'm not certain yet. If I could, I'd find a way to get the smallpox vaccine to him, but I don't think that'll be possible."

"My former servant has taught him and your grandmother a technique that should help," I said.

"Variolation." He shivered. "While it's not the form of prevention I'd choose, it seems better than the alternative. In any case, I think we can save some of the people who died before."

After standing on my tiptoes in order to kiss him on the cheek, I smiled. "My son, the cunning man."

"I only hope that I can help."

"You shall. Of that, I'm certain."

Mist surrounded us, and Jaysen vanished from my view. Back in the hovel, I took comfort in the fact that the circle *would* complete. Jaysen's death wasn't necessarily imminent, if I could solve the puzzle.

36

Wind Talker

1630

WEEKS PASSED SINCE I HAD LEFT Phoebe and Jaysen. Each night, I tried contacting her through the dreaming, without success. I worried what might have happened and continued to try and reach her. Anytime I entered the misty world, the white crow appeared. The epidemic was near. Not only did the crow signal the warning, I felt it in my bones.

At night, I had trouble sleeping. Even during my days as a cop, I had found waiting the most challenging thing. After hours of lying awake, I moved quietly so as not to disturb Elenor or Silver Eagle and made my way over to the fire. Since it was considered bad luck if the fire went out, I stirred the embers and added a log. The wood flared, and I concentrated.

Through a hazy mist, a blinding light appeared at the end of the tunnel, moving closer and closer. I squinted and realized the brightness wasn't caused by a light, but the white crow flying through the fog toward me. She settled on the ground several feet away from me. *The time is near.*

"I had guessed as much."

Do you recall what Bess has taught you?

"I do, and I'll have Elenor's help."

Good. You shall save some who would otherwise die.

"And Walks Through Mist? Her voice has gone silent."

From more than one realm, she seeks you. To her, your voice has gone silent.

Cryptic, but then what did I expect from a spirit? "I've been trying to reach her. I keep seeing you, but for whatever reason you won't let me pass through. Is it because you represent death?"

Crow cackled. *You have much to learn, Wind Talker. You may now see Walks Through Mist.*

The mist parted like a curtain, paving a trail through a forest. Crow failed to take flight. "Aren't you coming with me?"

Not this time.

"Thank you, Crow." As a breeze blew, I stepped forward. The path was the familiar one along the James River, but... I sucked in my breath. At the end of the trail, no palisade existed, and the house was brick. That's what Crow had meant by Phoebe seeking me from more than one realm. I took the path to see my wife, not the younger woman.

As I got closer to the house, I called for Phoebe. I looked in every direction. No one. I tried again, "Walks Through Mist..."

"Wind Talker?" came a feeble voice from behind me.

When I faced her, I gasped. Her red hair had gone white and deep wrinkles covered her face. A walking stick helped support her emaciated frame. I swallowed. "Phoebe?"

She held out a bony hand. "Wind Talker, I've been trying to reach you."

I grasped her hand. No matter how much time had passed, she remained the woman I loved. I gently hugged her. "I had almost given up hope seeing you again."

"And I, you." Her face was lined with sorrow. " 'Twill be the last time we meet as such."

"Last time? Why?"

"You know I can't answer your questions, but your mission lies ahead."

"My mission? You mean the epidemic?"

She shook her head. "Nay, the smallpox is merely but one factor of what must come to pass. I cannot share with you for I would risk you making a different choice." She reached a shriveled hand to my arm. "During the pestilence, you shall save a few—some who died afore. 'Twill not be easy in the weeks ahead, but be at peace with what you are capable of doing, my love."

A smile crossed her face, making the wrinkles around her mouth more pronounced. A gleam registered in her eyes, and I had no doubt that her wisdom had only expanded with age. As the wind picked up, leaves rustled. I grasped her hand and gave her a quick kiss on the lips. "Time grows short."

"Aye. We shall meet again in the next realm as the circle shall repeat."

The circle shall repeat. Crow cawed and gusts blew. Mist surrounded Phoebe until she was engulfed. I blinked and stared into the fire where I had entered the dreaming. Sapped of energy, I shuffled to my sleeping platform. This time, I had no difficulty falling asleep.

By the time I woke, Silver Eagle and Elenor had already risen. I started the morning by cleansing myself in the river and welcoming the new day. Yet I couldn't shake my encounter with Phoebe. Seeing her as an elderly woman had unnerved me, but I was pleased to learn that she would live well into old age.

In my life among the Arrohateck, I had expanded on many of the tasks I had learned while living with my own tribe and the Sekakawon. In many ways, I still felt like a novice, but later in the day, I was able to return their hospitality when the chief asked me to translate for him.

Three colonial men had approached the town. I recognized two. They had been among the five who had visited months before, trading goods with the town. Something gnawed at my gut. I sensed something wasn't right, but I shook hands with the traders and exchanged pleasantries. The men had brought many goods—frying pans, kettles, shovels, and axes. The steel tools were coveted items among the Arrohateck as they made many laborious tasks easier. In exchange, they received animal pelts and corn. Nothing seemed out of the ordinary. *So why did I have a sense of doom?*

The man I hadn't met before dressed plainly in breeches, a waistcoat, and a felt hat. Like most colonial men, he had a sword at his left hip and a pistol on his right. All carried flintlocks. Unless an army lurked outside the town, their weapons weren't a risk. So few men could hardly overcome a group of warriors.

After the conclusion of business, the chief invited me to stay and continue to be the interpreter. The traders stayed as guests for a feast, while the goods they had brought were distributed among the people. Smiling faces surrounded me. At the conclusion of the evening dancing, the men were escorted to a guest house. For the night, my duties had concluded.

In the morning, the colonists loaded the supplies on their boat and waved goodbye. Could one have been unknowingly sick? Was smallpox transmitted like a cold or did it require physical contact? Growing up, I'd heard tales of the armies in the west giving infected blankets to the plains tribes, but the only trade goods I had seen were hand tools. Too many unknowns. I watched them as they rowed downriver.

"What's wrong, Wind Talker?" asked Elenor.

"They've brought smallpox."

"We shall be ready."

I recalled Phoebe's words that I would save a few who had died before. I hoped her mother and Silver Eagle were among them.

"Wind Talker, it's begun."

Two weeks later, Elenor's voice woke me. I blinked back the sleep, and her face came into focus. "Smallpox?"

"Aye. Our vigil begins."

Immediately awake, I stretched and got to my feet. She showed me to another house. A young girl around seven years old lay on a wool blanket. "The traders brought this?"

"Aye."

"When? I only saw hand tools."

"In the morn, afore they left. They said they had forgotten to give them to the people."

Now, my misgivings made sense. The traders had brought infected blankets. "We need to gather the blankets that the traders brought and burn them. They're infected with smallpox."

Circle in Time

"I should have seen it myself."

"History is plagued with infected blankets being given to the Indians." Elenor eyed me in confusion, and I continued, "Let's not worry about the should haves right now; we have work to do."

"Aye. That we do."

"Make certain that no one touches the blankets with their bare hands." She sent me another perplexed look. "Trust me," I said.

"I do trust you as you must trust me. We need to isolate those who have the smallpox from those who don't."

Not having extensive medical knowledge about epidemics, I hadn't thought of that tactic myself. With our resources pooled together, we might be able to keep the disease in check. "If you see to the girl, I'll take care of the other tasks." She nodded that she would. "How soon before we inoculate like Bess showed us?" I asked.

"Once the pustules begin to show. Should be no more than a few days."

"After I see that the blankets are burned, I'll check on the others for symptoms. What should I be on the look out for?"

"Fevers, aches, exhaustion, vomiting."

"Flu symptoms?"

"Flu?"

Even after spending years in this time, I still managed to find words that people from the century didn't understand. "Influenza."

"Aye. In the beginning, it oft looks like influenza. Now go. There is much to do."

She was right. First, I went to the chief and explained the situation. "We have our own ways of treating ailments," he said when I had finished.

"I realize that, but the *kwiocosuk* will be at a loss. This disease was brought by the *tassantassas*. Our people have no . . ." How could I explain immunities and disease resistance when the people believed such illnesses were spread by spirits? While the colonists failed to grasp what caused disease as well, they had enough experience with smallpox for some precautions. Even if he would believe me, there was no time for such details. "The blankets and clothing the *tassantassas* traded are tainted with curses."

To this, he nodded. "We will proceed with your request."

"No one must touch the goods with their bare hands or put them near their faces. We must also burn anything used to collect them as a precaution."

The chief raised an eyebrow in confusion.

"It's necessary to put the spirits at ease."

"I will summon the *kwiocosuk* for further strength."

As spiritual leaders and medicine men, the *kwiocosuk* needed to do their job and give the people belief in what Elenor and I were doing. "That would be most welcome. I must see if anyone else has the illness and separate them from those who remain well."

"Why do you separate them?"

"Again, to keep the spirits at ease."

My answer satisfied him. "Thank you, Wind Talker, for all of your help. May we appease the spirits before they become angered further."

Before checking on who else might have the disease, I oversaw the gathering of the infected blankets. A huge bonfire was built. The *kwiocosuk* shook rattles, sang, and danced in front of the flames. Blankets and clothing were tossed onto the burning mound. Satisfied the chore was being taken care of, I went from house to house to check for other diseased victims.

Most people attended the ritual of burning blankets, but a few lingered behind. The first several houses were empty. In the next one, a mother hugged her child. Both were sick. "Please come with me." I explained why and afterward escorted them to where Elenor could watch over them. As the day went on, I gathered ten more individuals. Women and children were mostly affected. I rationalized that men were in the minority because the blankets had been given to the children first, and the women oversaw ailing children the most, therefore making them the most susceptible. Only time would tell if I was right.

Each day, I made the rounds, finding more individuals who had become ill. Rashes formed. Elenor opened the first child's mouth for my observation. "See the spots on her tongue?"

I nodded. "They're throughout her mouth and throat."

"Aye, soon they'll become raw sores and break open."

I winced, thinking how painful such a development sounded. But the symptoms could be a fate that all of us looked forward to. I blocked such negative thoughts from my mind. Elenor was taking the time to teach me how to help others. I focused on that.

When the sores erupted as she had described, I had a strong feeling the unfortunate victims were highly contagious. Again, I shoved this from my mind and did the best I could to help those in need. For fevers, we administered willow bark tea as well as making certain the afflicted drank plenty of water to prevent dehydration. Soon, rashes appeared on their faces, quickly spreading to their arms and legs. Within a day, the rash would cover the entire body. Many fevers dropped and the stricken began feeling better. In my naiveté, I thought the worst was behind us.

"Do not be deceived," Elenor warned. " 'Tis only the beginning of what is to come. If only I had some medicinals from home to ease their suffering. I know not which native plants might help."

Elenor rarely spoke of England, and I detected sorrow in her voice for not having access to the plants that might help. The *kwiocosuk* possessed the knowledge of the local medicinal plants, but they had no experience with smallpox. "We're doing the best we can," I said, attempting to reassure her.

A pinched smile crossed her face. "I fear I will not be able to carry out Bess's treatment."

"You will—successfully."

On the third day after the first rash broke out, raised bumps developed. Another day passed, and the protrusions filled with fluid, often with concave centers, making them look like blisters with navels. Fevers climbed again.

"Shouldn't we inoculate?" I asked.

"Nay, not yet."

Trust worked both ways. I had to believe Elenor knew what she was doing. Once again, the bumps on the afflicted changed. They raised sharply and became firm to the touch, as if there were BB pellets embedded beneath the skin.

"Now, is the time," Elenor said.

A chill crawled up and down my spine. "I'll be the first."

"You're aware I have ne'er performed this procedure afore."

"I am, which makes me the logical choice to go first."

She picked up a sharp knife and clenched the handle. Her face scrunched as if she were in pain. She shook her head. "I cannot."

"Elenor, it's the only hope we have. Many will die if we don't try."

"My daughter will ne'er forgive me should anything go awry and you . . . you succumb."

By caring for the sick, I had purposely avoided thinking of my own demise. Like most Natives of the seventeenth century, I probably had little to no immunities for a disease that had been wiped out in the century I had grown up in. "If I'm not inoculated, I'll be more at risk. Should it come to that, Phoebe will know you tried your best."

"Aye, I'll proceed, but then you will do the same to me."

Maybe she could survive in this realm by being inoculated. "I will. Let's get it over with."

Elenor collected a small thread and took a deep breath. With the knife, she approached a woman covered by the blisters over her body. She made a small slit into one of the bumps on the woman's arm and ran the thread through the open wound. After packing the wound with moss, she faced me. "Roll up your sleeve."

I shoved up my sleeve and held out my arm. She raised the knife and her gaze pierced mine. I nodded that I was ready.

In her expert hands, she made a slit in my arm that I barely felt. Blood flowed, and she buried the infected thread in the scratch. She placed moss over the wound. "Hold it in place 'til the bleeding stops, then you shall do the same to me. Afterward, we will inoculate as many as we can who do not have the smallpox already."

When the tiny wound on my arm had clotted, I said, "I'm ready. I've never done anything like this before."

"Which is why I'm your first subject. You shall do fine. I'll prepare the thread, but aft tending to me, you must carry out the procedure on your own, or we will not have sufficient time to inoculate e'ryone."

"Agreed."

I watched carefully as she went to another smallpox victim—this time a young boy around five years old. She made a small slit in one of the blisters and buried the thread in his open wound. After packing the wound, she gave me the thread and knife. She pushed up her sleeve and held out her arm.

My hand shook. *She would certainly die if I didn't proceed.* I poised the knife and sliced into her skin. My incision wasn't the nice, neat cut Elenor had made in my arm, and she winced. I immersed the thread in the wound. After removing the thread, I cared for her wound.

She nodded that I had performed the task to her satisfaction. "Now, we shall inoculate those who have not already been stricken."

As we set out to perform our task, I wondered how long before we acquired the symptoms of the disease ourselves.

37

Phoebe

1674

WITH TEARS STREAMING DOWN my daughter's cheeks, Elenor bowed her head by the freshly dug grave, for she had become a widow. Her sons lowered the coffin into the sandy ground. She said a prayer, and we gave a round of amens. I alone sent a silent prayer to Ahone. Was I the only one left who remembered the Paspahegh god?

At fifty-five, Elenor's black hair had become streaked with gray, and her sons were grown men with families of their own. The eldest, Christopher, would now become the master of the plantation. With the aid of a walking stick, I turned towards the house. Afore long, Elenor accompanied me.

Once inside, she served corn pone and wine to the gathered guests, consisting of her sons' wives and children. When the task of burying their poppa was complete, Christopher and Nicolas joined us. When the gathering ended, I found Elenor outside, looking in the direction of the cemetery. She placed her hands to her face and sobbed into them.

"Elenor, I had hoped you'd be spared."

"Momma, I can't complain. He lived a good, long life, and we were together for most of it. Unlike you and..."

Circle in Time

I kept quiet about my recent encounter with Wind Talker through the dreaming. Though I was frail with age, I drew my daughter into my arms. "This is your time of grief. Wind Talker and I will be together again soon."

With a tear-streaked face, Elenor looked up. "Nay, Momma. I've lost my husband. I can't lose my momma so soon after."

"We don't decide when the time arrives that we must walk on. I'm not long of this earth, but I will always remain with you in spirit, as does your husband."

Her tears renewed, and I embraced her as best as I could with my withered arms. She cried upon my shoulder. When her tears were spent, she wiped the dampness from her cheeks. "The last time he sailed for England," came Elenor's soft voice, "I ne'er thought I'd see him again."

As she poured out her sorrow, I listened and wondered what life would have been like if I shared a similar time with Wind Talker. Though we had connected through the dreaming on occasion, I had kept my vow to Momma, and we had remained physically separated. My visits to Lee had brought my only solace. E'en then, I had stopped seeking him more than a couple of years afore. I believed he was ready for what lay ahead. My tears mixed with Elenor's in my own grief.

After Elenor rejoined the others, I decided to make a trek that I had not done in years. With each step, I winced, but I was determined to reach my goal. My movements were slow going, and after awhile, I needed to rest. On and on I journeyed through the forest 'til I required more rest. A black woodpecker, with a red crest and loud call that sounded almost like someone laughing, flew o'erhead.

Most of the day passed afore I neared the area where I had rarely traveled. I shivered. O'er the years, the trees had matured to full growth. Unlike the first time I had ventured to the sacred place, no arrowheads lingered on the ground, nor clay pot pieces. The bones had been covered by the sandy earth long ago. Though time hid the evidence, this place was where the Paspahegh had been annihilated.

No longer affeared of unsettling the spirits as I had been in my youth, I ventured closer.

Walks Through Mist.

The wind echoed Wind Talker's whispers. 'Twas here where Crow in the Woods had traveled to the twentieth century, only to return as Wind Talker. *Soon, my beloved, I will join you.*

As mist surrounded me, my hound barked. No longer did my aged body drag. I followed the dog with the alacrity of my younger years. When the fog cleared, I bent o'er my poppa. He alternated betwixt shivering and sweating. I ministered yarrow tea for his fever.

'Twas the time of the smallpox pestilence. The days in the dreaming blended, yet I knew I was here for a reason. A deep red flush spread across Poppa's countenance. I isolated him from the rest of the household, making the sickroom in the loft and tending him there.

I envisioned the days as I had in my youth. Bess inoculated her son and me from Poppa's pustules. Because of my servant's actions, all in the household had survived, except for Poppa. I felt the knife in my hand and cut into my daughter's arm. Elenor winced afore letting out a cry when I sliced into her skin. I placed the small thread in the cut. I patched her, dried her tears, and hugged her. Bess held Jaysen out to me. I repeated the procedure. My son wailed and I hugged him close. Jaysen was the reason I had been brought to this realm.

From the loft, Poppa groaned. I climbed the ladder and went to his side. The sweet odor of death surrounded me. The pustules on his countenance had shrunk and turned to rosy spots. "What would it take for you to forgive me?" he asked.

The years had softened my misgivings about him. 'Twas not the time to bear malice. "Can you accept Elenor and Jaysen as your grandchildren?"

A broad smile spread across his countenance that I had ne'er seen the likes of afore. "A brush with death reveals to a man the error of his ways. I'm honored to have them as my grandchildren."

"Then you admit that Lightning Storm is Elenor's poppa and Wind Talker, Jaysen's?"

"Aye," he said, lowering his voice.

By that eve, Poppa's spots had darkened to purple with angry red rings. His breathing grew labored. Throughout the night, I sat with him. In the morn, he choked and coughed up blood. I recalled the horrors of the bloody pox. I helped him drink. He weakly patted my hand. "For...give."

Ne'er afore had I wanted to embrace him, and during this time, I could not. To do so would bring him agony. "Poppa, I've already told you that I forgive you. I meant it."

His head moved slightly. "El...enor."

"Momma?"

"Tell...her."

"I will, Poppa." The sickly, sweet odor of death strengthened. "Poppa..."

He coughed and sprayed blood upon me. He choked. Unable to catch his breath, he gasped and sputtered. I closed my eyes, but naught shut out the sound of him drowning in his own blood. After a long while, his muscles relaxed. He was dead.

When I blinked, my body ached. Once again, I was an old woman. The forest surrounded me. I had ne'er been able to relay Poppa's message to Momma for she had also died from the smallpox. And now? With the aid of my walking stick, I got to my feet. Darkness had settled. A shrill scream echoed deep within the trees. At first, I thought a woman had been assaulted, but when the high-pitched shriek repeated, I realized the cry belonged to a fox.

I shuffled along the path towards the house. "Wind Talker, Jaysen will survive the smallpox. Pray save Momma and Silver Eagle."

In the darkness, I tripped o'er a root. With a bone snapping in my leg, I struck the ground with a sickening thump. Moaning, I sprawled, hoping that someone would find me afore 'twas too late.

38

Wind Talker

1630

AFTER USING BESS'S TECHNIQUE, Elenor and I treated those who had already contracted smallpox. Many of the children barely got ill. The adults were less fortunate. In some cases, we hadn't inoculated in time. In others, they died anyway. The *kwiocosuk*, at least those who weren't sick themselves, performed rituals. Sweat house ceremonies weakened some individuals. I had participated on several occasions myself. All the same, I had difficulty convincing those who viewed the activity as a sacred rite that it could endanger their lives further.

When Elenor became feverish, we both knew she had the disease. In the previous time period, she had died. I only hoped she had been inoculated in time to change the course of history. In the beginning, she insisted she was well enough to make her rounds, but between the aches in her head and back, as well as her fatigue and vomiting, she gave up and rested. I continued tending the stricken.

Day and night, I went from house to house. Oftentimes, there was nothing for me to do except hold a hand while a patient or loved one cried hysterically. Although I didn't possess the gentle touch of Elenor or Phoebe, the gesture was usually enough for a calming effect. Throughout my visits, I maintained my stoic face—the one I had perfected so well in my former life. Inside, I shed my tears.

Yet, we had been successful. More people survived than died. For that blessing, I was grateful. At the same time, the deaths haunted me. I had witnessed it often enough as a cop but had never grown used to watching the dying breaths or viewing dead bodies. The most gut-wrenching deaths were those of the children. Thankfully, there were few, but I had no way of explaining to the weeping mothers why their children were among the stricken.

On one evening after checking on everyone else, I finally returned to see how Elenor fared. The white crow flew ahead of me and I trembled. The meaning was crystal clear. I went inside where Elenor moaned in delirium. I moved toward her. A rash covered her body. I checked her pulse—irregular, but she was most definitely alive. She muttered under her breath, but I couldn't quite make out her words.

"Elenor?" I asked.

She mumbled again, and I leaned closer. "Silver Eagle," she whispered.

I peered across the *yi-hakin*. Like most houses during the outbreak, the fire had gone out. Without the flame, the lighting was poor. I squinted. A prone shape lay near the far wall on his stomach.

"Silver Eagle?" I rushed over and bent down to help him. Even in the dim light, I could see his body was covered in bloody blisters. I gently turned him over, and his limp form splayed out on the floor. My fingertips went to his neck. *Too late.* I slumped down beside him and slammed my fists to the ground. "You bastard! You were supposed to survive this time."

From the pallet came sobs. Struggling to my feet, I made my way back to Elenor and apologized for my outburst. I held her in my arms as she wept on my shoulder. For a long while, neither of us moved, and my back ached from remaining in the same spot for so long. Finally, she drew away and wiped her tears with the side of her hand. "He was proud to call you a son. He only wished—"

What I wished as well—that Phoebe and I could be together. I shook my head. No, I didn't wish for her to be with me now and view all of the death surrounding me. She'd know soon enough that Silver Eagle had died. I stood and sang his death song.

* * *

By the time Elenor regained her feet, I was flat on my back. My head felt like it had been split open, and sweat poured from my body. Around me swirled a heavy mist. I stumbled through the thick fog. The sound of flapping wings approached me. Closer and closer—until Crow settled in the branch of a tree. He gave a panic-stricken caw, and darkness surrounded me. I found myself behind the wheel of a car—my old, trusty Thunderbird—navigating a road. I slowed the car, pulled off on the shoulder, and came to a complete stop. From a pocket in my jeans, I withdrew my wallet. Driver's license, police ID, and my badge—Detective Lee Crowley. A Glock was holstered on my hip. Had the seventeenth century been nothing more than a dream?

I took out my cell phone and dialed home. A sleepy voice answered, "Lee?"

I *was* home. "Phoebe, I'm on my way."

"Thank you." She sounded more awake. "Jaysen wanted to wait up for you, but I convinced him 'twould be best to take his rest afore then."

Jaysen? He hadn't been born in this time frame.

"Lee?"

I blinked. "I'm here." Whispering my love, I bid her goodbye. But where was I? I put the T-Bird into gear and returned to the road. The twists and turns seemed familiar—Route 5, heading toward Richmond. A sleek animal darted across the road. I slowed. *A fox.* This was the night I had traveled to the seventeenth century. Up ahead, a deer would dash across the road, and I would hit it. Instead of increasing speed, I crept along. Almost a mile later, the car's headlights picked up another shape on the edge of the road. I braked, and a deer darted across the road a few inches in front of me.

I breathed out in relief. I *had* changed time. Once again, I pressed the gas pedal, but another deer shot in front of me. The T-Bird slammed into the animal, which rolled off the fender, over the hood, and up the windshield.

I braked to a halt. Thankfully, the windshield held and the deer slid off the hood. *Not again.* My whole body shook. Grateful the air bag hadn't triggered, I checked for any injuries. Like the time before, I was numb but seemed to be in one piece. I grabbed my flashlight and hauled myself out of the car.

Expecting to find an injured deer that I would need to relieve from its misery, I reached for my Glock. Behind the car, the deer lay dead. *The events aren't the way the night happened.* I holstered my piece, when I thought I overheard a woman's voice. Phoebe's daughter, Elenor would lead me through the woods. I'd enter a mist and return to the seventeenth century.

"Lee..."

But it wasn't Elenor. "Phoebe?" I shined my flashlight in the direction where I thought her voice had come from. Nothing. Not only that, it couldn't be her. I had just talked to her on the phone. My head hurt. Maybe I had imagined her voice. *Get a grip.* After a deep breath, I took out my cell phone and called in the accident. Out here between major cities, a couple of hours were likely to pass before anyone would arrive.

The time before, I had assessed the damage before calling Phoebe. Unwilling to make that mistake again, I dialed home.

Her sleepy voice answered once more. "Lee..."

"I've hit a deer. It's going to take a little longer than I thought to get home."

"Are you all right?"

"I'm fine, but it wasn't so great for the deer. Should I get a permit to keep the carcass? We could dine on venison for a few months."

"Pray no jokes."

"Sorry. Right now, I'm waiting for a tow. I'll give you another call when I'm on my way." After another quick goodbye, I hung up.

"Lee..."

Raising my head, I made a wide sweep with the flashlight to no avail. "Phoebe? It can't be you. I just talked to you on the phone."

Unless she had called to me from the seventeenth century. If I followed her voice, I'd enter the mist. I wanted to remain in this time and stayed where I was. Clammy dampness on my skin chilled me. Pain in my chest. I couldn't breathe. From a distance came the sound of flapping wings. Crow hadn't left me, but I gasped. I struggled for another breath. Then, he was above me, cawing at me.

Once again, I was flat on my back. Though my vision blurred, I spotted a man standing over me. I felt as if I should know him. He placed a cool cloth to my forehead. The gentle feeling spread down my neck to my chest. "The rash has begun," he said.

Crow cawed. I followed the sound and stood near the pitched-roof house. "Phoebe?"

The door opened, and she stepped outside, holding a child's hand. Jaysen's eyes held no hint of recognition of who I was. I was as much a stranger to him as Heather. "Wind Talker," Phoebe said, "except for Poppa, all of us have survived the smallpox."

Smallpox. I thanked Ahone that my family had survived. Before I could respond, Crow cawed madly—the white crow. I suddenly felt dizzy. I swayed on my feet and could barely breathe. The man who had stood over me earlier helped me to a sleeping platform. "Who are you?"

He hushed me. "I'm White Bear, a healer among my people. You've been having hallucinations because of your illness."

As I laid back, I shivered between hot and cold. Once again, I entered a foggy realm. Hallucinations? The experience was much like the dreaming. Had my entire life been nothing more than a delusion? Crow cawed.

Hunched over a table, I stared at human bones. For an instant, I thought of my tribe. I blinked back the vision to discover I was in an exam room. A partial skull, a backbone, a few ribs, an intact arm, and hand bones lay on the table, while a coppery-haired woman examined them. "Because the remains are pre-adolescent, I can't determine the sex," she said.

What was I doing here? This event wasn't one I had ever experienced. I glanced at a paper in my hand—a pathologist's report. A homicide? The woman had to be a forensic anthropologist, but I didn't recognize her. "DNA results state the bones belong to a boy," I said. I pointed to the conical depressions and tiny parallel channels on the skeleton's arm. "Knife wounds?"

She shook her head. "Tooth marks from rodents."

What next? I had no idea what sort of investigation had been carried out.

"Detective Crowley?" the woman asked.

"I think it might be best to discuss the case a little later."

"You appear confused?"

I am. I glanced at my watch and pulled out my cell phone. "If you'll excuse me a minute, I need to make a call."

"Certainly. Feel free to use my office, if you like."

I muttered my thanks and headed for the nearest door. Once in the hall, I had no idea which way her office was. I scanned through my cell phone directory.

"Dad?"

At first I didn't look up, then I spotted Jaysen's name in my directory. A man in his early thirties with a definite family resemblance stood across from me.

"Was Sarah able to help?"

"Sarah?"

"Dr. Sarah Cameron. That's why we came here. I thought she'd be able to help you with your case."

For a moment, all I could do was stare. *My son, Jaysen, was here with me.* And I wasn't in the seventeenth century. Somehow, I would return to the twenty-first century. My hands had wrinkles that I had never noticed before. Future time—where Jaysen was grown. Then I realized something else. "You're White Bear."

Unable to breathe, I gasped. The wind picked up. Branches creaked and the leaves rustled. The wind grew stronger and a mist formed. Soon, I was engulfed. *Not again—I refused to move.* The wind howled, nearly bowling me over. Stronger and stronger—why couldn't I talk to it? Another gust sent me sailing, and I landed flat on my back. I struggled to regain my feet, but the wind pushed me over again.

From somewhere within the swirling storm, a crow cawed. Groggy, I opened bleary eyes. My mother stood in the distance, waving at me. Beside her was Swimming Beaver. Hadn't they both died in the massacre? The pure white crow fluttered before me. I suddenly understood the true meaning. Crow wasn't foretelling someone else's death, but my own.

Sweat dripped into my eyes, blurring my vision further. Blisters covered my body. Each one felt like a shotgun pellet was buried beneath my skin. I wanted to scream, but the crusty boils filled my mouth. I couldn't breathe. *Phoebe.*

39

Phoebe

1674

WIND TALKER. I searched and searched but could not find him. The pain in my leg was agonizing. In my delirium though, I walked through endless mists. Stumbling along, I was lost in the forest and could not find my way. Waving my hands afore me, I struggled through the brambles as they tore through my flesh. Aside me was a small lad. *Jaysen.* I picked him up.

"Phoebe..."

From a nearby branch, a crow cawed. I smiled to myself. *Wind Talker was near.* "Follow the light," he whispered.

Torches—e'erywhere, blinded me. I pressed a hand to my face to blot them out.

"Follow the light."

My hand fell to my side, but I could see naught through the light. "Wind Talker, where are you?"

"Follow the light," he repeated.

I stepped into the thoroughfare. More lights chased me. I froze in my path, deafened by a piercing sound and sudden screeching. The earth trembled. I went flying and struck the pavement. Not moving, Jaysen lay aside me, not breathing.

"Phoebe..."

I awoke with a start and his voice was gone. 'Twas no longer Wind Talker's voice, but Jaysen's. "You survived," I said.

"Mom, yes, I'm here. Dad is fine. I tended him. He survived smallpox."

His voice came from e'erywhere and nowhere at the same time. I staggered through the fog 'til my feet grew weary and sore. How far had I come? When I feared I could go no farther, my spirit dog appeared afore me. He would guide the way. I gripped his collar and continued walking. The hound stepped surely and soundly through the forest. Ne'er afore had I traveled so far without the fog clearing. Again, I stumbled and fell to my knees. The hound waited 'til I recovered to my feet.

Finally, the mist lessened slightly. Up ahead, I could make out a shadow of a man. As we got closer, I saw that he wore a suit. 'Twas Lee. E'en though I hadn't seen him in years, he hadn't aged. My body was no longer ancient as well. I let go of the hound's collar and ran towards him with my arms outstretched. "Lee..."

He reached out and called my name.

My arms went round his neck. Unable to contain myself, I whispered my love in his ear. "You must be there for Jaysen as he was for you."

"Momma? Thank God."

Once again, I awoke. Elenor bent o'er me.

"Elenor?"

She touched my forehead. "The fever's broken. I've set your broken leg. The break was just above your ankle. When the fever set in, I thought I was going to lose you."

I looked past her, trying to find Lee. "Elenor, where is he?"

"Who?"

"Lee. He was here a moment ago."

"Nay, Momma. 'Twas the fever."

I cast my eyes about the room—but he was gone.

As the days passed, I grew bored. Elenor had soaked cloths in comfrey paste and wrapped them round my leg, rendering me immobile 'til the bone mended. My only escape from tedium was through the dreaming. On one occasion, I spoke with Jaysen. I thanked him for helping Wind Talker and me. During another journey, I encountered Heather. Though pleased to see my children as adults, I longed to rejoin Wind Talker. Forgetting my vow, I sought him. When I walked through the mist, I traveled on a familiar path through the forest. In the past, I recalled wearing leggings and fine doeskin. On this trip I wore a skirt and leather shoes, and Henry walked aside me. A breath caught in my throat. 'Twas the time after the pestilence. Was I viewing the realm I had originally lived through, or the one with Wind Talker?

As we got closer to town, Henry readied his musket. I spotted fear in his eyes. "They will not harm us," I assured him.

He lowered the musket. " 'Tis been a long time since I've traveled in Indian country."

" 'Twas once all Indian country, but I speak Algonquian. You need not fear."

The closer we got, the more uneasy I grew. When we approached the town, warriors greeted us. *Some had survived. I viewed Wind Talker's realm.* After telling the warriors who I was, they let us pass. Children scurried about without a care, but no women sang whilst making pots or tanning hides. Here and there were cooking pots with solemn women stirring them. No one smiled nor laughed. Mats on longhouses were falling off. Other dwellings were in equal disrepair.

With Henry aside me, I peered in the first house. A woman bent o'er a man, covered in a rash. In another house, a mother hummed, whilst cradling her babe in her arms. Spots spread along the woman's forehead. I asked how her babe fared. She smiled and said, "She'll live." She returned to humming.

More houses revealed much of the same. All round me, the faces were gaunt and weary. Those who were healthy tended the sick, but many survived. I searched further, 'til coming to Momma and Silver Eagle's house. 'Twas empty.

In the next house, a man comforted a woman in his arms. Though years had passed since I had last seen him, I recognized my brother's broad shoulders. "*Mat,*" I said. Brother.

He cast his gaze in my direction. "Walks Through Mist?"

"Charging Bear." From my own experience, I had known he would survive, but I couldn't help cry my relief. "Where are Momma and Wind Talker?"

He blinked and motioned to a pallet in the corner. "Over here."

I barely noticed Henry leave the *yi-hakin,* and with some hesitation, I inched towards the pallet. A figure slumped on it. In the previous realm, she had died. Wind Talker had helped save her. "Momma?"

"Phoebe?"

I rushed o'er and hugged her. "Momma, I'm so glad to see you."

She buried her face in the folds of my dress and sobbed. "He's dead."

My heart pounded. Jaysen telling me that he had tended Wind Talker might have been naught more than delusion during my fever. "Momma..." My throat closed and I could barely breathe. Unable to hold back, I mixed my tears with hers.

"Silver Eagle is dead."

I drew back. "Poppa is dead?"

"He died two moons ago."

"And Wind Talker?"

"He lives."

I looked round, searching for him. My heart thumped so fast I thought 'twould pound straight out of my chest. "Where?"

"I know not."

Bolting from the *yi-hakin,* I called for Wind Talker. I searched e'ery house but could not find him. Nearly giving up my frantic search, I stopped at one more house. A warrior bent o'er a pallet, speaking words of comfort to a small lad. "Kesutanowas Wesin," I said.

He looked o'er at me as if not knowing who I was. Though his frame was gaunt and his countenance sallow, he stared at me. Then, he blinked. "Phoebe?"

Tears filled my eyes, and I hastened to his side. His arms went round me, and our lips met. "Jaysen said you had survived." More tears spilled down my cheeks.

He escorted me outside and we kissed again. "Jaysen?"

"He tended you when you were ill."

"I remember now." He hugged me. "We tried to save Silver Eagle. I'm sorry, Phoebe."

The past had been changed. This time, Momma had survived. I grieved for Silver Eagle afresh. When I had no tears left to cry, Wind Talker's fingers brushed my cheeks. Then, he stepped back abruptly, breaking our embrace. I followed his gaze to Henry, standing behind us. "Henry?"

"You need not worry. I will no longer keep you apart." With his shoulders slumped, he skulked off like a cur that had been kicked in the side.

I ran after him but he kept walking away from me. "Henry!" Only after I had shouted his name several times did he stop. "I ne'er meant to hurt you."

His green eyes glistened as he faced me. "I know. I should have ne'er tried to change you. You belong with the Indians. When you're through tending those who are ill, return to the plantation, and I'll surrender the children to you and Wind Talker."

My children. He was willing to let them go. This was the time frame where Wind Talker and I would be together. We could be a family. "Henry..."

He shook his head. "Pray say no more."

I watched as he shirked off in silence. He would eventually find another and marry her. She would return his love. For that measure of peace, I took comfort. He deserved to find happiness.

Mist captured me, returning me to my bed site. Recoiling in pain, I gripped the sides 'til my knuckles turned white.

"Drink this, Momma."

With Elenor's help, I sipped the tea. After awhile, the pain in my leg grew more bearable. "Wind Talker and your grandma survived the smallpox."

My daughter hugged me close. In the other time frame, I would see my children grow to adulthood.

40

Wind Talker

1630

A MONTH AFTER MY RECOVERY, CHARGING BEAR ACCOMPANIED Phoebe and me downriver in a dugout. Fully aware that she faced the prospect of an upcoming witch trial and being whipped again, I had hoped to have a contingent of warriors along with us. Too many had yet to completely recover from the epidemic to turn that possibility into a reality, so we made do.

As we rowed closer to Henry's plantation, I thought of my tribe and how all of the surrounding land had once belonged to the Paspahegh. Except for a few of us, all had been killed outright, diseased, or displaced by the colonists. Phoebe exchanged a glance with me, and I instantly realized she had similar thoughts. *Focus.* I needed to concentrate with clarity in order to keep time from repeating itself.

Charging Bear and I brought the canoe up on the river bank a few miles from Henry's land. I helped Phoebe from the boat. Alongside the river, we set out. In the short time that Phoebe had been with the Arrohateck, she had taken to dressing in deer hide and moccasins.

As we made our way through the forest trail, I couldn't help but think she must be more comfortable. I recalled the pinching leather shoes and had no desire to return to such painful footwear. I easily imagined women's clothing being even more restrictive than men's.

Charging Bear pointed to the sky. Black clouds furled ahead. We continued walking, but soon the river rolled to a rapids and thunder roared. As rain pelted us, I placed my arm over Phoebe's shoulder to try and protect her. Wind gusts nearly blew us from the trail, and we no longer had a choice but to seek refuge in a hollow. We covered ourselves with leaves to wait out the storm. In my arms, Phoebe trembled.

In another place and a future time, the three of us would face a similar situation. Only then, we would be pursued by bloodhounds. Since neither Charging Bear nor Phoebe had lived through the experience yet, I wondered if I had changed time to where the event would occur at all. Or were we caught in an endless circle? Was that what was meant by the warning?

When the storm passed, we returned to the trail. Phoebe picked up a quick pace. "I can't wait to see the children."

I grasped her arm to slow her down. "Phoebe, there's something I should tell you."

She halted. "Pray continue."

Charging Bear stood nearby. While he was aware that I wanted his help if we ran into trouble, he didn't know the entire story. I motioned for him to come closer. "If history repeats itself, a group of soldiers will be waiting for your return. They'll try you as a witch."

She swallowed. "Why do they think I'm a witch?"

"I don't remember all the details." I lifted her left hand to where her conjoined fingers were apparent. "According to them, you bear the witch's mark."

She withdrew her hand. "Do you believe the same?"

I shook my head. "You know I don't and never have."

"Then how can we change it?"

"I had hoped Charging Bear's and my presence would help."

"If we met in some future time, I presume I shall survive this witch trial."

For some reason, I didn't like the direction the conversation was heading. "You do."

"You must make a vow." She glanced from me to Charging Bear, then back again. "Both of you. Do not endanger your lives unnecessarily." She sent us a piercing look. "Vow to me. If I survive, then I don't wish to risk our chance of being together. Now vow."

My head said one thing and my heart another. She was right though. It wasn't fair to risk Charging Bear's life as well as my own. "I promise."

She stared at Charging Bear and he made the same promise. "Wind Talker, I understand the warrior's heart, but if I must face a trial, I shall. Naught can change the fact that we shall be together soon."

I hoped she was right. Once again, we continued our journey. Before long, we stood on the perimeter of the forest outside the palisade. Smoke drifted from the chimney. Everything seemed peaceful, but my gut shouted a warning.

"Wait here," she said. As she stepped toward the gate, I notched an arrow to my bow and joined her. She met my gaze and halted. "You vowed."

"Phoebe—"

"Wind Talker..." She sent me a soft smile. "I feel it in my heart. We *shall* be together soon."

Against my better judgment, I lowered the bow and allowed her to proceed unhindered. All of my muscles remained at the ready as she crept forward. The guards were absent. She hesitated before the gate, then peered through. With a quick about turn, she retraced her steps toward Charging Bear and me on the forest edge.

Without any coaxing, she sought the safety of my arms and breathed out in relief. "Soldiers—drinking ale."

"Let us go with you."

"Nay, I must face it on my own, but aft darkness has settled."

Once more, I nearly argued with her, but her mind was made up. She would face another witch trial. I held her and comforted her until darkness fell. She gave me a parting kiss, then crept forward. I stepped alongside her.

"You vowed," she reminded me one more time. "I *must* go alone."

"Phoebe—"

"You pledged a warrior's vow."

I merely nodded and stepped back. Once again, I watched her negotiate the path. Only moonlight guided her, and I lost sight of her as she slipped inside the palisade. *Think of it as a stakeout.* Wait patiently until we could make a move. Charging Bear and I would know when the time was right. Except by that time, Phoebe would have been arrested as a witch. Feeling helpless, I clenched my jaw and watched. A stakeout, I reminded myself.

Throughout the night, Charging Bear and I took turns keeping watch. The vigil reminded me of waiting inside the house for a group of attacking warriors. That event would take place far into the future, and Henry would die as a result. How could I know for sure? Time had already changed. What if Phoebe or Jaysen lost their lives now? I inched forward.

Charging Bear's hand clamped around my arm. I instantly halted and waited.

When the light of dawn appeared in the sky, the palisade gate opened. Charging Bear gripped me once more, but I managed to hold steady. Soldiers led a chained Phoebe through the gate toward the waiting boats on the river. I called out in the voice of a crow to signal Phoebe that Charging Bear and I watched over her.

She looked around in an attempt to locate me but dared not respond. *Pray keep your vow.*

Her words were as clear as if she had actually voiced them. The soldiers led her to the dock. One man climbed in the first boat, then wrenched Phoebe's arm to pull her in. I nearly sent an arrow in his direction. *Not yet.* Two more soldiers climbed aboard the boat, and they shoved it from the dock. Others filled the remaining boats, and they set out on the river.

As they sailed downriver, I called after Phoebe in the crow's voice. Charging Bear and I watched the boats sail downriver until they faded out of sight. When I heard footsteps, both of us readied our bows. Henry held out his hands with his palms up. "Kill me if you wish. I wouldn't blame you, but I had hoped we could work together."

I lowered my bow and motioned for Charging Bear to do the same. "I wouldn't hurt you, Henry. No matter what's come between us, I honor your friendship."

"First, come and see your son, and we shall make plans." He waved the way to the palisade.

As we walked through the gate, the guards remained absent, and James walked toward us. His brow pinched. "Is there a way to get my Bess and the missus back?"

"That's what we'll discuss, James," Henry replied. "Tend to the livestock, and I'll let you know our plan aft we've formed it."

James frowned but did as he was told. Henry ushered us into the house where Jennet cared for the children. A young boy strode across the floor with greater sureness than a toddler. Had his third birthday already come to pass? Like Elenor, he wore a shift—a common garment for boys until they were toilet trained and breeched. My throat constricted. "Jaysen?"

He looked in my direction but showed no hint of recognition.

"This is your poppa, lad," Henry said.

"Poppa?"

"Aye, now give him a proper welcome."

Unsure what to do, he shoved two fingers in his mouth and sucked on them. I knelt down, but he remained where he was. "It's all right. He doesn't know me. Let's find a way to help Phoebe." I stood.

"I understand your ache," Henry said.

His gaze met mine. After having been away from Virginia for over two years, he *did* know what being separated from loved ones was like. "Henry—"

"Nay, don't say it. Let us focus on freeing Phoebe and Bess."

"Why have they been accused of being witches?"

" 'Tis because the women inoculated for the smallpox. Some in Jamestown followed suit, and those infected died. The governor believes 'twas due to the devil being involved. I will go into Jamestown and find a way to help her escape."

Superstition—something that couldn't be overlooked during this era. "I'd like to go with you."

His eyes widened. " 'Tis obvious that you're an Indian."

"I've done it before. If you have some clothing I can borrow, I can blend in as long as I don't let anyone get too close."

"Aye, I can help there." He held out a hand.

I shook it. He *was* the man I called a friend.

41

Phoebe

1674

For days on end, my body raged betwixt chills and fever. Elenor removed the comfrey dressing and watched o'er me in worry. My leg was riddled with black patches of skin. Afore long she'd have no recourse but to lop it off. My mind wandered, and I found myself walking through the mist. Why did I always navigate the same path? My hound led the way, and I emerged on a familiar street.

'Twas the one where I had been hit by the car upon my arrival in the twenty-first century. In the daylight, the street was peaceful, but the vision of Jaysen haunted my mind. I calmed myself. Lee would await me in the restaurant. I carefully crossed the road, and once inside, I caught a glimpse of myself in the mirror. My hair was reddish-blonde, and I had no wrinkles in my skin. I wore a cotton shirt and trousers.

"Phoebe!" Lee waved at me from a table afore coming o'er to me. "You look baffled about something."

Looking in the mirror, I touched my face. The wrinkles were definitely gone. "I'm young again."

"You're the way I've always seen you." He escorted me to the table.

O'er the years, he *hadn't* been trying to comfort me. "Lee, I've experienced the turn of sixty-three seasons."

He held out a chair for me to sit in, then sat across from me. "I don't care how old you are." A waitress stopped at our table and asked what we wished to drink. With a smile, Lee glanced at me. "A fine wine, or do you prefer a beer?"

"An ale is fine," I replied.

After Lee ordered the drinks, the waitress scurried away. "I wanted to let you know that I've taken the job."

"The job?"

"I've been assigned to the cold case team, effective at the beginning of next month. While my pay remains the same, I'll generally have shorter hours."

When we had been a married couple, I would have relished having him home more often. Had my actions somehow changed the flow of time? But how would we help Jaysen?

"Well... aren't you going to say something?"

"I'm pleased, if you are."

He cracked a grin. "Because you showed me the dreaming has made it all possible. I can find leads that I wouldn't have been able to otherwise."

I reached across the table and gripped his hand. "I'm pleased, and we met for the second time in this very place. 'Tis symbolic."

The grin vanished from his face. "How do you mean?"

"Search the dreaming, and you shall find your answer."

After our meal, we stopped at Wingfield Hall, a seventeenth-century manor house that had been shipped piece by piece from England in the 1920s. Lee had brought me years afore when he hadn't fully believed that I was a cunning woman from the seventeenth century. I recalled being immersed in the great hall, and John Gerard's *The Herbal* resting on a table in the parlor. 'Twas the only book Momma had owned, but she was far more knowledgeable in the ways of healing than any book. Notably absent from the bed chamber was a pisspot. I chuckled at how sensitive many were in this time about natural body functions.

After the house tour, we ventured to the kitchen in a separate outdoor building, which had been closed for renovation on our previous visit. Afore entering, a cool breeze swept o'er me. *I had been here afore.*

"You all right?" Lee asked.

I nodded and we stepped inside. The feeling only grew stronger, whilst our tour guide spoke about how the servants often spent much of their time in this building. "This building is from Dorset, not Lancashire, like the main house," I said.

The guide sent me a pinched smile. "Why, yes. How did you know?"

I shook my head.

"The kitchen belonging to the main house was unavailable at the time," she explained. "The original owner brought this one over instead. I detect an accent. By any chance, are you from Dorset?"

"Aye, I am."

She smiled again, this time a sincere one, and continued with our tour.

I glanced about the room. The remake was true to the period, with a stone floor and a wood table with benches, yet it differed from the way... A chill spread along my arms. O'erhead the fireplace, I noted a circle with six flower-like petals etched into the wall.

"I see you've noticed the graffiti," our tour guide said.

"Graffiti?" I looked to Lee.

"Drawings or messages inscribed in areas—often illegally," he replied.

I reached towards the drawing. " 'Twasn't illegal. My poppa etched it to keep witches away."

Our guide knitted her brows together as murmurs spread amongst the others taking the tour. She examined the engraving. "I'd heard of hexafoils before but had never seen one." She shook her head. "There's no way that it could have been made by your father. Like the rest of the house, it dates to the seventeenth century."

I knew not what a hexafoil was, but my chill had grown to icy cold. Seeing my difficulties, Lee grasped my arm and escorted me outside. I breathed in the fresh air.

"You'd grown mighty pale in there."

"My poppa feared the wicked tongues that said Momma was a witch. When they wagged I was growing up just like her, we sailed for Virginia."

"The circle in time. I think I'm beginning to understand." He drew me into his arms and held me as if the act could keep me from leaving this realm. "Phoebe, I don't want you to leave."

"I'm not meant to be here. 'Twas only possible because of the dreaming."

He closed his eyes and kissed me on the lips. I returned the kiss in all of my earnest. So close, yet so far apart. Pain surged up and down my leg.

"Momma, I need to cut off your leg."

Through blurred eyes, I saw my daughter standing o'er me, not Lee. I could not put her through the anguish of severing my limb. "Nay, Elenor, you mustn't."

"You'll die."

"I wouldn't survive it. My time is near."

"Momma..." She choked back a sob.

Though weak, I held her hand and closed my eyes. I dreamed of holding my hands to the sky and facing the four winds. E'en when Henry and Poppa had forbidden me, I had secretly carried out the ritual. By facing east, I thanked the light of each new day. As I faced south and west, I made vows to honor and aid my tribe. When I faced north, I reconciled with my past, bringing me back to the east.

Like Lee had said, 'twas the circle. I wished a *kwiocos* was near to see me through my final days and into the afterlife. Elenor would aid me, and I'd find my own way.

Elenor made a tincture from poppy seeds to help me with the pain. I drifted in and out of awareness, sometimes knowing where I was, other times naught. My white hound trotted o'er to me and licked my hand. I dreamt I was a lass again, and he hastened away from me. Faster than the wind, he raced through the woodland with his feet barely touching the ground. I marveled at his swiftness. He had led me on many journeys. Once again, I followed him.

At the sound of the drums, I halted. Momma and Silver Eagle stood near the fire. "*Nows*," I said. "And Momma." Momma's hair was blonde, and Silver Eagle's black crown hair stood upright. They were as I remembered them when first coming to Virginia. I stepped towards them and hugged each in turn.

"There are others here that you may wish to see." Momma motioned to the others dancing round the fire of the drums.

A warrior stopped dancing and walked towards me.

Upon seeing my first husband, my heart fluttered. "Lightning Storm."

He embraced me. "Walks Through Mist."

As a young lass, I *had* loved him with all of my heart. He was Elenor's poppa, and naught could e'er change that he had been my first true love. "I missed you."

"And I, you. There's someone over here that I think you'd like to see." He moved towards the dancers. Another warrior halted. He had blue-green eyes.

My son. "Dark Moon?"

"I am now Soaring Hawk."

Soaring Hawk. As the Arrohateck had taught me, my son had come of age in the afterlife. Was that where I was now? The drums pounded a final rhythm, and the dancing halted. Many poured towards me. I spied my childhood friend, Singing Woman; my brother Charging Bear and Meg, and the babe they had lost so long ago; Henry and Bess; Crow in the Wood's mother Snow Bird and his father Black Owl; Elenor's husband Christopher; Lee's adoptive mother Natalie Crowley; and my trusty companion Caleb. They all greeted me in a warm welcome.

"Momma..."

Elenor's voice called me back. "I saw Christopher," I said weakly.

A cool cloth went to my forehead. "I thought I had lost you."

My daughter's gentle hand could not erase the radiating storm from within my leg. I gripped the sides of the bed and bit my lip to keep from crying out.

"I'll get more poppy tea."

I had no idea how long had passed afore Elenor returned. Holding the cup, she helped me sip the tea. She spread some salve on my leg, which helped cool the fire from within. I laid back and finally slept. Mist captured me. I looked for my hound but could not find him. Instead, I waved my arms afore me and navigated the forest path blindly.

From somewhere o'erhead, a crow cawed. Wind Talker was near. Of that, I was certain. Out of the fog, the black bird swooped towards me, then flew in the opposite direction. As best as I could, I followed. Mayhap, he would lead me to Wind Talker. Too slow to keep up, I sat near a tree. When the crow doubled back and made a frightful racket, I got to my feet and went deeper into the forest.

A young lad sauntered towards me. "Crow in the Woods?"

As if not seeing me standing on the path, he walked on past. I turned to a bright light shining through the mist. He forged ahead. The light beckoned me, but I was frozen in place. Crow in the Woods stepped through an invisible door and vanished.

The crow cawed. The beacon had formed in another section of the forest.

Follow the light.

I finally understood. Crow in the Woods had traveled to the future. I was now being led to Lee. I picked up my pace and raced to the light.

The crow squawked a frightening scream, halting me in my tracks. *You must be careful, or what you seek will not come to pass.*

For a moment, I knew not whether to proceed. I had no choice. "I shall be careful."

With caution, I proceeded towards the light. The closer I got, the brighter the light became 'til 'twas nearly blinding. I stepped through and found myself in a maze. I groped my way along.

Follow the light.

A man stood in the middle of the light, waving me towards him. "Lee?"

I passed a darkened passageway. I ignored it and continued towards the figure. Soon we'd be together. My heart pounded, then the man vanished into the light. I raced ahead to join him. When I reached the spot where he had been standing, I looked e'ery which way. The light formed in another distant corner, but my leg hurt. I limped along.

Follow the light.

I entered another passageway. On the ground lay a dead crow. I collected the lifeless body and cradled the bird in my arms. I gazed upon the light and understood its meaning. *Wind Talker.*

42

Wind Talker

1630

P<small>HOEBE</small>. I heard her calling to me loud and clear, but her voice vanished as quickly as it had come upon me. *Concentrate*. We needed to rescue her from Jamestown before she faced trial. Unlike the time before, we held no purification ceremony in a sweat house. Neither Charging Bear nor I had the experience to conduct one by ourselves. As promised, Henry lent me some old clothes. Even though he was considerably smaller than me, the linen shirt was baggy on him, therefore trim on me. When Henry handed me a doublet, I shook my head. The previous time warned me that the garment would never fit.

Henry shoved a pair of brown breeches in my direction. Even before I tried them on, I knew they would fit snug. Thank goodness for loose-fitting garments. Though the breeches were tight, I managed to shimmy into them. A woolen coat went over my shirt, but Henry's shoes were way too small. James loaned me a pair, and they were as god-awful as I remembered.

Gloves and a broad-brimmed felt hat finished my disguise. This time, I didn't need to look in any mirror. All too aware that if anyone got a good look at me, they would *know* I wasn't a colonist. I sighed.

Henry handed me a pistol in a leather holster. While I had fired a flintlock musket on occasion, I had never shot a pistol since being in this century.

"Can you use it?" he asked.

I removed the pistol from its holster. About a foot long with floral patterns decorating the pommel and barrel, the weapon looked elegant. I replaced the pistol in its holster and strapped the gun to my waist. "If necessary, I'm a quick learner."

"Good." He secured his weapon around his waist. "Shall we be off?"

I nodded and Henry bid the kids goodbye. Jaysen still wouldn't come to me. In time, I hoped he would. Once outside, I intertwined my index finger with Charging Bear's. "Safe journey, brother," he said.

With a parting smile, I patted him on the shoulder. "We'll do our best." James lingered a few feet away with a worried frown. "We'll bring Bess back safe and sound," I said.

"Thank you, Wind Talker."

Henry and I stepped through the palisade toward the dock. We climbed aboard a vessel that resembled a rowboat. Henry shoved the boat away from the dock, and we headed downriver toward Jamestown.

"Wind Talker," Henry said, breaking the silence that had descended between us. "For the duration of our journey, I think we should use a Christian name. Do you have one?"

Taken unaware, I hadn't realized Phoebe had never told him. "It's Lee... Lee Crowley."

"For the rest of this venture, that is what I shall call you."

With a nod, I focused on rowing. After several hours, we neared Jamestown Island. Having been to Jamestown in this century more than once, I no longer expected to see the Colonial Parkway or a bridge spanning from the mainland to the island that I had grown up with. The town was notably smaller than it would be in the 1640s, but boats were on the river, and near the port, sailing ships were anchored. The first time I was in awe that they had sailed from England to Virginia. After being abandoned on West Island, no such fascination remained. "Are we going on the Back River?" I asked.

Henry studied me with curiosity. "You know your way around, don't you?"

"I've been here a few times."

"Aye, makes sense. Fewer will take note of our presence if we come ashore from the Back." Henry guided the boat into the bay. The current lessened and rowing became easier. On the left, I spotted mud flats. Henry was a skilled seaman and purposely avoided them. We skirted other sandy shoals; then the bay narrowed, and we turned onto Back River. Less than a mile later, we rowed toward shore. Near the bank, we got out and splashed through the water, bringing the boat ashore. After covering the boat with ferns and branches, we traveled through the cypress and pine forest.

I remained haunted by Jamestown. The Indian exhibits in the twenty-first century showed little of what my people had truly suffered. My father Black Owl had most likely hunted and fished here when he was younger, but I kept visualizing the enclosures where the colonists kept Natives penned like livestock.

We slogged through the marsh and frightened a heron from its fishing. The great blue spread its vast wings, flying away with its legs stretched out behind it. Once we reached dry land, a gray fox darted in front of us. Unlike the time I had traveled the route before, the double-pitched governor's house had yet to be built. No brick houses existed, and cattle, goats, and hogs roamed throughout. Fences surrounded planted fields to keep the livestock out.

People wandered the riverfront. A black woman shrieked and ran toward us. Tears streaked her cheeks as Bess halted before us. "I couldn't believe 'twas you."

Henry grasped her arm and led her away from the main activity. "I have someone you can stay with 'til we're ready to depart."

"They have the missus."

"That's why we're here."

Bess looked at me as if seeing me for the first time. "Wind Talker?"

"Master Crowley," Henry replied sharply.

"My humble apologies." The tears returned to her eyes.

"Bess," I said, after we got a distance from the main body of people. "We're here to help. Tell us what happened."

"They released me aft they brought the missus in. She said she was responsible for overseeing those who had the smallpox. I wasn't certain how I'd find my way home, but I didn't want to leave the missus either. They've searched her body. I know not what they found, but her trial is on the morrow."

"We'll wait 'til dark," Henry said.

As I cast my gaze to the sinking sun, a crow cawed. The white crow flew overhead in warning.

"Lee?"

I blinked and looked in Henry's direction.

"You look as if you've seen a demon."

"Not quite. Henry, if anything should happen—"

"Nay, naught will happen 'less we don't get moving." He waved the way until we arrived at a frame house. Not wanting to be seen, I kept my distance while Henry left Bess with a farmer and promised to return for her before dawn. Then, we waited for the sun to set. Even after darkness had settled, we waited. Finally, we moved.

Few candles illuminated windows, so there was very little light. Except for the soft bellow of a cow, even most of the livestock slept, and the path along the waterfront was empty of people. We came to a wattle and daub building. Before stepping inside, we readied our pistols. No one sat at the desk, but lantern light came from the adjacent room. We edged toward the door with Henry on one side and me on the other. I peeked around the corner as the jailer set a bowl on the floor near Phoebe's feet. Crow cawed in my mind.

"I told ye I'd have ye, witch," the jailer said to Phoebe.

I clenched my fists and nearly rushed forward. *Not yet, Wind Talker.* Phoebe? Crow rattled as if sending a message between us. For the moment, I stood firm.

Phoebe sent the jailer a smile. "You said you would help me."

"Ye must make it worth my while."

I took a step, but Henry held me back. *Patience, Wind Talker. You know when the time will be right.* Phoebe lifted her arm and rattled the chain. "Unshackle me."

The jailer stepped closer. His back faced me, which was probably a blessing. If I saw the lewd gestures he was likely giving Phoebe, I would have never been able to hold my ground. He bent down to unshackle her ankles, then drew her near and kissed her. Crow cawed. Unable to contain myself any longer, I hit him over the head with the pistol butt. He slumped to the floor.

I made a fist to strike him, but Henry gripped my arm. "Lee, you've done enough."

I glanced at Phoebe and my anger faded. "Phoebe..." She clung to me and I patted her back. "It's all right now. We're going to get you to safety." After I led her from the cell, Henry helped me drag the jailer into the cell. Resisting the temptation to punch him, I shackled him to the wall. "They'll find him in the morning."

While I helped Phoebe toward the door, Henry locked the cell. Outside, the moon cast dim light.

"I'll fetch Bess and meet you at the shallop," Henry said.

"Be careful, Henry."

"I will, but if I don't show up within an hour of your arrival, take off without us."

"Henry—"

"Bess and I can blend in amongst the people here. You and Phoebe cannot." He vanished into the darkness.

Keeping a firm grip on Phoebe's hand, I continued forward. We passed the remaining houses and headed into the swamp.

"He called you Lee."

"He thought it was best that I use my English name. If it wasn't for the darkness, I'd never be able to hide my heritage."

"Aye, 'tis true."

For so long, I had wanted to see and touch her again. She hesitated a minute as if sensing my thoughts, but I tugged gently on her hand to get moving again. We reached the swamp. Mud sucked on my feet. Phoebe stumbled in the muck, but I managed to keep my grip on her hand to prevent her from falling.

When we reached the river, I removed the ferns and branches from the boat. Then, we waited. Where were Henry and Bess? Phoebe shivered, and I drew her near. My arms went around her, hoping to lend her some warmth.

"They searched my person."

At the sound of her shaky voice, I hugged her tighter. If only my arms would be enough to keep her safe, but we weren't out of danger yet. "I'm sorry we weren't here earlier."

"I thought I might die there." She sobbed again.

I held her until she had no more tears. A branch snapped. I stepped in front of Phoebe to shield her and reached for the pistol in case someone besides Henry had tracked us. Another fox—only this time a red one. I reholstered the pistol and hugged Phoebe once more. With her next to me, I didn't fall into the habit of pacing. Had an hour come and gone yet? I looked to the sky. Only the moon gave me a hint as to how much time had passed, and I certainly hadn't become adept at calculating the hours by watching the sky.

Phoebe withdrew from my embrace. "I thought mayhap that I had desired too much."

"Too much?"

"Us. Living together—as a family."

I drew her near again. "You haven't desired too much. We will be together." For a long while, I simply held her. Her muscles finally relaxed. I had no doubt that more than an hour had slipped by, but I remained in place. When the first streaks of light appeared in the sky, I could no longer ignore it. We had already stretched the limit.

"We can't wait much longer," I said. *Where are you, Henry?* I hated the idea of leaving him behind, but as he had said, he and Bess could blend in. If Phoebe were recaptured, she might face more than a trial and whipping. Her safety came first. "Only a few more minutes."

"He does know how to keep Bess and himself safe."

"I have no doubts about that." I helped Phoebe into the boat. Before I shoved off, I scanned the woods one last time. Due to the poor lighting, I really couldn't see much. With some hesitation I got into the boat.

"Wait!"

Bess? I needed no prodding to halt. A shadow stepped out of the woods, and I went to meet her.

"The master needs help." She showed me along the trail until we came to a large tree where Henry lay sprawled on the ground.

"Henry?" Worried that he might have been shot, I bent down.

He groaned. "I twisted my bloody ankle."

I pulled his arm around my shoulder and helped him to his feet. "I thought it might be more serious." We returned to the boat, and I helped everyone in.

Finally, we cast off. In spite of his ankle, Henry helped with the rowing. A short time passed before we left the Back River and entered the bay. Early morning light spread, and I hoped we'd make it to the James before the colony woke for the day. As dawn broke, we entered the stronger current of the James River. With the growing light, it was much easier to hug the bank and keep from running aground.

I concentrated on the task at hand and kept rowing. By late afternoon, we reached the plantation. As I tethered a line to the dock, a crow cawed—a white one. We weren't out of danger yet.

While Phoebe rushed into the house to greet the servants and children, I changed into my loincloth and leggings. Thankful to be rid of the scratchy colonial attire, I went inside and caught Phoebe scrubbing herself from a wash basin as if trying to rid herself of the grime and grit from the jail. "Charging Bear will take us to the Arrohateck, where your mother will be waiting."

"I can't leave the children behind."

"They will slow us down. We can always—"

"Nay, we bring them now."

Against my better judgment, I nodded. "We'll bring them."

"Thank you."

"I want us to be a family too. Rest up a bit. Come outside when you're ready." I gave her a quick kiss and left the house.

In the yard, I met Henry dragging his right foot. "There's no need for vexation," he said. "I have already assured you that I will not stand betwixt you and Phoebe."

"Will you be all right?"

"Aye. Wind Talker, I knew when I helped Phoebe escape that you would make your life with her."

"Thank you for helping us."

"May God go with you. I'll tell Phoebe that you wait for her."

I thanked him again and he went into the house. Charging Bear joined me. Before long, Phoebe came outside with the children. I gave Henry and James a parting handshake. After another round of goodbyes, and with Charging Bear in the lead, we followed the trail alongside the river. As I had warned Phoebe, the children slowed our progress. Jaysen refused to come to me, and Elenor buried herself into the folds of Phoebe's skirt.

When we reached the riverbank, Charging Bear and I uncovered the dugout hidden among the shrubs. We helped the children and Phoebe in and shoved the dugout into the water. Phoebe rowed alongside us, taking frequent breaks to tend to the children. After awhile, they screamed their hunger, and Phoebe shared some of the rations that Bess had prepared.

In the fading daylight, Charging Bear pointed across the river at a colonial shallop. We hugged the dugout near the shore and hid beneath an overhanging branch. Instead of sailing past, the boat moved toward us.

"It's time that we observe them from land," I said.

Charging Bear agreed and we brought the dugout onto the bank. Phoebe hugged the children to keep them quiet, but Elenor cried. Phoebe tried comforting her in order to silence her. Though she quieted some, she continued to whimper.

The shallop failed to change course. "They've seen us," I said. "I think we need to put some distance between us."

"I concur," Charging Bear replied. "There appear to be six men." He gathered his bow and arrows together. "Follow me."

Phoebe struggled with the children. I attempted to take Jaysen, but the boy withdrew. "Go to him, Jaysen," Phoebe whispered. "Your poppa will help keep you safe."

With some hesitation, Jaysen took my hand. I smiled slightly, but there was no time to rejoice in the breakthrough. Charging Bear grasped Elenor's hand.

Free of the children, Phoebe climbed from the dugout. Charging Bear led the way along the narrow path through the tangled woods, with Phoebe in the middle. I brought up the rear. Phoebe carried Jaysen, and Elenor gripped her skirt.

When Jaysen squirmed in Phoebe's arms, I held out my hands. "I'll take him."

Jaysen clutched Phoebe tighter. "Pray go to your poppa. Momma's arms have grown weary."

Thankfully, he seemed to understand Phoebe's urgency and came to me. After another mile, Elenor whined that her feet hurt. Phoebe hushed her, attempting to explain the importance that she remain quiet. We pressed on. When we had gone another mile, Elenor stumbled, and Phoebe picked her up.

Charging Bear halted. "Rest the children." Then to me, he said, "Watch over Walks Through Mist and the children. I'll see if we're still being followed."

"Be careful," I said.

He nodded and doubled back on the trail we had come. Phoebe gathered the children together and rested beneath an oak tree. Elenor and Jaysen lay upon the ground in exhaustion. "I should have listened to you," she said. "I've endangered the children unnecessarily."

I sat beside her and held her hand. "You wanted to be with your children. No one can damn you for that. Everything will work out in the end."

She squeezed my hand. "You're right. Soon we shall be a family."

More than anything, I wanted to believe. *Reassure her, you fool.* "I know it in my heart."

"Wind Talker?"

I shook my head that I didn't want to talk about it. "Are you okay? Charging Bear keeps a breakneck speed. I have a hard time keeping his pace. After what you've been through, I'd think you'd have a worse time."

Before she could answer, Charging Bear sprinted toward us. "They're about a mile behind—with reinforcements."

I stood. "Damn." I picked up Jaysen and helped Phoebe to her feet, while Charging Bear carried Elenor. Both of us struggled to keep his pace. He pressed onward, even after sunset. By the time we rested, the children cried in hunger. I had difficulty watching when Phoebe overturned a rock. Crickets and grubs lay underneath. She fed them to the children to relieve their hunger. Afterward, she rubbed their backs until they fell into a fitful sleep. She sank to the ground beside the children but tossed and turned as if she couldn't sleep.

The wind creaked nearby branches, and I had that sinking feeling again. Phoebe bolted upright. "Wind Talker..."

My arms went around her. "I'm here."

"When you had the smallpox, I was certain I would lose you."

I hugged her closer. "You're not going to lose me."

She leaned her head on my chest. In my arms, she finally slept. Before long, I dozed as well. I dreamed of the wind circling me, carrying me through the mist. "Follow the light."

With a start, I woke. Phoebe was still in my arms. But I had heard *her* voice.

"We need to be moving again," Charging Bear said.

My heart sank. With reluctance, I helped Phoebe wake the children. They huddled in her arms, weeping from hunger. In the early light, she collected grasshoppers. She twisted off their heads and the entrails came along with them. Though not satisfied, the children stopped their whimpering after consuming the insects. Jaysen came straight to me. For my son's acceptance of me, I took small comfort. Charging Bear offered to take Elenor, but for now, she could walk. He led the way. After a couple of miles, we came to a stream. Charging Bear picked up Elenor to help her cross, and we sloshed through the water.

"I shall see if our pursuers are nearby," Charging Bear said.

Yet again, I warned him to be careful. He assured me that he would. Phoebe collected earthworms and more grubs. I sat beside her and buried my revulsion. We all shared the seemingly small delicacy. We held each other as well as the children. Before long, Phoebe's head bobbed and she fell asleep on my shoulder.

Scanning the horizon, I remained alert. As time passed, every bone in my body screamed the enemy was near. I gave Phoebe a slight shake to wake her. "Get the kids to safety."

"Wind Talker...?"

I readied the pistol Henry had given me. "Now."

Two bearded men stormed from the cover of nearby trees, blasting their flintlocks as they charged. I returned fire. One flailed to the ground. The other continued forward and slammed into me with his entire bodyweight, throwing me to the ground. Although stunned by the blow, I managed to regain my feet and punch him in the face. He struck me in the chest. When blood spurted I realized I had been stabbed. The bearded face laughed and struck me again.

Dizzy. As I sank to the ground, I thought of Phoebe. I hoped she had gotten safely away with the kids. I drifted. *Follow the light.*

In the distance, a baritone voice sang.

"Wind Talker!" Someone grasped my hand. "Wind Talker, pray be all right."

Her face flickered in and out of focus. *Phoebe,* I gasped for breath. While she removed my shirt, the voice continued to sing. *A death song.*

She applied pressure to my chest, making breathing a little easier. "Stop singing. Wind Talker isn't dying."

Follow the light. The white crow flew overhead, and I now understood. "Phoebe..."

She continued to use pressure to slow the bleeding. "Don't try to talk."

"Phoebe..." Struggling for breath, I clamped my fingers around her wrist. "Stop."

"I mustn't." She met my gaze. "You vowed we would be a family."

I coughed. More blood. I fought for another breath and choked. Finally, I managed to take in a breath of air.

Phoebe stroked through my hair as she hugged me. "Pray don't give up."

One more breath—I fought for it. I encircled my hand around hers. "Follow... the... light." I choked and gasped. Phoebe stood before me, not the Phoebe beside my physical self, but my wife. I moved toward her in the endless circle of time.

43

Phoebe

1630

I CLOSED MY EYES, HOPING AGAINST HOPE that I was living naught more than a nightmare. Finally, Wind Talker's muscles relaxed, and his heart stopped beating. Once again, Charging Bear's baritone voice sang.

"Wind Talker! Wind Talker!" Sobbing, I pounded his chest, then shook him. "Wind Talker, pray wake up. Now's not the time to sleep." Unable to rouse him, I embraced him and wept.

"Walks Through Mist..."

Not knowing how much time had passed, I blinked back my tears to my brother's face.

"We mustn't stay here. There's still danger."

I caressed Wind Talker's cheek. "I can't leave him."

"I'll return later with help, and we'll see that he receives a proper resting place."

Resting place? "But he's not dead. He's sleeping."

"Walks Through Mist..." Charging Bear gently grasped my arm and helped me to my feet. I cast my gaze to the children. Elenor had tears in her eyes. Too young to understand, Jaysen stared at me as if unsure of what had come o'er his momma. "They need you, Walks Through Mist."

My children needed me? I cast another glance at Wind Talker, resting on the ground. Not e'en a finger had moved. "Wind Talker—"

"Walks Through Mist, we need to make haste. Wind Talker gave his life so that you and the children may live. We were only successful in fending off the first wave. There are more colonists in pursuit. They still believe you to be a witch."

Trying to make sense of his words, I stared into Charging Bear's eyes. I bent down to Wind Talker and kissed his already cooling lips. "I'll ne'er forget," I whispered. "Goodbye, my love."

For my children's sake, I would remain strong 'til we had reached safety, then grief would consume my soul. Charging Bear carried Elenor on his back, and I, Jaysen. E'en as darkness shrouded o'er us, we trekked onwards. Closer to the Arrohateck we traveled.

Behind us came loud voices. I nearly bolted, but Charging Bear gripped my arm to keep me in check. I e'ened my breath, and we pushed deeper into the forest. Branches scraped my arms. My skirt protected my legs from the brambles. Still, we pressed on.

When we traveled far enough to elude our pursuers, we sank to the ground in exhaustion. The children fell into a restless sleep, but I remained wide awake. *Wind Talker.* Only numbness kept me from falling into a weeping heap. His words of following the light haunted me. Then, I spied the light of torches. I nearly rose and moved towards it, but I caught myself. Behind the light were our pursuers. I shook Charging Bear and woke him.

"Come," he said.

On our hands and knees, we scrambled along the forest floor. Like afore, Charging Bear carried Elenor, and I, Jaysen. When the torches grew distant, we regained our feet. No moonlight alighted our path to aid us. I focused on the night sounds. Branches, with rustling leaves, creaked in the wind. A screech owl trilled a mournful melody, and midges hummed past my ear. We moved towards the sound of rushing water and would follow its course to escape. Unless the hounds were sent after us, the advantage was ours. Unlike our pursuers, we had been taught to move swiftly and silently through the forest.

Upon reaching the bank of the stream, I kicked off my shoes, for they slowed me. I dipped my toes into the water and felt the cool and slippery moss-covered rocks. A fish splashed near me.

On the path behind us, Henry's voice called out. "Phoebe, come back. I assure you, no harm will come to you."

"He's with others," Charging Bear said in warning.

Henry called once more. I quivered with uncertainty, when a voice inside me urged me to continue forward. I feared what lay ahead, 'til hearing *his* voice. *Do not fear it. You will be reunited with what once was.*

Tears sprang into my eyes, and I called out in Algonquian. "Wind Talker, where are you?"

"Walks Through Mist," Charging Bear said. "Wind Talker isn't here."

"This is why I kept hearing his voice. He'll lead us to safety."

"What does he say?"

Any of the colonists, including Henry, would have been skeptical with my words, but my brother believed me. I turned in e'ery direction. "Where are you? Guide us."

A gentle wind rustled nearby leaves. *Forward.*

I gripped Charging Bear's arm and stepped forward, fording the stream. The water churned round my feet. Near the middle, the water swirled about my waist, and I feared the water would encompass Jaysen afore I could reach safety. I fought the current and arrived on the far bank. Suddenly, I was lost.

Trees were e'erywhere. We stumbled through the gigantic roots. "Are you certain this is the way?" Charging Bear asked.

I halted. "Where my love? Where are we to go?"

Raging shouts of the mob came from the opposite bank. Their torches formed bright flames. My heart pounded at their nearness. In the breeze, Wind Talker whispered, "Walks Through Mist, follow my voice, and be certain you have both of the children within your grasp."

We traveled through the forest, 'til my hound stood afore me. A thick mist surrounded us. I gripped Elenor's hand, and the fog swallowed the children and me like a ship. "Charging Bear!" No matter which direction I turned, I could not find my brother. The dampness on my skin raised the hairs on my arms. I finally understood. Wind Talker was leading us to the afterlife. We would be a family after all.

The wind picked up, and I gripped the hound's collar. A crow floated on the currents ahead of me. Together, we sailed on the wind. In this place, time had no meaning. All periods existed side by side with no division betwixt them.

On and on, I faltered through the fog, tracing a huge circle. A ship rocked and swayed neath my feet. A wave of nausea overcame me, and I clutched my stomach with my free hand. The hound failed to break stride. Onwards.

From a nearby branch, the crow cawed. I thought of Crow in the Woods, and how he had vanished in a similar mist. Yet, he had returned to me as Wind Talker. As I passed beyond my own lifetime, I spied men attired in tailored coats with tricorn hats and powdered wigs. Cannon roared, and women wore bell-shaped skirts. Men charged o'er a hill, firing muskets. On the other side of the hill, horseless carriages sped about. I recalled seeing them in my dreams.

The mist grew thinner. "Follow the light," Wind Talker whispered.

Up ahead, torches were e'erywhere. As I stepped out of the fog, the hound and crow vanished. I blinked in disbelief. How could so much light be possible in the night sky? I looked about me. Lights upon lights, swarming with people. And clattering noise. Jaysen and Elenor cried from the onslaught. The thoroughfare had a surface the likes of which I had ne'er seen. *Which light should I follow?*

I clutched the children's hands and stepped into the road to escape. More lights chased after us, blinding me. I froze in my path, deafened by a piercing sound and sudden screeching. A man shouted. He grasped my arms and flung the children and me aside, out of the glaring light. I struck the pavement and closed my eyes to the pain.

"Ma'am, are you and the kids all right?"

'Twas *his* voice. We had arrived in the afterlife. I opened my eyes. Though his hair was shorter than I remembered, and he wore strange garments, I had no doubt of who he was. "Kesutanowas Wesin."

"Phoebe?" He finished inspecting Jaysen, then Elenor. "Except for a few scratches, I think the kids are fine." He held out his hand to aid me to my feet. "Are you all right?"

I couldn't help but stare. "I'm ... I'm fine."

He returned my gaze. "You don't recognize me?"

"I do, but you differ from the way I knew you."

"I'm Detective Lee Crowley. That passing car nearly hit you."

"Lee?"

He nodded. "Lee Crowley."

'Twasn't the afterlife. We had arrived in the twenty-first century, and the man standing afore us was Wind Talker. "This is Elenor," I said, introducing my daughter, "and my son's name is Jaysen."

He glanced from Elenor to Jaysen. For a moment, he studied the lad. "Jaysen?" he said weakly, then his gaze met mine. "This isn't the dreaming?"

" 'Tis not."

"Then, we haven't met before. I had better have a doctor examine all of you, but I'll drive you home afterward."

"Lee, I have nowhere to go in this time."

He examined my dress as if seeing it for the first time and smiled. "You followed the light?"

"Aye."

"That explains why I had the feeling I should be in this spot tonight. You told me while in the dreaming that I needed to be here."

Our son went o'er to him and stretched his arms to be picked up. Lee studied the lad but obliged. "Poppa," Jaysen said.

Lee looked at me in puzzlement. "This is going to take a bit of getting used to."

"We have much time afore us now." As Lee met my gaze, I knew I was where I was meant to be.

44

Lee

Through the dreaming, I discovered what Phoebe and I had been through together. Although I had learned about Jaysen and Phoebe's daughter with her first husband in the past, my mind boggled at being an instant "Dad." I had always wanted kids, but my ex and I had never gotten around to seriously considering having a family before our divorce. Shae and I were still friends, and I suspected she was even more surprised when Phoebe and I married within a month of our "meeting."

As the weeks went by, I relived my experiences about my heritage and how I had become Wind Talker. The death screams of my family would always be a part of me. Yet oddly enough, I found myself at peace. The knowledge of who I was and where I had come from silenced the questions that plagued me growing up.

But then, I contemplated whether I was destined to return to the seventeenth century and repeat my experiences yet again. If Phoebe and our future daughter had followed me, hadn't that created a paradox? What if they had become trapped there as a result?

Phoebe noted my stress. At first, I blamed my tension on the job, but she saw right through me and I admitted the truth. She had her own unanswered questions of what had happened to her family and friends. We joined in the dreaming. The mist became an impenetrable fog, engulfing us. Flying overhead, the crow guided the way, and the wind was at our backs. Never wanting to let go, I grasped Phoebe's hand.

On the other side of us was Phoebe's greyhound, tracing a large circle. Lights filled the night sky, and I found myself on an urban street. A voice called to me and I moved forward. I hustled through the crowds of people. Up ahead, a car honked and headed toward a woman with two children. Without bothering to stop and think, I shouted at the woman and charged into the road. I grabbed her arms and threw her and the kids out of the car's path, barely escaping in time myself.

"I ne'er thanked you."

Phoebe's voice drew me back. This was the dreaming, and we continued walking. "I was meant to be there."

As the mist thinned, my gait became smoother with moccasins on my feet. I found myself attired in a loincloth, leggings, and a wool shirt. The garb felt completely natural, and Phoebe was dressed in a long skirt. When we emerged from the fog, we stood on the bank of a river. I had already experienced the dreaming enough to know exactly where we were. "It's the James. We're always brought back to this place."

Phoebe cast her gaze about, then bolted, following the river downstream. I easily caught up with her, but she didn't stop running until she was winded.

The palisade had been torn down, and the pitched-roof house was no longer built of wood, but red brick. Out front stood a man. His dark brown hair had some gray, and wrinkles surrounded his eyes. I felt as if I should know him.

"Henry," Phoebe said.

He blinked in disbelief. "Phoebe? How is this possible? You look the same as when——"

"As when I vanished?"

With tears in his eyes, he kissed Phoebe's hands, then glanced at me. "Wind Talker?"

For some reason when he called me by that name, it seemed right. We shook hands. "Henry."

Phoebe craned her neck, attempting to peer over our shoulders. "I need to know what happened to Charging Bear."

"He lives with the Appamattuck now," Henry responded. "He brings us venison and fish in exchange for tools. Phoebe, there's something else you should know."

She bit her lip as if fearing the worst.

"Elenor has returned to us," he said.

"Returned to you? I don't understand."

"This is her time where she wished to raise a family."

"Raise a family?"

"Aye. You'd be proud of her. She cares for me now. Come." He waved the way inside.

A hall with wooden floors divided the house. A table was to one side with candles atop it and a mirror above. A ladder no longer led to the loft. Instead, a staircase with a wood handrail wound the way to the second story. In the parlor, a black-haired woman bent over a spinning wheel. When we entered the room, she looked up. "Momma? Poppa?"

Phoebe ran over to Elenor and hugged her. "Elenor, I ne'er expected to find you here. What happened?" They embraced.

" 'Tis a long story, but Jaysen helped me return."

"Jaysen?"

She sent the two of us a beaming grin. "You shall discover the depth of his capabilities when he comes of age. E'en now, he looks in on me from time to time."

I exchanged a glance with Phoebe, then returned my attention to Elenor. "Does that mean the rest of us remain in the twenty-first century?"

With her grin widening, she nodded. "Aye. The cycle was broken."

"And Heather?" Phoebe asked.

"She'll join you at the proper time. Now, let me introduce you to the grandchildren."

I had barely gotten used to the idea of being a father, but a grandfather too. Phoebe's eyes lit up as Elenor introduced the children. Tall and gawky, Christopher was nearly seven and named after his father. He had Elenor's black hair. At five, Elsa had blue-green eyes, reddish hair, and freckles. She was a lot like the way I imagined Phoebe at the same age. Nicolas was the youngest at two. He had light brown hair and blue eyes. Elenor said that he resembled his father.

When Bess entered the room, Phoebe's face brightened. The two hugged. Before their greetings ended, another woman stood in the door frame. Although her blonde hair had gone gray, I recognized Phoebe's mother from the dreaming. "Elenor?"

"Aye, Wind Talker, 'tis me."

After another round of hugs and kisses, we sat in chairs, where the family brought Phoebe up to date. Henry had remarried, but she had died a few years before. He had a son, a merchant, who was presently in England along with Elenor's husband. Not only did Phoebe's daughter take care of Henry these days, she also looked after her mother. Both Elenors often traveled between the Indians and home life along the James River. Phoebe had received one wish—her daughter had gotten to know her people.

As they chatted away, I had a longing and excused myself. Outside, I wandered the trails. I negotiated my way along the path through the forest with an uncanny familiarity. After several miles, I halted by a section that had smaller growth than the surrounding trees. Chills ran up and down my spine. No one needed to tell me that I stood in the spot that I had barely escaped from as a small child.

Lying on the ground was part of a femur and a bony hand. Ribs, jaw bones, and arms were partially buried in the loose soil. The bones were all that was left of my people. I choked on my breath and sank to my knees. Only because I had walked through the mist had I not died along with them. Phoebe had saved me. But my mother *had* died. She would be buried here along with the others. I called for her.

No response returned, but I remained in place. Why had I bothered coming here? Still, I waited. I had no idea how much time had passed. Minutes? Hours? When the wind blew, I suddenly understood. Voices whispered through the trees. I could hear them loud and clear. They were my family—and ancestors—for I was on Paspahegh land. My name, Wind Talker, I clearly comprehended where it had come from, and my people would always be a part of my soul.

"Wind Talker... Lee..."

The wind faded and along with it, so did the voices. Phoebe stood beside me. " 'Tis time," she said.

I got to my feet. "I heard their voices—here, in this place."

"Aye, I knew you would."

Before leaving, I gazed out on the site of the massacre. With my hands out and palms facing up I extended my arms. At long last, I understood the sacrifice my mother had made so that I could live. As fog engulfed us, Phoebe smiled. Overhead, Crow cawed and the greyhound stood nearby.

Children's voices guided us through the mist. A moment passed before I got my bearings. We were in my apartment, not the forest. A candle flickered on the table where we had entered the dreaming. A child babbled from the next room, then another one laughed.

"I think Elenor may have woken Jaysen from his nap," Phoebe said. "I'll fetch them."

Content since Phoebe and the kids had entered my life, I got to my feet and helped her with our family. Afterward, we all hopped into the T-Bird and drove to the local park. Beneath shade trees, we strolled hand in hand, while Jaysen and Elenor romped ahead of us. From behind us, a woman shouted.

A black woman most likely in her late teens, gripping a two-year-old girl's hand, struggled to join us. Out of breath, she handed Phoebe her purse. "I believe you dropped this."

"Meg," I said.

Her mouth dropped open. "How do you know my name?"

"Long story. Why don't we let the kids play, and we can talk."

She glanced from Jaysen and Elenor to her own daughter. "Sounds like a plan. I have the strange feeling that we've met before."

Phoebe couldn't help but giggle. "Aye, we have. 'Tis the circle of time."

With her words, several crows cawed from a nearby tree. Their racket greeted me, and I knew the circle was complete.

Author's Note

As in the previous books of The Dreaming series, *Walks Through Mist* and *Wind Talker*, the dreaming is not meant to represent the belief system of the Virginia Algonquian-speaking people, who were composed of approximately thirty tribes commonly referred to as the Powhatan. Instead, I chose to portray it as a rite of the cunning folk. The cunning folk were the healers of seventeenth-century European societies, who used herbs and magic and often had guardian spirits.

In 1645, the year following the organized attack of paramount chief Opechancanough, the colonists retaliated on the Native tribes. They captured and prosecuted many captives, mostly from the Pamunkey tribe. The women and children were sold into slavery. In order to prevent the men from returning to and strengthening their respective tribes, Governor William Berkley's ship was used to abandon boys over the age of eleven and the men on Western Island. Today the island is known by the name of Tangier Island, which differs considerably from what it was like in the 1600s.

While my story surrounding the abandonment is fictional, I attempted to portray a possibility of what might have taken place. In reality, the men's fate is unknown. The conditions represented in my story are real. There was no fresh water, so unless another tribe saved them, they would have likely perished.

Throughout the seventeenth century, the Native Virginia tribes were in turmoil. The English continually squeezed them for more land. Many died in land grabs, and their crops were stolen. Others moved west, infringing on the territories of other tribes. Chief Ottahotin of the Kiskiack, along with many other leaders, were given poisoned wine during a so-called "peace" meeting as mentioned in my story. As a result, many died on the spot, but Ottahotin was a survivor.

The smallpox epidemic that I have portrayed as being caused by English colonists is totally fictional. The first-known intentional epidemic with infected blankets was recorded in the eighteenth century. Many epidemics abounded during the seventeenth century, but the actual records were either lost or specifics never written down. Therefore, I took liberties with an idea of a repetition throughout history that began taking place long before documented instances.

As for time travel, scientists state that we may live in one universe among an infinite number of parallel universes. Many authors use this theory in their works of fiction. Some genres commonly superimpose the concept that every decision, every branch, every choice made by an individual causes a fork with two subsequent universes.

I preferred to view the hypothesis in another manner with each universe remaining a separate realm. While some time travel takes place in *Circle in Time*, the realms are not normally connected, and the characters in each realm live out their lives separate from the other universes. The connection between the universes occurs predominantly through the dreaming. As a result, I hope I have created a more vibrant story with more possibilities than in a conventional time-slip story.

Acknowledgments

A special thank you goes to my editors, K.A. Corlett, Catherine Karp, and Kate Stephenson, and my cover designer, Roberta Marley. And of course, I wish to thank my family: my son Bryan, and especially my husband Pat; both are now hopeful that I may have rejoined the twenty-first century.

Made in the USA
Middletown, DE
25 August 2021